HAWKS & HARRIERS

Also by Page Stegner

THE EDGE

ESCAPE INTO AESTHETICS:
THE ART OF VLADIMIR NABOKOV

NABOKOV'S CONGERIES

Hawks &

Harriers

by Page Stegner

THE DIAL PRESS / NEW YORK 1972

5/1973
Genl

Hawks and Harriers
Library of Congress Catalog Card Number: 75–163588
Printed in the United States of America
Book design by Thomas Clemens
First Printing
1972

To my oldest and closest friend, Sherrard X. Gray,
who shares with me a certain nostalgia
for that long, lonesome train whistling down,
and to my children, Rachael *and* Page,
who, for reasons beyond their control,
may find themselves dancing
to a different tune,
this book is dedicated.

Part 1

JOURNEY TO THE EAST

1

Highway 66 leaving Flagstaff. Night. The canary perches on its little wooden peg and peeps at the dashboard lights. Ringworm's hairless skull looks like a round of moldy cheese, and Earl Scruggs and the Foggy Mountain Boys sing "When the Angels Carry Me Home" out of station XERA in Del Rio, Texas.

A bump in the road and Crowe woke to the risen moon, and he watched, for as long as he could bear the weight of his eyelids, the rock formations that loomed like phantom citadels from the floor of the plain, bathed in pale light, surreal, eternally cold. Then he slept again and dreamed he hid from a band of gaudily dressed Navajo whose sheep he had slaughtered, or was about to slaughter. They rode along the rim of a wash in which he crouched, their unblocked Stetsons bobbing above their red and purple shirts. When they passed he stood. Discovered himself surrounded. A brave who looked, oddly enough, like his old friend Aristotle Papanikolas rode up, raised a shillelagh, and smacked him square on the figment of his imagination. His head cracked and he found it lying on his pack between his feet.The driver, Orange, swerved off the road onto the shoulder, bounced over a drainage ditch, and skidded to a stop with the car sideways across the road. Lois Dishman took shape in the darkness, climbed off the floor, felt herself for broken bones, let out a long wail as she peeled the canary from her kneecap. Likewise Teeterass Smith took shape and picked himself off Ringworm, who was gibbering "I knew it, I knew it, I knew it," and then everybody began hollering at once, except Orange, who had his head out the window and was looking back down the highway. "They is a guy in the road," he said. "I almost run him over."

J. D. Crowe held his palms over his eyes and wondered what was real. A thousand miles from home, he thought, and I'm right back where I started. Is there no escaping the lunatic fringe? Earlier in the day when he had been standing beside a field of wild flowers watching a group of children playing baseball he had been admiring himself for his great good sense in finally leaving California, for having finally had the courage of a conviction that told him it was really a death trap, psychologically speaking, and not only for the transients who populated it but for the native who was born and raised on its unstable soil. He had congratulated himself for having the wit to invert the migratory process and to look for a quiet nesting ground as far from the Pacific as he could get.

He was, of course, willing to admit that had he not lost control of himself completely he might never have left. But that recent night sitting on the beach when he had had a vision, a genuine hallucination, of an angel who had appeared out of the surf and told him in a perfunctory and not very supernatural voice that some were going to fly and some were going to die—that had done it. He had imagined himself metamorphosing into a bird, wattles growing on his lip, a pain between his shoulder blades where the wings began to sprout, and he had clucked and scratched an hour in the sand, secure in the knowledge that he was one of the saved, before flying off along the railroad track that runs up the coast from Salinas to Santa Cruz.

Fortunately he had come to his senses a few hours later, in a hen house near Watsonville, trying to roost on a foul and crusty pole with twenty or thirty hostile birds. That had scared him badly. Shivering with cold, his clothes smeared with filth, chicken-shitting it home through the early morning mist, he had realized his only hope for salvation was in a different kind of flight, a complete repudiation of everything he was, a total change of scene. He knew he had become the victim of the same myths he had tried for two years to illustrate in a tiresome novel he had been writing. California had consumed him somehow, though he didn't quite know how or why. His father's death, for which he now and then held himself accountable, had a little to do with the urge to escape, but there was something more basic than that. It had to do with a question that people occasionally asked about where he was from, where his home was, and he could never decide. Born and brought up in Monterey, his father a salmon fisherman (by choice, not tradition or heritage or even need—a curious variation on the gentleman farmer theme) he could not find any real identification with the town or with his family's acreage along the coast or even the kids he grew up with, and he had come strongly to believe that if you couldn't define home you couldn't define yourself. He found it an utterly absurd position for a man of twenty-eight, unencumbered by family or relatives, and reasonably educated (the gentleman fisherman had sent his son to Andover, where he had rather quickly been expelled for disciplinary reasons, not serious enough to keep him from being accepted by a less aristocratic, less reputable school in the southwest. And so he had packed up and left in search, as he told himself, of the Holy Grail. The impulse to simply fly to New York had been overcome by the impulse to conserve his limited savings, and hence he found himself now in the demeaning and third-rate position of thumbing across the country.

At the outset there had been a Greyhound bus as far as Bakersfield and a middle-aged lady with the sweats and a son named Lonny at USC. He had heard about Lonny on the track team, Lonny on the debating team, Lonny on race riots, black power, and coastal ecology, and when he had been asked "Are you a college grad, young man"? his mind had tripped and he had replied "I am a nut, crank, soup-slurping, card-playing, baby-raping deviate on my way out of Atascadero; a tablespoon surgeon on my way to perform hysterectomies on middle-aged ladies with offspring named Lonny." That outburst had been bad enough, but less frightening than the reappearance of his angel who had advised him this time not to go out in the rain. The rain, it said, was contaminated. And in a luggage store in Bakersfield a clerk dug up an umbrella from the back room and he opened it and went tap-tap-tapping out into the desert, away.

Rain. It did rain, he believed, and if he believed it, it did. Watching the downpour through a large window without glass, sitting on what appeared to be bales of hay, and when he awoke from that dream it was dawn once again and he was sitting on his rucksack behind a Dairy Queen in Needles, eating a fifteen-cent chocolate dip and looking at the Dead Mountains. A young Mexican floated up in a pale blue suit and wingtip shoes, narrow brimmed straw hat with golf tees in the band. Asked the way to Las Vegas.

There was a pickup truck, and a delivery van, and a semi full of cold-rolled steel, and then in Flagstaff, just as it had started to rain again, three men and a girl had picked him up in a 1959 Ford sedan with a luggage rack on top and a water bag hanging off the hood ornament. Full display of window stickers—wonderful Wyoming, the Beehive State, the Royal Gorge, Cave of the Winds, The Lost World. Plastic Christ on the dash and a hula girl under a palm on the rear deck. Angora dice hanging from the mirror. A real bird cage with a live parakeet in it hanging from its own pedestal between the occupants of the front seat. They were on their way, they said, to New York City. Crowe had thought he must be hallucinating again, but he squeezed into the back next to a fat kid named Smith that everybody called Teeterass (get your ass over Teeterass, they said) because, as Smith had been quick to explain, he'd played country piano for two years in a honkytonk in Oklahoma City.

"I see," Crowe had told him, though he did not.

"Neither do I," Teeterass had agreed. "Would you care for a cocktail?" He'd passed a half-empty bottle of El Toro tequila and Crowe had suddenly perceived that it was not only the car that was loaded. Everybody was juiced, including the orange-haired man behind the wheel.

"No lemons," Teeterass had apologized. "No salt neither. Ringworm ate the salt while we was getting gas in Kingman. The whole frigging box." He cocked a thumb at the creature sitting next to him, a hairless young man, maybe nineteen or twenty with red-rimmed eyes and a brow like a six-ply tire. "This here is Ringworm. Ring-a-ding ain't altogether bright."

"I knew you gonna tell that." Ringworm had looked down his nose and closed his eyes, then jerked forward, leaned over and told Crowe in an exclusive interview tone of voice that salt helped him pee. "Anyway," he'd said, giving Teeterass a feisty glance and jerking himself back against the seat, "I'm as bright as that shit-bird is. He's so dumb he can't chew gum and walk at the same time." Crowe had smiled politely and wondered to himself how far it was to the next gas stop where he could lock himself in the men's room.

The orange hair driving the car everybody called Orange, and Orange, Crowe had soon discovered, was one of the strong, silent types whose jaw muscles worked constantly in place of a mind. Short skinny legs, so that he had to slide down on the seat to reach the pedals; huge torso with sloping shoulders. Teeterass had informed Crowe in a loud voice that Orange was the worst driver ever to lay hand to wheel. In the three thousand miles they had all been wandering around together he had hit a deer, a parked car, a dog, a half-dozen cats, two skunks ("Oh, the dreaded skunk," Ringworm had piped in), and an unrecorded number of jackrabbits.

"An' a turtle," Orange added. "We cold cocked a big ol' turtle in the Beehive state."

"He does it on purpose," Teeterass said. "He thinks it's funny. Don't you think it's funny, Orange."

"Up yours," Orange said. "Fault's with the car, not me. Shimmies like a dog shittin' peach seeds. Can't be drove in a straight line."

Crowe had sat back against the seat and closed his eyes. The girl next to Orange, Lois Dishman, a vaguely pretty but completely taciturn and stupid chick, fiddled with the radio until she picked up the gospel hour from Del Rio, Texas. Earl Scruggs and the Foggy Mountain Boys singing "When the Angels Carry Me Home," and the static suggesting that they may have already got there. Del Rio, Texas. Ten minutes of music, fifty minutes of posthumous panegyric for Jesus Christ the Redeemer, and twenty-seven ads for guaranteed baby chicks, inspected, selected, sent in a sturdy box, posthaste, postpaid. You can't escape it, Crowe had thought. The tyranny of the egg.

For a while he had watched the last of the day fade from the desert. A few mesas still visible in the distance, black projections soaring out of a vast loneliness of sand, mesquite, and stunted piñon. A single wisp of cloud still flushed against the dark sky paled to the faintest salmon ember, went out. Two horsemen materialized out of the dusk and rode along an improbable fence for a half-dozen frames before the camera panned once again across the distant plateau. Teeterass and Ringworm asleep. Lois in a bluegrass trance. Only Orange and Crowe remained conscious, and then Crowe, numbed by the tequila and too worn-out to struggle anymore, had dropped off before the film was half over.

Bump. Slam. Bang. Two elbows and some bad breath on his face and the sound of Orange's voice saying "They is a guy in the road. I almost run him over." And then everybody struggling to regain a sitting position. "I don't get why a guy would lie around in the road," Orange said. "That's a crazy thing. I don't get that."

"Might be dead," Lois Dishman said, groggily.

"Dead, dead, dead," Ringworm accused. "You run him over, you hair brain. I knew it. I knew it. That such should come to pass, I knew it."

"Shut up, ding-a-ling," Teeterass said, taking charge. He turned to Orange. "You sure you didn't hit somebody?"

"I don't get that," Orange repeated. "That's weird."

"I mean you do have a tracking instinct for warm flesh."

"So what," Lois said, already bored with the whole thing. "If you didn't hit anybody, let's split. If you did, make like the speeding bullet, man."

"That ain't Christian," Ringworm said.

Orange swung the car around and they rolled back in first gear for a hundred yards until the headlights picked up a shape in the road. It was indeed a man, on his stomach with his scalp like a night-shade over his eyes. Orange cut the engine, and then everyone was outside, forming a circle around the corpse while the wind blew a fine spray of sand across the road and periodic gusts whipped the mesquite. Crowe bent over and saw it was the body of an Indian; from the unclotted blood around the nose and ears, recently dead. Probably he had fallen asleep and bounced from the back of a truck and had never been missed. Crowe remembered reading somewhere that Indians working on road crews and returning to the reservations late at night sometimes had that happen to them.

"So now what?" Lois said. She had seen many a Hollywood red man bite the dust and was unmoved by the current spectacle. "We going to choose up sides and smell armpits?"

"*Quel sentiment exquis*," said the bilingual Smith. Then turning to Orange, "sixty-six is a main route. If we wait a few minutes somebody will come along . . . unless you'd rather they didn't." He looked musingly up into the sky.

"We ain't on sixty-six," Orange answered sullenly. "We're on sixty-one. I wanted to see a Zuñi so I turned off."

Teeterass quit looking at the stars and glanced at Orange in disbelief. "A *what?*"

"A Zuñi. The sign said there was a preservation of them out here."

Teeterass continued to fix Orange with a contemplative gaze, as if he had just discovered a new and rare animal with lots of teeth and wondered how best to capture it without getting bitten. "You know what a Zuñi is, Orange?" he asked.

"Sure," Orange lied.

"What is it, Orange?"

"It's like a . . . whatchamacallit . . . a antelope."

Ringworm, who had been following this exchange with great interest, perceived that Orange had goofed and burst into a raucous series of gulps and guffaws. "If you ain't the perfect fool," he said, mincing around and clutching himself because he had to go to the bathroom. "Everybody knows a Zuñi don't come out except in the daytime."

"How do you know, dip-shit?" Orange said belligerently.

Teeterass sat down on the bumper and put his head in his hands. "I don't believe it," he muttered. "I just don't goddamn believe it." He was about to appeal to Crowe for confirmation of his disbelief when the soporific Lois suddenly woke up and came to Orange's defense. "Hey listen, you lames," she piped. "What's it to ya, anyway. It's his car and he can go see what he wants. So fuck off, buckwheat."

"Yeah," Ringworm said, confused, turning toward Smith. "It's his car, fuckwheat."

"I was including you, stupid." Lois gave him her most withering glance and began to adjust her breasts, which had slipped down under the elastic of her empire-waisted dress. (Like a rock in a sock, Crowe thought.) The wind continued to blow, stirring a few strands of the forgotten Indian's hair. No light in any direction. The moon had hidden its face behind a scurf of cloud to the south. They all seemed frozen in their places, leaderless, unable to begin an act. Crowe told himself he was only a hitchhiker in a dream; who was he to butt in?

It was Lois again who broke the stalemate. "Well, come on. What are we gonna do with this thing, anyway?"

"Right," Ringworm agreed.

"Put him in the car and take him into Gallup," Teeterass offered from the bumper. His face was still in his hands. "Can't be too far."

"You put *that* in the car," she replied, "and you leave this kid behind."

"You promise?" he asked. He'd done it again. Lois exploded.

"Listen you," she said, turning on him and doubling her fists, "fatso. You just cool it. These aren't your wheels, they're me and Oranges, so just watch yourself or you'll be thumbing like him (pointing at Crowe). One more crack like that and your ass is grass and I'm the lawn mower."

"We could put him in the trunk," Crowe said, thinking if he didn't add something practical they'd be there all night.

"Trunk's full," Orange said.

"How about on top?"

"Mess up the luggage."

"We could tie it on the fender," Ringworm said.

Teeterass looked at him with contempt. "Oh hell yes," he said. "Maybe we could find some of those antelope horns to rig on its head and make out like we're hunters."

"I tell you we leave it right here," Lois insisted.

"I knew you were going to say that," Ringworm howled. "I just knew you'd come on like that. That ain't the right thing. That ain't Christian." He darted around to the driver's side of the car, reached through the window and removed the keys, popped them in his mouth. "If we don't do the Christian thing," he garbled, "I swallow the keys."

Lois glared at him and apparently decided that Ringworm was crazy enough to do it. "Okay," she said, coldly, "then we'll zip it up in your sleeping bag and put it up on the rack. And you can do it, too."

While they unrolled Ringworm's mummy bag and tied the body up on top, Crowe returned to the back seat to have another blast on the tequila bottle, thinking *why me? Why have I been singled out to witness this witless confrontation between red man and white? Why am I so cursed?* And he was about to send a silent request up into the sky when the doors opened and the rest of them piled in. Orange started the engine and they went shimmying off toward Gallup.

Somehow, either because the difficulty of explaining his cargo caused him to lose his nerve or because he wasn't paying attention, Orange managed to miss Gallup, and by the time the others discovered it they were eighty miles east, back on 66, and getting close to Albuquerque. Twenty miles short they stopped for gas and Crowe decided he'd cut the knot. "I got an old friend around here," he said. "I think I'll look him up."

"You wouldn't like company?" Teeterass inquired.

"He's got a very small place," Crowe said.

"Ah well," Smith told him. "Another time then."

"Just a minute," Orange said. "Nobody's leaving until we get rid of what's on top. Might be problems. I might need witnesses."

Crowe, who was by now standing outside the car, and who had five inches and thirty pounds on Orange anyway, merely smiled and said "thanks for the ride."

Orange smiled right back. "Look in your back pocket, friendo. You might want what you ain't going to find there."

Crowe checked his pockets and discovered his wallet was gone. The two hundred dollars that was in it was supposed to hold him until he found a job in New York, and he could hardly afford to walk about without it. "Hand it over," he told Orange. "You'll get it in Albuquerque. I ain't taking any chances. And it's hid, so it's no use trying to get it off me." "What's the pitch, Orange? You've got witnesses enough, and if you didn't hit that man you've got nothing to worry about. Come on, hand it over." Orange just shook his head and started the car, and Crowe, although he was exceedingly weary of the whole insane situation and mad enough to become homicidal, decided he had little choice for the moment. "Get your ass over, Teeterass," he said, climbing in.

In Albuquerque there was another long and absurd argument about who constituted the proper authority to receive a corpse; the police, the local hospital, the morgue, the Bureau of Indian Affairs. Lois was still for finding a quiet alley and disposing of the problem there. Orange opined that if they went to the police department some pig would arrest them and they'd be detained with a lot of questions, and Ringworm declared himself in opposition to all suggestions that didn't include the clergy. He furthermore informed Orange that he found the term "pig" offensive: that he had once had an uncle who had been an officer of the law (employed, it turned out, by the Board of Education to help children across the street at a school crossing), and that far from being a pig he had been the sort who offered candy and rides home to little boys and girls when he was off duty.

Orange responded to the confusion by driving through Albuquerque and out the other side—an option that seemed to satisfy everybody—and nothing more was said. Crowe's incredulity had become by this time amused curiosity. He really wanted to see how far the whole thing would go and how it would all turn out, and he spent most of the morning before he fell asleep trying to think of literary antecedents to the situation, since both characters and plot had all the verisimilitude of a third-rate detective story. Third-rate detective stories, he had long ago decided, were the best kind. They required only the most passive kind of participation.

Late in the afternoon Orange pulled in behind a filling station and diner in a little town outside of Amarillo. "I can't drive this heap another inch," he said. "I'm gonna crap out." Offers to replace him at the wheel were rejected. Orange was clearly worried that others beside Crowe might be looking for an opportunity to mutiny, and the only one he could trust, Lois, couldn't drive.

"You go ahead and crash, sweety," she said. "I'll keep an eye on these pricks."

Crowe, who had already slept for three or four hours, asked Orange's permission to go into the diner for a cup of coffee. Orange looked doubtful, but remembering that he had stashed away two hundred dollars of the man's money, finally relented. "Here," he said, handing Crowe a fifty-cent piece, "have yourself a time."

Who knows, Crowe told himself, how things come to pass? A heat wave, an empty stomach, a fishy burp in the void, a tiny tickle by fate, you're on your way. Little chances that determine the course of a private history. Our hero forgets to roll up the windows of his car. A thunderstorm comes up. He rushes to close them, and *kawhap*, a bolt from the firmament welds him to his maker. From the shock of so freakish an extinction his wife loses her baby. The soul of a future hero is flushed down the drain.

"You see," he said (the rest stop had dragged into its second hour), bending over his coffee cup and peering into the muddy eye of a waitress with whom he imagined himself in conversation regarding his predicament, "I am neither poet nor philosopher. I can no longer roll with the punch. I am, or I have become, madam, a nudnik, and that, in the parlance of those of the tribe of Judah, is a man whose sole virtue, indeed, whose only *raison d'être*, is to bore the living shit out of the rest of humanity."

The waitress, who was cleaning her fingernails with a fork, allowed her game eye to wander in his direction for a moment before it slid away sharply to the left, toward the clock above the toaster. "Let's watch the language, Charley. You're not talking to just anybody." Her tone suggested that she had seen a good many like Crowe in her years behind a lunch counter, and that while he didn't look like a nut, there was only one way to deal with the funny talkers and that was to keep them in line. Don't let them get away with too much familiarity. They'd spend twenty cents on coffee and fifteen more on a sweet roll and sit on your stool for three days telling you their history. The mistake had been hers. Seeing him come in with a knapsack and the weathered look of one who had been recently burned by wind and sun, she had asked where he was from and where he was going. She hadn't thought he'd talk about it forever, he looked so nice with his short hair and rangy build, sort of like Paul Newman in *Hud* which she'd seen for the fifth time on "Tuesday Night at the Movies." Not like the hippies that were always coming through and stopping in her place because it looked cheap. He may have looked like Paul Newman, but he talked more like hippies.

"You see," Crowe went on, warming to his subject, though in truth he had forgotten precisely what his subject was, or whether he had had one. "I think it's important to take a long, hard look at reality, however trivial, obvious, and dull, and the reality is that out of the mysterious and impenetrable instinct for self-preservation which I share with others of my species, I had to evacuate California. I'm from that coast, madam, the land of milk and honey, and the reality of California is that all the clichés are right. It has no reality; it's of the mind."

He pointed at his coffee cup and raised his eyebrows to indicate he'd like some more. "It's all shifty and vague, a sneaky concept when you get right down to it, no traditions, no social customs, no heritage, everything borrowed from someplace else." He sipped, holding the bitter heat in his mouth for a moment before swallowing, and then peering into the eye of his audience, said, "Did you know, for example (now get this), that the whole coast line is moving, north, along the San Andreas fault. One of these days Los Angeles is going to wind up in San Francisco, which for your average San Franciscan is going to be something of a culture shock. And I won't even mention the political implications thereof."

"Amazing," the waitress said, wondering why nobody ever came through from North Dakota or Maine who could tell her something she didn't read about every week and see four times a night on TV. Who the hell cared about California? "Just amazing. So you're getting away from it all, huh? On the road, huh?"

"Wrong," Crowe told her. "Wrong. On the road implies aimlessness, wandering about, thumb tripping. I, on the other hand, am making a pilgrimage to the east where I intend to find a respectable job and stimulating social intercourse among the cultured and established gentry of old America." He wondered, vaguely, why he was talking like such a horse's ass; why his mouth always got away from him and turned what was an entirely serious ambition into a joke. "My problem is that I can't seem to clear my head. I've got this imagination, you know, that won't give up. Would you believe, for example, that right now I am being held captive by four lunatics and a dead Indian?"

"No," the waitress said. "I sure wouldn't believe that."

"Well, I wouldn't either," Crowe agreed, "if I weren't from California. Things like that happen there."

"This here's Texas," she said.

"Yeah, but they started in California."

"California, California. Big deal. Everybody thinks that's a big deal. You're just running from the frying pan into the fire, kid. California's got no patent on screwballs."

"No, no," Crowe said, "you're missing the point."

"It's easy to miss."

"The point is, it's like this. If you were born in California you were born nowhere. You grew up with no sense of who you were in terms of the place you were. Like there was no protocol, no definition of your role as citizen, no expectations about what you'd become or do. People figured that when you got out of high school you'd split for parts unknown. I mean, your California product has no moral or spiritual investment in his community; he doesn't think of it as home, and if he leaves it for six weeks he can't even recognize it when he comes back. Somebody has thrown up a tract and a shopping center and a new freeway. Half the houses on the block have turned over and he finds himself with fifteen new neighbors, none of whom he'll ever know, and the orchard that used to be just south of him has suddenly disappeared and surveyor's stakes are sprouting where the noble apricot once grew. I could go on and on, lady, it's like that, it really is."

"Every place is like that," the waitress said.

"Every place is *not* like that," Crowe argued. "Sure you have change, but not overnight. Listen, I went to this school once, Andover, it's in the east, and on vacations I used to go home with guys with names like James Henry Peabody the 4th and William Prescott Otis the 10th, and they lived in houses that their grandfather's grandfather had lived in and they had attics in these houses with two hundred and fifty years of the past all stuffed in boxes and chests, and genealogy tables that went back to some schmuk who had been knighted by William the Conqueror for having scaled the walls at Burnham Castle during the battle at Maiden's Head, and I mean when those guys looked at the record they knew who they were. It was all defined. They knew what walls they had to scale, so to speak, because everybody in the history of the family since Sir Schmuk had scaled the same ones. In California nobody even has an attic. No basement either."

"And you're on your way to find yourself an attic." She offered a bored smile.

"With a basement underneath. I'm going to find me a fertile hole into which I can stick my root. And I want to tell you, madam," he said, lapsing into his demented, W. C. Fields routine, "since you have been such a patient listener, that there are some concessions I will not make." He banged his fist on the counter. "I don't accommodate relativism, polygamy, the transparent self, and the dreaded Zuñi. I believe in the essentials of rhetoric, the elements of style, the worlds of fiction, and a missing wallet with two hundred clams."

"Listen . . ." the waitress began, glancing at the clock, obviously growing tired of the conversation.

"Mnemosyne is my muse and mistress," Crowe went on, really starting now to ramble. "I follow her vagrant whims, I hop at her command, without transition, without reference to real life where things occur in an endless succession of moments ticked off one after another by the sweeping hand of an imaginary clock, a fraudulent artifact constructed by a limited imagination . . ."

The screen door on the diner banged and Crowe, turning slightly on his stool as he paused in mid-sentence, watched Tee-terass Smith come in out of the glare of a hot Texas afternoon and plop himself down with a fat man's sigh at the end of the counter. "'. . . a fraudulent artifact,' Crowe repeated, "constructed by a limited imagination, a constricting and constipated mechanism that serves no bloody purpose but to remind the possessor that he is an illusion, a random, irrelevant, unconnected memory. You think not?"

"How's things?" Teeterass said.

"Things are all right. It's people that eat it."

"I'll have a grilled cheese and a chocolate malt," Smith told the waitress.

"I'll have a brillo pad and a turkey shake," Crowe said. He made a pair of binoculars out of his hands and looked down the counter through them at Teeterass. "How long you figure this is going to go on?"

"Until the pinprick of an idea stabs Orange in the mush that passes for brain."

"I don't get it. The whole thing is so simple. Or it was simple. It might be a little hard now to explain why we hauled Arizona litter all the way to Texas, but it *would* have been simple."

"Well, not altogether," Teeterass said. "You see, Orange is an ex-con, having done a stretch at the state farm in Chino for felony assault with an automobile, and he might have had a little trouble explaining why he, of all the world's citizens, happened to be the one to find our, ah, silent companion."

"How do you commit assault with an automobile?" Crowe wondered.

"What Orange did was he ran over a guy who had put the hustle on Lois, and as he chased him halfway through a corn field to do it there wasn't much doubt in the jury's mind about malicious intent. Orange doesn't have the brains to blow his hat off, but he's smart enough now to be afraid of the law. But what I figure is we'll jettison this cargo somewhere before too long, you'll get your wallet back, and that will be that. I wouldn't worry about it."

"I won't give it another thought," Crowe promised.

Oklahoma City, Tulsa, St. Louis, Cincinnati. The farther east they got the farther they were from a solution. Orange was obviously perturbed, sighed a good deal, and gnawed at his cuticles in an attempt to think of something, but nothing seemed to occur.

Then, outside of Wheeling, West Virginia Teeterass, who had been silent for two days, leaned forward and put his arms on the backrest of the front seat. "How much is it worth to you Orange if I tell you how to get out of this?"

Orange looked sideways for a moment and then back at the road. After a while he said, "I dunno. What dya want?"

"That all depends," Smith said. "See, I can't think of any reason in the world why you would carry a body on the top of your car for fifteen hundred miles and across a half dozen states unless you did, in fact, hit it. Now if I'm wrong we can stop in any town along here and explain the problem and I imagine still get out of it clean. If I'm right, then I'll sell you my solution for, say, a hundred bucks, and I'll guarantee it."

"Hey," Crowe said. "Do a buddy a turn. Make him give me my wallet too."

"A hundred bucks and his wallet too," Smith said.

"You know I got a record," Orange grumbled. "I can't go to no cop."

"But you can't carry it around forever. You're going to have to do something."

"It'll come to me."

"It's going to smell."

"Fifty bucks."

"Seventy-five."

"Whats the plan?"

"No dice. I'll do the whole bit. You just come along for the ride."

"If it don't work," Orange said, "I'm gonna make a stain out of you."

Teeterass directed Orange into New York through the Holland Tunnel and then across town to East 10th where a musician friend of his had an apartment. He continued to refuse to divulge his plan except in stages, and the first stage, he told them, was to unload everything from the inside of the car and everything from the luggage rack except Ringworm's sleeping bag which they would cover up again with the tarp. The stuff in the trunk would be O.K., but he kindly suggested they make room for Crowe's pack since he might want to be on his way after phase two had been completed.

Smith drove uptown because he knew where he was going, and Orange sat next to Lois, chewed his cuticles some more and expressed the profound hope that whatever Teeterass had up his sleeve was going to work because he certainly didn't look forward to the mess he was going to make out of Smith if it didn't.

"When I die," Ringworm said, "I hope they bury me face down."

"How come?" Crowe asked.

"So the world can kiss my ass."

Somewhere on the upper west side Smith parked the car in front of a run-down laundry about a half block from a liquor store whose neon advertisements were the brightest lights on the street. The area seemed deserted except for an occasional figure who would emerge or disappear into one of the tenements, and Smith pronounced it perfect. "Everybody out," he said. "We're going to take a walk."

"What the hell," Orange said. "What is this, Smith?"

"You want to ditch the evidence?" Smith answered. "Take a walk."

They locked the car and headed down the street away from the liquor store. "This may take a while," Teeterass said, "but it shouldn't be more than twenty minutes."

"*What* shouldn't be?" Orange insisted, trotting on his short legs to keep up.

"The heist."

"*What* heist? What the fuck are you talking about? You tell me what's up or I'm gonna crease you right now."

"Patience, patience. It's guaranteed, Orange. Relax." He continued to walk, stopping now and then to look in a store front at the displayed merchandise. The others simply followed along. Eventually the strain became too much and Orange boiled over again.

"Listen, you fat shit, you tell me what's going on. I've had enough of this walking around in the middle of the night."

"All right," Teeterass said, "time's about up anyway. Here it is. Anybody who's ever lived in New York knows that if you leave anything in your car, or *on* your car in our case, that somebody coming along thinks might be worth stealing, it'll get stole. It's like gravity and the laws of motion. Put an empty cardboard box in your car and lock it up tight and in ten minutes somebody will come along and rip it off." He turned at the intersection and headed down the street. "Now back there on our block, out of some shadowy crack, there are two little Puerto Rican cats eyeballing that luggage rack and they're figuring on the best way to get it off quick and get gone before anybody sees them. Pretty soon one of 'em is going to saunter by like he's on his way home, and he's going to groove on those canvas tie-down straps that can be cut with a knife quicker than you can blink, and the next thing you know him and his rat-faced buddy are going to be out there, slash, slash, yo ho heave ho, and away she goes. End of problem. We let *them* figure out what to do with a dead Indian."

They had been making a wide three-block circle of the car, and Smith's projected twenty minutes was just about up when they turned back onto their street. The car was there, and sure enough, as Smith had promised, the rack was gone; so recently removed, Crowe noticed as they came up, that the hula girl on the back deck was wiggling her rubber hips beneath her palm. Jesus Christ had fallen from the dash. Orange took the keys from Teeterass, opened the door and then, noticing Crowe standing expectantly by, the glove compartment out of which he handed the wallet. "That was pretty smart, Smith," he said, "only the Goddamn luggage rack cost me twenty-seven fifty and I'm taking it out of your hundred. You should have thought of that, wise guy."

Crowe had gotten his pack from the trunk and put it on. As he started to move away, back-pedaling slowly as if he were half afraid he might be stopped again (or was it a curious reluctance to leave even *these* people?), he heard Teeterass pleasantly reply. "That's O.K., Orange. You'll probably get it back—on account of I scratched your name and license plate number on it, both sides," and then all he heard was the pounding of feet, whether his own or Smith's he could not, and dared not, tell.

2 Faded red carpet on the foyer floor, color-matched wallpaper with embossed fleurs-de-lis on the walls, plastic table made to look like marble set under an enormously useless mirror —the whole place in hopeful imitation of a better address uptown. He pushed the button under the mailbox reading Papanikolas, A. F., and after a short wait the door rattled. In the tiny elevator that smelled of vomit and pomade and took twenty minutes to rise seven floors, he was advised by a shirt-cardboard taped to the wall not to throw "airysol" cans into the incinerator and that, furthermore, an anonymous gentleman would like to suck his, yours, our joint on the roof, Tuesdays and Thursdays, seven to eleven, by appointment only. At apartment seven a surprised St. Francis, unshaven, sleep drugged, and wearing only his skivvies admitted him to the sanctuary with a surly, if not wholly displeased grunt, a "where in the hell did you come from?" and after a short inspection of the new hide-a-bed couch and the well-stocked icebox—proof that Paps had not yet turned off the tap to his ample trust fund—a dilapidated and completely exhausted Crowe confessed his willingness to stay.

"My lucky day," said Paps.

An uneventful trip. Really, Francis, I'm in no shape to retell it. In fact, I'm not sure it happened because, you see, my head is a little upset, not seriously, you understand, but a head, like a stomach or a bowel, goes off its feed now and then, clamps up, you know, and there's really nothing to do but give it a rest, let it soak for a while, trust nature to put everything back in the proper place at the proper time. A little sleep, I need, and if I could perhaps touch you for a fiver just to tide me over until I find a job, a loan, you understand, I don't intend to sponge. A little sleep first. And tomorrow I'll seek my fortune.

Sitting in Paps's apartment looking out the dirty window at the snow that spits into the canyon below. Not a tidy man, Paps. Litterbug. Clothes and papers and books and a half-eaten sandwich on the sill. Coffee cups here and there growing beasties along the bottoms. The ash tray dumped on the rug. Snow? Why not snow? Did it not rain in the San Joaquin Valley in June? Just because things never happen is no guarantee. Dirty snow through a dirty window. And the paperback open on the table is dirty. Not pornographic. Not obscene. Dirty.

Read a hundred pages to keep from going out again to hunt a job. Its soul is dingy and it sweats. Written in the muck, in the slime, in the snot and broken hair collecting in the sink trap of a public toilet. Pubic toilet. Its pathetic protagonist scrawls invitations on washroom walls and waits in his dingy, rented room for callers. No one ever comes. He fiddles and dreams and lives in a protuberant depression where men and boys escape across fields of Brussels sprouts. No one ever comes. That's the saddest thing of all. Nothing so dreary as a wallflower pasted on the cracked and peeling walls of a rented flat. The air is stale and sour as a buzzard's breath. Demeaning, actually, the job-hunting game. One really should have connections.

"The wallflower," said mock-jovial Crowe, addressing the shaving mirror on the morning of the second week, "is a noxious weed I cannot bear. Onanistic fantasies I cannot get with. The quicksand is pulling me down, chum, and the oppressiveness of my own isolation is too real to allow my imagination to be sodomized by a faggot."

I'm with you, the mirror told him. *Hurray for an opinion.*

"And yet I have been sodomized, by Christ."

By Christ?

"Sodomized comma by Christ. Somewhere along the corrugated toll-road of my life I was had."

That's a good one. Corrugated toll-road of my life.

"By what or by whom I'm not quite sure, and that, of course, is the trouble. Feel like the woman from Killnape, humped in her sleep by an ape. No wonder she found the results horrid."

All ass and no forehead.

"When you don't know who has put it to you, you don't know where to lay the blame. Think, in off-colored moments, that you might have done it to yourself. *Va te faire enculer,* as the French says."

The front door slammed and Paps came in, threw his tie on the bed, entered the bathroom and urinated while Crowe was shaving. "You might have the good taste," Crowe said, "to wait until I am finished. I am, after all, the guest."

"You're more like the camel that the Arab allowed to put its head in the tent during the sandstorm."

"And?"

"Pretty soon the Arab was out in the sandstorm."

Crowe feigning hurt. "Pappy, am I crowding you? Am I underfoot? Do I make noise?"

"Yes. All of those. And worst of all you talk to yourself continually. What were you saying when I came in? I bet you don't even know."

"I was saying as you came in that I have always been vague and without purpose, an aimless thought wandering along passageways that other men have cut through the mountain, an empty handcar rolling down the track, always moving over for the train, left to rust on a forgotten siding in the great windies of the terrible Southwest . . ."

"Wandering through iceboxes other people have paid to fill with food and drink, I see," Paps said from the kitchen. "You consumed all the beer."

Crowe ignored him, continued the self-analysis. "I am not so silly, Francis, my buddy, to think that there is any special merit or even interest in my particular case. I am, one might say, simply a footnote from underground, a parenthetical aside, a symptom, not a disease. But I have as much right as the next man to scratch, and because I am supremely indifferent to your stifled yawn, your rasping snore . . . you bastard . . . I shall continue to do so as long as I itch."

"What have you done with the Scotch?"

"I am ignoring, Francis, your overbearing manner, your boorish inhospitality . . . but if you must know, the maid drank it. Incidentally, how's the portfolio these days? It occurs to me that if I had a tenth of your ill-gotten, ill-earned, and completely undeserved private income, I wouldn't be so fucking cheap with my Scotch."

"For Christ's sake, Crowe. When are you going to get a job?"

"Soon. I'm waiting for a call."

It was incredibly hot on the street. Smog blanketed the city and clung to the buildings with the tenacity of paint. Crowe looked down Fifth Avenue from 13th Street and was barely able to make out the arch portal into Washington Square through a heavy sulphurous cloud. It was, he thought, like peering into a snowstorm through yellow lenses.

He ruined the borrowed summer suit with sweat stains. His shoes looked as if they belonged to a tar-worker. The soles of his feet blistered and burned long into the night in remembrance of pavements past. He had, unfortunately, little to offer in the way of skills, and in mid-June everybody was thinking of getting out of town and up into the Adirondacks or the Catskills or the White Mountains. He went through his spiel to a hundred different flunkies in tight pants and pinched coats. He explained to a collage of seersucker, khaki, and olive wash-and-wear that he needed a job, any kind of a job, that he had just come from the west coast as a kind of exchange student, one might say, or a D.P., or maybe just a boll weevil looking for a home, but nobody was amused and nobody was hiring.

Home. To hell with it. Try again tomorrow. Or maybe call Parker Prince up in Connecticut and pull a few strings. Owes me a few favors that shall not go unrecorded, and his wife, whom I have never met, sends Christmas cards, so he has not forgotten. Took his Latin 5 exam for him and won him a B in the course. Wouldn't have graduated without me.

Paps gone and the apartment empty. Probably with some lus-

cious chick, eating out. What was the old joke? Eating out at the
Y. Oh, but you must try the bearded clams, the tube steak, the
rolled roast. Terrific wits, my high school cronies. Back in a flash
with a sash for the gash, and crusing the drag for poontang that
never existed, and hanging around the burger pit on a Saturday
night waiting for another carload to show up with a crate of fruit
to split up and heave at each other as we speed around the residential areas of Monterey. Burning crosses in the old men's lawn
bowling green. All the good times now past and gone.

Dark in here, but cooler with the lights off. The world completely cockeyed. It's snowing up as hard as it's snowing down.
Somewhere around the third floor the flakes get caught in an
updraft and they go back past the grimy window with the same
velocity at which they fall. Somewhere in the pattern of their rise
and fall there seems the hint of a solution to my puzzle. Somewhere in those few thousand flakes that have stuck in the center
of the center pane and are building out slowly, pushing their
perimeters toward the frame that will contain them forever until
they melt and die—somewhere in that sooty crystal world there is
the answer to my melancholy riddle. It snows up and it snows
down, and I'm the little man in the ball of glass that some monstrous child is shaking in his sticky fist. He sets it on his desk and
watches the flakes settle to the bottom. When they do he turns us
upside down and I read the writing on the floor. *Today is the first
day of the end of your life.* Tell me, if you know, what is real.

3

Who knows just how things come to pass? A heat wave, an empty stomach, a fishy burp in the void, and you are on your way. Eventually, once upon a time, during that summer of meditations and excursions, it occurred to Crowe that he might wear so thin that Paps would repress his grudging but natural generosity and ask him to move the hell out. Fasting, and he had been more or less fasting since Francis had begun quoting supermarket prices over the breakfast table, was a second cousin to what he would be doing if he didn't quickly find some source of income, and although he had been holding the prospect in reserve—a last-resort possibility—he called Parker Prince and invited himself to Prince's house in New Canaan.

He had first met Parker during his brief sojourn at Andover. They had shared a course in beginning French, a semi-final position in a round robin golf tournament, and an excessive hatred for a house master named Fish who had, in place of a wife, a bow-legged cocker spaniel named Sheba. One of the reasons for Crowe's eventual dismissal had been his loud announcement to Parker one night on the stairwell just before lights out that the reason Fish's cocker was bowlegged (Crowe knew the door to the master's apartment was standing wide) was that Fish was a retired pederast who had converted to sodomy. From then on Fish had obviously gone out of his way to issue demerits to both boys, and had finally had his moment when the fate of Crowe's probationary status (on academic grounds as well as inappropriate personal conduct) had been turned over to him (as Crowe's house master) for a decision.

Three years later (he had done time in a prep school in Arizona and had been a model prisoner) he had run into Parker again during registration week on the steps of Sproul Hall at Berkeley, and they had renewed their friendship during freshman football practice that fall. Crowe played in the Blue's backfield, Parker in the Gold's line, and when a trap or a cross-tackle would go through Parker's slot, Crowe would yell "bend over, Sheba, baby, Massah Fish comin' atcha," and Prince would convulse and often miss his tackle. Their relationship had cooled a bit by the second year when they both made the varsity squad and for the first half of the season were regular starters. Parker took his football very seriously and believed what he was told about team effort and the sacrifice of the individual for the good of the whole. Crowe did not. He became something of a prima donna, and it was fatal to his career as a ballplayer. He practiced indifferently, he broke training continually, he refused to "give it all he had," and by mid-season he was second string. When, in his junior year, he missed a week of fall practice on the grounds that he was ill and it happened that his picture turned up in the Sunday Chronicle among the grinning crew of the Morgan yacht *Windswift* that had just won, on corrected time, the San Francisco to Ensenada race, he was dropped from the team without a hearing. Parker had been truly offended. Crowe, whom he thought should have been the leading ground-gainer in the Pacific eight, had let the boys down. And worse, seemed to regard it as a joke.

After college Parker had married a bank and a blond cliché named Elaine whom he had met briefly at Mills College before she flunked out and returned to the east to finish her education at Bennett. Millbrook-by-the-Leary. Unfortunately no such culture shock as Leary had ever touched Elaine.

Parker, Crowe noticed as the handshaking was going on, looked prosperous and suburban in his eleven-room stone and clapboard house four minutes from the New Canaan Yacht and Tennis Club. The good life had cost him some hair, and the top of his pants had a tendency to fold over his belt, but it was a deterioration that Crowe decided he would happily join in if he could also join in Parker's economic environment.

On the whole Parker seemed pretty much the same old good-fellow joker who had once, before big game, managed to shove a cow into the Hoover Library elevator at Stanford University and ride her to the top where she died during the afternoon carillon concert and had to be removed in pieces; the same Prince who had once in pre-med anatomy filled a plastic sack with hamburger, stuck it in his cadaver's stomach cavity, and eaten a handful during a nurses' auxiliary tour; the same chump whom everybody had called "The Prince" and whom Crowe had honestly never much liked. But Prince had money and eastern textiles in his family, and Crowe managed to confuse his admiration for the one with his faint dislike of the other.

In the den where they retired for drinks after a swim, there was a coffin that had been made into a couch and Parker had a real shrunken head on a small pedestal on his desk. "Elie refuses to come in here," he said. "Which suits the hell out of me."

They had several Pimms Cups and then Prince clapped Crowe on the shoulder and said, "What's on your mind, J. D., old buddy?"

"I need a job, Parker," Crowe told him. "I'm flat. I thought maybe you'd know somebody."

"Sure, I know lots of somebodies. What can you do? Besides read. Ha Ha." Prince had a low opinion of literature.

Crowe shrugged. "I can write."

"Ho-boy. I mean what can you do that somebody might conceivably want? Can you sell?"

"I doubt it."

"Bookkeeping, accounting, anything like that since I last saw you? What'd you do in the army? Communications? Intelligence?"

"I was a sign painter," Crowe said.

"Christ." Parker poured another drink and sliced a piece of cucumber into the glass. "A sign painter. In defense of his country."

"It wasn't bad duty," Crowe told him. "No shit details, no slogging around in the boondocks. I'd misspell every sign a couple of times and have to do them over. I kept busy."

"What else you got in your curriculum vitae?" Parker pronounced it "witty."

Crowe scratched his face. "Well, now. I spent a year in a fire tower in the Lassen National Forest perusing the horizon for smoke signals. When they finally had a fire, I was off fishing. Then I was training to be an air traffic controller in Hayward for about six months, but that didn't work out either on account of I tried to land a 707 and a Piper Apache at the same time on the same runway . . . simulation, right? I pointed that out to the instructor. No damage. Just a lot of blips on the screen. But they figured I didn't take the whole thing seriously. So after that, let's see, odd jobs, this and that. Sailing instructor, bartender. I was writing and I just took part-time gigs to keep alive."

Elaine announced dinner and they sat down to a prime rib that Crowe thought he probably could have lived off for the next six months. Parker was not one for conversation when there was food in the vicinity, so the question of Crowe's future was delayed. Elaine picked at her plate and told about Bobby's (her son's) swimming lessons, what she thought of a Mr. Wentworth's proposal to raise the club dues, and where she wanted to spend Prince's vacation. "That Vermont place of your folks, Parky," she said, "is an absolute drag. I mean there is *nothing* happening up there, and besides, it always rains."

Parker stopped chewing. "Hey, you just gave me an idea," he said through his peas with onions. He shook his knife at Crowe and swallowed. "My folks got this place up on a lake in Vermont —you remember, I must have told you about it, they had it for years—anyway, it's empty and it needs some work, painting, a few new shingles, one of the cans leaks, stuff like that, and I was supposed to get somebody to do it—sent them the bill." He put another fork load of peas in his mouth.

"So?" Elaine said.

"So now I got somebody."

"Who?"

"Him." He sighted down the barrel of his knife at Crowe.

"Him?"

"Yeah. He needs a job."

Elaine gave Crowe a look that said down three points. He belched into his hand. "Unemployed poet," he told her. "Any port in a storm."

"Listen," Parker said. "You can take my old man's car, he's in Europe for six months. And I got a load of junk to store up there that you can take along. My old clubs, stuff like that. What say?"

"No, thanks, Parker. It sounds great, really, but it's not in the master plan. I've got to find something with a future to it; something with a little stability."

"Yeah, but from what you tell me, the market's down."

"I haven't exhausted it."

"Look, temporarily, take a vacation and see what turns up. The lake's full of guys with connections. You hang around the club a couple of days and show the boys that three-hundred-yard tee shot of yours ('The kid could have been a great golfer,' he said to Elaine), and I wouldn't be surprised if you didn't just find what you're looking for. There's a lot of old money up there. Advertising, publishing, you name it."

All of a sudden it didn't sound bad. He obviously hadn't done any good so far, and a month or two in a New England spa (Crowe imagined all Vermont lakes and villages to be patterned on Saratoga Springs and Woodstock) could certainly not produce less. He pretended to vacillate for a bit, and then said in his what-the-hell voice, "O.K. What the hell. You give me a list of things you want done and a little advance," he paused, debated, decided to try it, "say a hundred bucks, and I'll do it."

"Terrific," Parker said. "Hey, I might even come up for a weekend or something and we'll tie one on like old times."

"Anytime, Prince," Crowe said. "Anytime at all."

Parker went into the den after dinner to find a bottle of special Port he had hidden away, and Crowe was left sitting in silence with Elaine. After a bit she said, "You were a friend of my husband's at college?"

He thought of telling her the truth. Put her down if she had decided his social status entitled her to be a snot. But Parker returned at that moment and, having overheard, said, "You bet."

Jack and I used to knock back quite a few together in the old days. He's the guy taught me to sail. You remember, I told you about Jack." He poured three glasses of Port into crystal liqueur glasses. "'Member the first time you took me out, Jack?" Parker turned toward his wife, chuckling. "The son of a bitch gave me a hand bailer and told me the centerboard trunk was leaking and to stick the hose down in there and start pumping. Must have sweated an hour with that thing before I looked around and saw him slumped over the tiller with tears running down his face and smoke coming out of his ears. You sure got me that time."

Elaine made no comment, did not smile, and Crowe thought, even Parker doesn't deserve you, but he smiled at her pleasantly and asked where she had attended college.

"Bennett," she said.

"Ah," Crowe said. "Is that two years or four?" Once again Elaine failed to reply.

At Parker's insistence, he spent the night and in the morning took the station wagon, golf clubs, tennis rackets, and old clothes back to New York, packed what few things he had, left Paps a note and by three in the afternoon was halfway between Danbury and Peekskill, lost, and hunting for the New York Thruway.

Three hundred miles north, near the Canadian border, there is a lake fringed with summer cottages, boat houses, docks, and floats. The Green Mountains are rolling there—except for occasional patches of hayfields—and heavily wooded with maple, elm, spruce, and cedar. The deer grazing through the lower branches of young and tender hardwoods are as thick as flies in June. Their ears twitch against the gnats as they stretch their slender necks upward toward the new growth. An inaudible something reaches them on the wind and they pause in their chewing to locate its direction and judge its potential danger. Chipmunks dance across a stone wall that has survived over a hundred years, and along an ancient split rail fence a porcupine waddles—an awkward, stupid collection of needles and guts whose reason for existence must be unknown even to its creator, a dim little brain in the midst of a pincushion that propels itself down through the woods in search of nothing at the end of nowhere.

A pileated woodpecker knocks holes big enough to put your fist through in a birch tree. The thrushes are singing in the chokecherry bushes: a creeper creeps up the trunk of an old and twisted elm. On the lake a Johnson Sea Horse snarls around in circles, towing a stiff-armed buffoon with boards on his feet.

In a cove along the northern shore there is a dock that sticks out over the water. Made of spruce planks and propped underneath by flat rocks, it has rings on its fingers for mooring boats. Underneath it there are minnows and a dead perch that has washed ashore. When it begins to rot, some editor will remove it.

A girl lies on a flowered beach towel, her face on her arms, her toes dangling over the side. Judging from the width of the dock, she is tall—nearly six feet—and from the darkness of her skin, she has been a long time in the sun. Her hair is copper and her two-piece suit is the color of her eyes and the water. Green as a fern in the middle of the woods, when the light is fading and the shadows have fallen long over the clearings. Green as the moss that grows along the brook through the pasture. Color so deep you can fall in and drown.

When the wake from the Sea Horse reaches the shore the swells wash up over the bottoms of her feet and waken her. She sits up on her towel and pushes damp strands of hair away from her forehead; fumbles around for sunglasses and looks out across the lake. She ties the straps of her suit and wipes perspiration from her squarish chin; reaches over the edge of the dock and cups water in her hands. She sloshes it on her face. The waving buffoon on the water skis gets no response from her as he planes by on one leg, and after a few minutes she gathers up her towel and sun lotion and walks up the path toward a shingled cottage hidden in the woods.

Around dinnertime Crowe reached Albany and stopped at a Howard Johnson's to get something to eat. The all-go-hungry hash house where a hamburger is a hamburger and the trimming is a bun. He settled for a tired-looking slice of rhubarb pie and a tepid cup of coffee that tasted suspiciously of detergent; lived to regret both. From Albany to Glens Falls they had an argument and left him with a cracked block in Rutland.

By midnight he was winding through a pitch-black forest somewhere in northern Vermont, headed, he hoped, for Montpelier. There were no cars on the road and every farmhouse was dark. His headlights would suddenly gleam back at him out of the vacant night and he would get a glimpse of glass and frame and weathered clapboards. A little fantasy kept running through his head. The houses were not only dark, they were empty. The whole northeast had been evacuated while he groaned his hour in truck-stop gents' rooms and he was now driving deeper and deeper into a deserted land toward the center of a defoliation zone that the military was soon (in fact, any minute now) going to transform into Nevada.

At one-thirty, twenty miles beyond Montpelier, he was sitting by the side of the road out of gas. The road map told him he was somewhere between East Cabot, South Cabot, Lower Cabot, Cabot Junction, Cabot, and Cabot's Corners. The fuel gauge told him he was a fool. It was cold. The engine heat was soon gone and the heater of no use. He yearned for New York City, that magnificent, overwhelming, suffocating, sweltering gas oven for people of all races and creeds. And when he exhausted that vision he yearned for California and a warm summer afternoon on the beach eating sandwiches and sand and watching the breakers smash against the rocks.

Never happy where I am, he thought. If I'm east, I wish I were west. If it's cold, I wish it were hot. If it rains or snows, I long for sunshine and soft winds. If I went to the Ganges, I would undoubtedly pretend it was the Mississippi and the greasy smoke from the burning ghats a steamboat 'round the bend. A phenomenon of displacement that has nothing of the greener pastures business in it. I know that the other side of the mountain is just as barren as this side, but logic and reason have nothing whatever to do with a footloose imagination. My mind is a hitchhiker and it has made me a perpetual exile. Prometheus has his vulture, Sisyphus his rock. I have excursions around my cerebral globe.

It was along this stretch of road, by the banks of a burbling brook, that he met Sandy. He could hear her coming for miles before he could see her lights in the trees, and he stood by the rear end of his defunct car and waved a thumb as she came into view. She stopped two hundred feet beyond him and backed up.

"I'm out of gas," he said when she rolled down the window. "Is there some place near here where I can get some?"

"Not at this hour." Her voice was husky and he thought she must have a cold. In this climate everybody must have a cold. "Where are you headed?"

"Cedar Lake."

She leaned over and opened the door. "Climb in."

"I hate to put you out," he lied.

"If you don't want to put me out, why'd you stop me? Come on, it's cold. I *live* on Cedar Lake."

In his somnambulistic state he wandered around shoving dream boxes into phantom cars, transferring fictitious canoe paddles and tennis rackets and golf clubs, thinking she must regard him as retarded or spastic as he stumbled in the shadows, dropping bags and trying in a slow motion frenzy to slam shut a dream vision trunk with his gossamer overcoat in it. His long-standing disagreement with rhubarb had left him weak and once they were on the road again he sank back into padded air and let his unconscious blur. A fuzzy line of trees blew past the car and the monotonous whine of her low pressure tires lulled him into an intense stupor. On the radio two Canadian politicians argued about slum clearance in Montreal, their voices rolling around in the warm car, and for a time he thought he was Helmut Dantine driving through the Harz Mountains in the bed of a canvas covered army truck. Its cleated tires droned on the asphalt and uniformed figures swayed on invisible benches . . . like corpses hanging from a beam. He peered through the little window behind the cab and saw Paps driving, Sandy seated beside him. Paps smoked a Mississippi Crook and his hand was up her dress. Crowe pulled his luger out of his rucksack and snapped in the clip, but when he turned to fire it he saw he was mistaken. The driver was only a corporal with a scar on his cheek and seated beside him a second lieutenant. Dreaming again.

Eventually lights glowed through the canvas and after bumping down a half mile of dirt road the truck stopped in front of a lake where they all piled out. Some truck. Another mistake. A three-month-old Cadillac Eldorado with everything in it but an auto-pilot. And there is no lake in Clausthal. These mountains are not the Harz.

4

Time and space without borders . . . a patch of sky, white bars beyond the glass, a curtain of green, a smear of metallic blue, a strand of cloud suspended in the morning sky. When Crowe woke he looked down a slight hill through a grove of birch trees to the lake. The bed, an ancient refugee from some farmhouse auction, was on a level with the windowsill, and he lay on his side, his nose nearly touching the glass. Along the shore the twisted wrecks of a half-dozen cedars canted at crazy angles over the stones—knocked cockeyed by a falling spruce. The sun rose behind the house and the birches just outside began to radiate like the coils of a heater, until the sun caught its outriders and turned on the day.

In truth, that first morning he missed all of this. In truth, he missed the morning altogether, and if it hadn't been for the racket a couple of boys made dragging an aluminum canoe down the path to the dock he might have forgotten where he was (a tiresome phenomenon) and lain searching in vain for peeling paint and cracked plaster. It was the temperature that put his subconscious at rest. He unquestionably was not in New York.

Off his bedroom he discovered a small bathroom with a bidet and a shower stall. The bidet came as a surprise. He stood staring at it for quite some time, his mind unmoored and drifting; turned one of its gold plated knobs and shot a geyser into the air. A fountain, he thought. Set to shaving his teeth and brushing his face.

In the kitchen he found some dry oatmeal left over the winter and forgotten by the mice, ate it dry by the handful, went outside

to look around. A woodpile along the north side of the house—
half of it rotten—a boat trailer rusting in raspberry bushes growing up along the side of the boathouse, a bunch of cedar posts
stacked in a neat grid by the path to the lake; everywhere low
growing vines and saplings that needed clearing. Crowe went
along the porch leading into the house from the drive looking for
tools and found a note from Sandy pinned to the door—an offer
to help retrieve the borrowed car. First things first. The weeds can
wait.

In a closet off the living room he discovered the phone, dialed
the number on the note, got no answer, went out again and
walked down to the lake. From the dock he could see the boys
paddling the canoe along the shore on the opposite side of the
cove. Main body of water some two to three hundred yards out,
takes a dog leg to the left, and if you strain memory and imagination you can just see beyond the tip of the point where a fleet of
Sunfish are sailing around a raft moored in the center of the lake.
They form and reform and cut across each other's bows and
sterns, and then the sound of a whistle floats out of time and
thirty seconds later the bang of a gun and you understand what
they are about.

In the cove the houses are all back from the shore and hidden
from view by an indiscriminate forest of spruce, white pines,
birch, and cedar. Here and there a dock protrudes into the lake,
and from the end of the point the corner of a boathouse peeks out
through a bramble of blackberry bushes. A sailboat is moored in
the pocket of the cove, the reflection of its hull wriggling in the
water.

A half mile away the Sunfish are beating down on an orange
course marker like a covey of bright-winged butterflies. Those
who have rounded the buoy merge with those still approaching
and all motion appears solidified for a moment, as if the flock has
paused to feed on a sticky piece of fruit. Then the line thins out
and they flee away to the south chasing a fickle breeze.

The day was deceptively bright with a strong wind from the
northeast and it was chilly on the dock. The water that had
looked so blue and inviting from his bedroom was the color of

gunmetal, and he went back through a clump of cedars along the path to the house. Buttercups in the short grass, and in the shadow of a fallen log a jack-in-the-pulpit with a ladybug perched on its stamen.

The porch was sheltered from the wind and he sat down in a drunken looking deck chair that someone had forgotten to put away at the end of the summer past. It wobbled badly and the canvas ripped a little when he eased back, but it held and he put his feet up on the railing to relax and think. The situation needed review. The sudden switch from sweltering city to cool pastoral was a bit disconcerting. No food in the house. Car stuck on the side of some road . . . didn't know where. Hadn't the faintest idea of where he was in relation to the village. Things needed to be done, but he couldn't organize himself to do them. Same old problem, he thought. In the midst of outlining his battle plan he fell asleep.

There should be here recorded a significant dream, preferably in technicolor; something full of portents, ominous rumblings in the background, flashes of lightning from a prophetic storm. Unfortunately most of Crowe's dreams occur when he is awake. When he sleeps he experiences the oblivion of death. He had no dream, no vision, but he did hear a voice rattling his tympanum . . . a husky voice . . . a woman's voice . . . and with a violent effort he jerked himself out of a murky swamp and into the sunlight. The canvas split with an obscene *FZZZzzz* and the rum-dum chair passed out. He found himself on his ass looking up at an amused Sandy from the wreckage of lath and cloth. "Sleep well?" she asked.

She was wearing a pair of Levis and a man's T shirt. "I was," he said.

"You want to get your car?"

"Not particularly." He lay back on the porch and felt the little stripes of coolness on his shirt where the air blew up the cracks between the warm boards. "Do you?"

Unamused. "If you want me to take you over there, let's go. I have a guest and I have to get back." She took her foot off the porch and started around the path to the drive in back of the house. Crowe was tempted not to follow just to see if she would come back, but he guessed she wouldn't, and after all, he thought, the car isn't mine. If I leave it laying around on the roadside, some derelict Vermonter will strip the tires off and I'll have to explain that to Connecticut. So he got up and pursued her.

Things didn't go very well at first. Sandy did not appear to be a great conversationalist and, as Crowe was to find out in the course of the summer, never felt the need to fill in silence with idle talk. She was moody, given to ignoring the answers to questions she would ask (and then re-ask minutes later), and she had an irritating habit of popping non sequiturs into any discussion at any time. "Sandy," he would say, "did you ever notice how when you are walking down a long, flat highway it gets thinner and thinner until it disappears in the distance and no matter how fast or how long you keep walking you can never . . ."

"What side of your face do you shave first in the morning?"

The profound analogy between highways and life is shot. Philosophy bows to trivia. He tries to remember whether he begins on the left or the right but he cannot. No matter. Sandy has jumped off the float and is swimming toward elephant rocks.

But that first day when she took him out to his car there was an additional air of hostility between them that Crowe thought strange for two people who hardly knew each other. Sandy made the offer of a favor sound a little like an obligation, and the plush enormity of her Cadillac Eldorado parked in the drive struck him as doubly ostentatious up in the backwoods of Vermont.

"Too bad about your car," he said.

"It runs."

"Maybe we could just send *it*," he said.

On the way to the village Crowe fiddled with the air conditioner, the heater, the radio, the power window, the power seat. He became obsessed with knobs and dials and levers. The radio had an automatic station selector; when he pushed a button it kept clicking through positions until it found a signal strong enough to suit it. "What's the matter with you anyway?" Sandy asked.

"Nothing. Just running through the pre-flight check. *Buurrr-*

zzzzz. Hello, control tower, this is Cessna three five eight alpha, requesting take-off instructions, altitude, temperature, and winds aloft. *Buurrrzzzzz.* Over. You certainly have green eyes, young lady."

"They come with the car."

If she had been unattractive he wouldn't have found it necessary to be snotty or to fool around with all the gadgets as if he were some kind of primitive tree dweller just witnessing his first machine. If she had had moles or hair on her lip or was skinny, he would have accepted the ride without worrying about his relations with the driver. He would have spared her the poor-relative clown act. But she didn't have moles or a moustache; and that T shirt. . . . Crowe could not keep his eyes off her chest, and did not. She had hair like polished cherry, and her eyes, her eyes . . . I have already described for you her once-upon-a-time eyes. He looked for flaws. Her front tooth was chipped . . . her mouth could be fuller . . . a bit more lobe to the ear. . . .

"What are you staring at?"

"I don't know," he said. "Nothing. Nothing at all."

"Boy, you make me nervous, you know that? I hardly know you and you act like you'd never seen another human being before." She skidded the Cadillac off the road and bumped in to the Shell station.

"Well," he said, "it's just that I'm not used to the surroundings, you see." He flicked some imaginary dust off the leather armrest.

"This car really bugs you, doesn't it?" she said, irritably.

"Well, I'm not responsible for my father's taste in automobiles, and I learned a long time ago not to crap in my hat if I still have to wear it."

"Really?" Crowe said, delighted. "Me, too. I learned that too."

When the attendant got around to them, she asked him, "Did you bring a can for gas?"

"No." She knew perfectly well he hadn't.

"What did you expect to put it in? Your shirt pocket?"

"My shoe. I forgot my money too, but I expect your credit is good." An inauspicious beginning. The embarrassing thing was that he *had* forgotten his money, left it in the glove compartment when he abandoned ship the night before, and he had to bum a dollar to pay for the gas. They drove out to the car without saying much and when she let him out he felt like a perfect fool. "Look." he said. "I don't know how we got off on this foot today, but I appreciate the help. How about stopping by for a drink on the way back?"

"Do you *have* anything to drink?" she asked, looking amused for a change. He not only had nothing to drink, he had nothing to eat either. Shook his head, smacked his brow, was smitten when she laughed. "You really *are* something else," she said, and backed over his toes.

On the way back to the lake he stopped at a market with a state store in the rear and bought three quarts of Beefeater's, a fifth of Noilly Prat, and a huge bottle of olives stuffed with pickled onions.

"I am a martini drinker," he told the clerk. "I have never been a martini drinker before, but I am inspired by the environment. I have acquired an image of myself, standing at sunset on the porch, staring across the lake as lights on the opposite shore wink on, one by one. Blue-blazered, tennis-shod, lonely, I stand swizzling my pickled onion in a long stemmed glass, reflecting on the eternal isolation of man in an alien and unregenerate universe. Sort of like Jay Gatsby, who in certain ways I resemble."

"A-yup," the clerk said.

Crowe bought, in addition, a quart of Scotch and one of bourbon; triskets, rye crisps, corn chips, several varieties of cheeses, including a Roquefort dip in a plastic container, liver paste, macadamia nuts, several cans of crab meat, maraschino cherries, and some napkins. In the grocery department he purchased two pounds of hamburger and a sack of potatoes. Then he went home and called Sandy. "The cocktail hour is a little gone by," she said. "We're eating dinner." He looked at his watch. Quarter to eight.

"What are you having?"

"Beef Wellington."

"I'm having worms and oatmeal. How about after dinner?"

"How about what after dinner?"

"How about coming over for a drink after dinner." Getting exasperated. She's playing stupid.

"Well, I told you, I have a guest up from Connecticut . . . staying the week . . ."

"Bring her along."

"It's not a her."

"Bring him along. He can have a drink, too."

Small pause. Then, "I'll take a raincheck if you'll give it."

"Don't go out in the rain," Crowe said. "It's contaminated."

He hung up, irritated that he could be irritated, drank a glass of gin, fell asleep on the couch. Bum dreams. No dreams at all.

Crowe did not see Sandy for almost a week after she took him to his car; then he ran into her in the local store one afternoon buying ice-cream cones for her two little brothers and a half-dozen of their sticky-fingered friends. He recognized by their squeals the kids from across the cove.

"How are you getting on at Prince's?" she asked. He said he was getting along fine, was about to add something on the virtues of isolation when one of her entourage dropped his double-decker on the floor and during the howling scuffle stepped in his own mistake. Crowe, on his way out the door, told the proprietor that when he had finished at the gas pumps there was a little chocolate ripple waiting for him inside. Then he went home.

From his front porch he could see her dock, and two or three times in as many days, when she was out there, he started to go down to the lake. Going to swim casually by as if he were on a marathon around the cove and just happened to notice her. But each day somebody would be with her by the time he had gotten his trunks on and he had to let it go. Somebody, he assumed, was her guest from Connecticut, though he later found out somebody was her father.

Burt Rinelander. Sandy's father. A World War II naval officer who had exchanged power for sail and who, judging from the number of expensive boats moored out beyond his dock, had been

unable to shake the call of wind and wave. Almost every afternoon the whole family would come down and go sailing, and
because Crowe had at one time spent a good part of his summers
racing on a neighbor's Star off the California coast, he took more
than casual interest in the way they sailed. The old man was crazy
for anything with a planeing hull that was bigger than a Sunfish.
Every Wednesday and Sunday afternoon the Rinelander fleet
(one Thistle, one 505, and a Flying Dutchman) went out to
compete in the local races. There wasn't anything on the lake that
could come close to them, so it was strictly a family competition.
Just as well. A good skipper could have beaten them with a
bathtub. Crowe had fantasies . . . appearing from behind the lee
of the cove in the old Star, sailing up to the starting line just
before the gun, striking terror in Rinelander's heart, beating him
so badly that he died of it and was given a Norse burial in his
flaming Thistle. He never became very fond of Burt.

Fantasy and fact did not merge. In fact, he just lay around the
house reading, eating, and sleeping. Did some work on the boathouse, as Parker had requested; sent him the bill. There *was* a
beautiful, wooden-hulled Thistle in there, but he couldn't find the
sails, and after the first inspiration to put it in the water and *really*
try to beat Rinelander, inertia overcame him and he went back to
the house to take a nap. The place was always quiet as death. The
phone never rang. No traffic, and only an occasional motor boat
or the shouts of the kids across the cove to interrupt the silence.
Great place for meditation, for writing poetry, for painting land-
scapes. Crowe was not really sold on it at first. Kept having an
itch in the bone marrow and no way to scratch it; a gnawing sense
of purposelessness that should hardly have surprised him but did.
If you work eleven months a year, he told the woodwork, and are
productive in some way, then goofing off for a few weeks doesn't
bother you. But an unearned rest is an unquiet grave, and when
there is no immediate prospect of its ending, things become even
worse. He was back in the sophomore doldrums, asking himself
over and over what he was going to do. Indirection is not strictly
a schoolboy's disease, he thought. The old man used to tell me
when I would go down to Monterey on the weekends that the

occupation didn't matter, only how well you did it. "Be a plumber," he'd say. "Be the best plumber there is. Don't be all the time worrying about who you are. Just keep busy and pretty soon you find out." Platitudinous Pop. Pretty soon you find out all right. Keep busy at what? I'd tell him I couldn't find anything I was interested in enough to keep busy at, and then he'd really start in. "When I was a boy," he'd say, "when I was a boy. . . ." I heard it a thousand times. "When I was a boy . . ." and then he treated me to the depression, to the price of a pork chop, to the nickel ice-cream cone Saturday night splurge and to how, when twenty-five years ago he had decided the tracks that had been greased for his wheels led in the wrong direction, he had left the office in which he had a fancy high-paying job and moved to Monterey, bought some land and a boat with the money Crowe's grandfather had left (and enough AT&T stock to keep the coin rolling in every quarter), and had become to his eternal peace of mind, a fisherman. "The thing is to not sit around and mope."

"Times have changed, Pop."

"Sure, sure. Times have changed. Too bad for times."

Sandy and her older brother sailed the Thistle and the two younger kids sailed the 505. They were all bad sailors and could have profited from a good book on fundamentals, but they at least got around the course without turning over or falling out of the boat. Burt and Hermina (bride of forty years) were something else again. Pretense, but very little style. From the porch Crowe watched them row out to the Dutchman in their little red dinghy —blue topsiders, foul weather gear, yacht caps, the whole shiteree. Hermina cranks up the mainsail without the battens, discovers her error, pulls it down, puts in the battens, hauls it back up as far as the spreaders—the crank falls out of the winch and the whole mess comes down on top of her. Eventually she gets it up. Burt steps into his little sling diaper so that he can hang out in the trapeze when the puffs hit, unfurls the genoa, and off they go. He forgets to unclip from the mooring and when the painter pays out they are suddenly snubbed short. Like hitting a reef. Burt goes in the drink. Sidesplitting.

Once they are away from the mooring the comedy begins in earnest. Burt crouches on the gunwale hanging from his trapeze wire, and shouts orders to Hermina about lifts and headers and approaching boats. When a puff comes he hikes out, legs stiff, body almost perpendicular to the deck, the water slapping at his behind. Does that part very well for a man of sixty-three, keeps the boat flat in the water so that it gets up into a plane. Spray flies from the bow, everything just dandy, but then the puff lets up or maybe Hermina loses the tiller and the boat swings around into the wind and he takes another bath. The trapeze clip doesn't let go and Burt is towed through the water like a water skier, inhaling the lake, shrieking at the old lady to come into the wind, slack the main, uncleat the jib sheet, turn him loose.

If at first you don't succeed, quit. But Burt never quit on anything. It wasn't in his blood. Or his genes.

The Rinelanders lived in an enormous house, Crowe discovered (by snooping through the woods); two stories of dark shingle with high peaked roofs and oversized dormers and a bedroom wing that looked as if it would adequately serve a small hotel. Around the house there was lawn on four sides that extended thirty or forty feet across to a low stone wall beyond which the woods served as an impenetrable shield to the less advantageous world outside. He also learned from a gossipy cleaning lady who came two weeks late to "open the camp" for him that the Rinelanders were among the oldest families on the lake. "He's from Boston, I believe, or thereabouts, and the missus comes from New York. Lots of money, oh, my. I wouldn't venture to guess."

"Where does it come from?" Crowe asked.

"I heard it was something to do with machinery, but I couldn't tell. 'Spect he inherited it, most of 'em do. He don't behave like he just got it yestiddy. Well, being as you're in, I'll go along."

"Good-bye," Crowe said, his appetite for the Rinelander daughter suddenly increasing until it gave him heartburn.

One evening near the end of July Sandy appeared at the porch door in some sort of wispy thing that fell from hip to knee in soft yellow folds. The sun was at her back, burnishing her hair, outlining her legs through the material of her dress, and as she stood there a moment waiting for Crowe, from the depths of an armchair, to offer some shock of recognition, his mind clicked, the photograph was taken and its negative catalogued in the overstuffed file of remnants and recollections.

That is how I first see her when I travel back. Copper and gold and indescribably lovely.

"Whatever happened to that raincheck you were going to give me?" she asked.

He pondered. "Don't know," he said. "I give up. What did happen to it?"

"Maybe you drank it?" she offered.

"No. Don't remember that. Come in and I'll see what I can dig up, like maybe a bottle of cream soda or a Dr. Pepper or something. Clam juice, ammonia, oven cleaner?"

"Did you ever have a Dr. Pepper?"

"I don't think I did."

"Did you ever *know* anybody who had one?"

"Come to think on it, I guess not."

"Did you ever know anybody who chewed Mail Pouch or used Burma Shave?"

"Sure. Practically everybody."

"Oh," she said. "Then I guess it pays to advertise. Can you come to supper tomorrow night? Burt's doing his Greek lamb thing for all his golf buddies, and he told me he didn't think he could get through it without you. He said he's absolutely frantic you haven't been over to see him yet."

"Who's Burt?" Crowe asked, not yet knowing his captain's name.

"Burt is . . ." she put her index finger between her eyes and gazed into the trees. "Well . . . Burt is somebody, I don't know exactly who. He lives at my house and we call him daddy, but other than that he's just sort of a puffy, inarticulate guy with grey hair and money and not too much sense."

"I believe I've observed the gentleman out there," Crowe said, waving toward the water.

"Yes," she said. "You admired his taste in cars, too."

"So I did. Tell Burt I'd be delighted. Tell him I thought he'd never ask."

"He'll be so pleased."

They were still standing by the doorway and Sandy turned to go. "What about your Dr. Pepper," Crowe said. "You can't leave yet; you haven't quite got here."

"You drink mine. You can tell me how it was tomorrow." She started up the path to the drive, high heels wobbling slightly on the uneven ground, then turned around and came back a few steps. "Incidentally," she said, "how shall I announce you when you make your entrance?"

"Announce me?"

"Your name, dummy. I don't believe I've had the honor."

"Lord Jim," Crowe said. "Tell Burt."

5 Lord Jim goes back to his armchair and his book, but his mind is restless and goes for a long walk where it is twilight at noon and the sea and the sky run together at the edge of an undelineated world. Foghorns croak across the cold, grey waters of Monterey Bay. The winds are from the northwest and they are piling up terrific swells that sweep down along the coast, battering the headlands from Cape Mendocino to San Simeon, nibbling away at the rotten cliffs until they avalanche into the surf and are ground to bits by the swirling waters.

He dreams of Monterey harbor where the fishermen are beginning to return to their moorings, unloading their catch, calling it a half-day and considering an afternoon at home puttering around their boats wiser than arguing with a churlish Pacific blow. He can see them as they take shape out of the fog and chug in past the breakwater, each boat with its perpetual escort of gulls. The gulls' cries are muffled in the heavy air.

And the house, old now, but old even when his father bought it at the end of the second world war, its shingles blackened by years of damp air. Near the ground they are rotted and the wood has turned to mulch. The rear porch sags. Screens are torn and rusty. A grotesque old place with cornices and gables and arched windows: three floors of Victorian gingerbread all gone to ruin. The paneling inside is dark wood and there are a half-dozen tile fireplaces whose chimneys have long been choked with soot and crumbling mortar and the nests of departed birds. In the kitchen the floor slopes toward the sea.

There is a sun porch along the western side of the building and it is from this vantage point that he can watch the boats return. There was a parrot out there once, and its droppings have stained the floor. His mother fed it sunflower seeds and taught it four or five phrases, but when she died it quit talking and after a year of silence died too. The sun porch is the emptiest part of the house now. All the other rooms are stuffed with furniture—heavy old couches covered in faded velvet with worn linen doilies on the back, cushions and arms, a ponderous chair of a similar design, lamps with fringed shades and sockets for three bulbs, corner shelves filled with china gimcracks that his mother collected and that has never been dusted or cleaned since her death seventeen years ago.

The old man cared nothing for the house after she died, let everything go to seed and expended all his energy on his boat. You could have eaten an egg off the deck of his boat, but his house he let fall to pieces as if he hoped it would eventually collapse and he would be rid of it, only he didn't live long enough to see that collapse, not the physical one, anyway. The human one he watched, but if it concerned him much he didn't say, preferring the isolation of his boat and the emptiness of the ocean to his depleted family, until his children drifted away like brush on the river and there was only one left to hate him and to bury him when his boat blew up one evening somewhere off Point Sur because fuel had leaked into the bilge from a faulty tank that his one remaining son had been told to weld, and had not. . . .

From the path, as you walk along the bluffs toward town, you can see the lights across the neck of the bay, a weird incandescence through the fog. The winds are inland and carry the sounds of Monterey away from the sea, and sometimes on a quiet night you can hear the clatter of dishes from the restaurants along the wharf and jukebox sounds from the bars.

And he dreams the cypress tree is full of cats who clamber about and build nests among its spiky boughs; dreams of parrots and musty furniture and windows without glass, and of a wind-chopped sea where there are bits of charred wood floating, a splintered mast, pieces of cork, all widely disseminated by a storm that has just blown over. A thermos jug bobs along like a drifted mooring, a foot of line still attached to its red plastic top. A herd of grey whales passes by on its way to southern waters, oblivious of the litter. Farther down the coast, almost to Point Conception, a bloated grey cat without fur floats like a fetus in the gentle cradle of the swells. A fisherman's boot washes in the foam off San Miguel Island.

6   Storm clouds in Vermont are another matter. The mountains around the lake are just high enough to give one the sense of enclosure but not high enough to detract, and the air so pure the edge of each billow is clean and precise. Seem to pile up forever, every stratum with its own particular light and velocity. Not at all like the California coast, Crowe told Sandy, as they sat on the sloping lawn in front of her house. Storm clouds there are without dimension. Low and flat and mean. No grand cathedrals, no fortresses, no Olympian anvils against the heavens. "The sky looks like a slab of moldy rhubarb pie," he told her. "Can't hardly tell it from the sea."

"I've never been farther than Lake Michigan," she said, "but I'm going in September."

"Consider yourself lucky," he said. "Stay home. Bad news out there. Pretty, but hard on the soul."

She lay back on the grass and put her hands behind her head and stared at the sky. "Home," she said, "is not my idea of a place to stay. Home is Brookline, Mass. and Brookline, Mass. is where we don't drink and we don't screw and we don't go with the boys who do."

"Chew, I think it is."

"Times have changed."

"Too bad for times."

"In Brookline nice girls wear tennis shoes and white socks and pretty little high-collared blouses with a pin at the throat, and they talk very softly [voice dropping to a murmur] and they all go to *caw*llage at places like Pine Manor and Briarcliff Manor after they finish up at Westover and Miss watch'ma-callit's and it's all so frightfully boring, da'ling [drawling through her nose] that it gives me a top drawer [her own voice] class A-one, pain in the ass." She sat up suddenly and fixed him with her big green eyes. "So I reject that advice, Lord Jim. I don't want to stay home. I want to go west. Tell me about the west."

"Yes. Well all I know is what I read in the papers," Crowe said with a shrug. He was beginning to wonder if they were ever going to be able to talk without turning everything into a joke. "What I read is that out there beyond the mighty wall of the Sierra Nevada lies a land of lemon and lime, loquät and lantana, love-in-a-mist and love-lies-bleeding; a land of every-day-fun clubs where folks gambol about in sun, surf, and sand, bikinis and beach walkers, and nobody works and nobody worries. Quiff and quaff all day long. All the girls are blond and all the sports got cars, and everybody drives around all day just trying to find where it's at."

"My, my," Sandy said. "Why on earth did you leave?"

"I found out where it's at," Crowe said, and then he lay back on the grass and watched the clouds drift by. "I found out when my house filled up with a collection of walking parodies who couldn't talk about anything but cellular consciousness and post-trip satisfactions, who couldn't read anything but Richard Brautigan, who couldn't listen to anything but acid rock, who dressed up like Navajos and neo-expressionist cowboys, who didn't look good, who didn't smell good, who weren't good; and I just got tired of all that love and flowers horse-shit, because when you came right down to it that crowd was about as mean and surly a bunch of sons of bitches as I ever met. I wasn't wild about my membership. I'm not wild about cults of any kind. I'd as soon join Kiwanis."

Sandy smiled and gave a tolerant look that made him suddenly feel rather old. "You just did," she said, waving her arm down toward the barbecue pit where her father and some of his cronies were gathered. Burt had on a large apron that said CHEF on the bib and below that a pop art hamburger with the instructions, EAT IT, in bold red letters. There were some other hysterical

quips printed along the fringe, like SOUP'S ON and COME
'N GET IT.

"That's the power elite," Sandy said. "You might think that
brown thing stuck under the nose is a cigar, but it isn't. It's a
plug, a bung, actually, for the bunghole. If you remove it the
stuffing falls out. And I'd rather join your cult than theirs, you
see, because I think it's better to be driving around looking for
where it's at than to have given up and died on the first tee. I'd a
whole lot rather be a parody than a packhorse for a bunch of golf
clubs. I mean, you ought to *talk* to some of those people. They're
really unbelievable."

The clouds were turning pink at their tops; the sky a pale
amber where Crowe could see it through the trees. A Mr. Somebody came up in a pair of yellow canvas shoes and maroon slacks
and began talking to Sandy. Said how-do-you-do and broke most
of the bones in Crowe's hand, and then Crowe tuned him out. A
blue, porky smoke rose out of the barbecue pit below and seeped
away through the maples surrounding the lawn, and there was a
distant barrage of thunder. The lawn tickled his neck. The bone
crusher gave a play-by-play of an eternal golf match. The Adi-
rondacs got a drenching. He lay there in the grass thinking of a
hill near the Carmel Valley, and of the squalls that blow in off the
Pacific and obscure it in sheets of rain. "Double-bogied the nine-
teenth," somebody said. "Ha, ha."

The fireflies were beginning to turn on in the closing twilight
and with the evening warm and breezeless the distant storm
seemed like some celestial prop to enhance the cookout, the
thunder background music to the clinking of ice cubes and
glasses, barks of laughter, voices mingling with the smoke up in
the trees. "Always a pleasure to meet one of Sandy's young men,"
the maroon pants said. "Think I'll go build myself another
drinky." Wafted away on yellow shoes. Firefly hung up in the
grass. Blinkety blink.

"Infuckingcredible," Sandy said.

"I don't know," Crowe said. "Everybody has his own style."

They took their plates down to the dock where they could
look at something beside the torch-lit assembly around the lawn.

From a washtub full of beer Crowe grabbed a couple of bottles and they went down the path to the boathouse and sat on a rock ledge just under its eaves. The sky clear overhead and indigo, though lightning still flashed in the distance. A half-moon had just made its way above the tree tops and was floating in the lake. Somewhere along the shore of the cove a bullfrog croaked and was answered in kind from a half-dozen places. "This is where it's at," Crowe said, settling back on the rock. "This is just *exactly* where it is at. This is nice."

Sandy stared out across the water, chewing slowly on an ear of corn and apparently oblivious to everything but the sounds of the night. An oarlock creaked out on the lake. Across the cove a porch door slammed and a dog barked for a few moments, then was silent. The bullfrog chunked once more "I've been watching you all sail this last week," Crowe said, opening two bottles of beer and passing her one. "It's quite a spectacle—all those boats."

"Burt's kick," she said idly. "He read somewhere that everybody should have a hobby so he bought ten thousand dollars' worth of boats and makes everybody go out and putt up and down the lake in them. He likes to win all the races."

"How can he lose? There isn't any competition."

A few bats flitted in and out of a clump of pale, luminous birches to the left of the oak, and Sandy put her hand to her hair. "If there were competition," she said, "Burt wouldn't like it so much. Oh, he'd go on, grimly, like a dog with his teeth in the seat of your pants, but he'd hate it. That's the way Burt is. Once he makes up his mind about something, it might as well be moored in concrete."

She turned toward him. "Actually that's not true what I said about it being a hobby. The 'sea' is in his blood, as they say. Great-grandfather Rinelander was a sea captain out of Gloucester, residing in Ipswich until he retired and moved to the Cape. At one time our family owned a good deal of Falmouth and some large chunks of Martha's Vineyard across the sound. This place up here is mother's, and he comes only because she won't go to the ocean. He says fresh water gives him an acid stomach."

"You don't sound properly respectful of daddy," Crowe said.

"Of Burt?" she laughed. "Well, that's not too surprising, is it? I mean the generation gap and all is fabled in story and song, right? Anybody who respects parents has got to be some kind of mistake. Except now I suppose you're going to tell me you had a marvelous relationship with your father."

"I always figured," Crowe said, ignoring her remark, "that if you're eating a man's bread you can't put him down too hard. And if you're going to put him down, maybe you ought to cut the cord."

For a while they sat without talking, then Sandy went back to the house to get some watermelon and Crowe took his shoes off, sat on the end of the dock, dangled his feet in the lake. Completely comfortable for the first time in what seemed like years, and totally unconcerned about anything beyond the outcome of one night. A little drunk from the beer and the gin-and-tonics, but knew with more than booze confidence that if he wanted Sandy he could probably have her. Just a feeling that with a little finesse, a little feigned indifference to all the hanky-panky and adolescent grubbing, the copped feel, the declaration of undying love—all that obsolete style from the faded '50s—he could make it. With a bang, not a whimper.

"And what if I do make it," he said quietly to the bullfrog. "What then? There is something about this girl that makes her seem considerably more important than the previous baker's dozen, but I have the feeling it might be her great-grandfather that excites me as much as she does, and that's a feeble reason to deflower a maiden. That's necrophilia, almost. On the other hand, why not? Why not indeed? That's what we came for, right? Up from the masses and into the classes? Let us not have any ridiculous scruples at this point."

"Chunk," said the frog.

Minnows were nibbling at his toes.

Sandy came back, slipped off her shoes, handed Crowe a slice of watermelon, and they sat side by side on the dock spitting seeds out into the lake. A little breeze came up and shattered the moon. Pieces trying to escape across the water, but the parent is watchful and snatches them back.

"How old are you?" Sandy asked.

"Three thousand," Crowe said. "How about you?"

"Younger than that," she said. She took a mouthful of watermelon and said with juicy amusement, "Not of your generation."

"To which do you belong? The lost, the beat, the angry, the love. . . ."

"I thought you said you read the papers," she mocked. "Teeny, micro, or mini?"

"It doesn't make much difference," Crowe told her. "I find children all pretty much the same in terms of their capacity to bore me."

"Ah, you're a hard old man," she said. "You know, it's not true that the human life span is longer now than ever before. It's shorter, and you're the living proof, sitting there, fat, dumb, and unhappy, putting down the young like a weary old Pharisee, gloomy, prophesying death and destruction, waiting for the end of time." She rocked back, hugging her knees, and laughed. "But you're a nice old man, anyway. A clean old man. Will you teach me, old man, the things I need to know before I venture forth into the cold unknown?"

"I might," he said, "if you let me eat the rest of your watermelon." She handed it to him and he grabbed her arm, pulled her over and kissed her, let her go and sunk his teeth into the rind.

"Well," she said. "For openers that was okay. A little wet, and you left a seed," she spat it into the lake "but it was not wholly without style."

"I always try to leave a little seed," Crowe said. "I would not deny my Lord and my Pope."

Shining out of the black fringe of pines on the opposite shores the lights from the houses warm and cozy, like something out of a child's picture book. Seemed vaguely familiar, as if he had been the child and the picture book had been him, but he couldn't give it a specific reference no matter how hard he tried. Sandy broke up the effort. "Before we go any farther with this, Father, I'd like a few vital statistics. I mean, I don't just accommodate every nut who comes along, so let's have the story of your life, please, and if you don't mind spare me no details. I can stand it."

"O.K.," Crowe said, though he was anxious to quit the banter and get down to something more serious. "Born: Monterey, California, Father: fisherman . . ."

"Really?"

"Don't interrupt. Mother: housewife. Both parents deceased; one from uterine cancer, the other in a fire at sea. College education: three and one-half years at the University of California . . .

"I applied to Berkeley. I don't know if I got in yet."

"Don't interrupt. . . . after which I quit with the intention of going back, but never did. Military service: two years in the United States Army, primarily as a sign painter; honorably discharged as a Specialist III. Twice busted for insubordination. After that: a wide variety of menial and uninteresting tasks interspersed with some attempts at sculpture and painting—talent mediocre—and the writing of fiction and poetry—talent also mediocre. Currently unemployed and, as they say, on the town. Future prospects: none. That's it. Knocks you out, doesn't it?"

"I especially liked the details," Sandy said.

"There aren't any details. That is the one beautiful thing about my private history. No details. It makes the filling out of forms very simple. I just write 'none' after everything. Occupation, education, ambition, parents, wives, children, place of birth, hits, runs, errors. 'None.' "

Sandy laughed. "You're the craziest freak I ever met," she said.

"Then you haven't been around much," Crowe told her, and in a whisper, "Anyway it's true. I jest not. Even the place of birth. My parents, you see, were not really my parents. I was one of those doorstep appearances you read about in corny, pulp stories. You know, where the kindly old lady comes out one morning to get the milk and finds the kid in the basket on the porch with a note, says 'Give this kid a nice home.' Well, the kindly old lady was *my* old lady."

"At least you have a fertile imagination," Sandy said, "even if the rest of your mind has atrophied."

"Indeed," Crowe said. "Certainly. You have at last inserted

your proctoscope into the heart of the mystery. A fertile imagination. A fecund imagination, one might even say. Beyond the imagination I do not exist. Therefore I am permitted to write 'none' after all questions of fact."

Of course most of it was a lie. But why tell the truth? Crowe thought. You're an aspiring writer, or used to be, and the imaginary is so much more interesting than the truth. Why tell her that you were a dull child who learned to read at the age of two; that you were passed out of the first grade after three weeks; that you were class president of the fourth, fifth, and sixth grades (with the attendant responsibilities of milk monitor and head of the safety patrol), not, as your mother and teachers were pleased to believe, because you were the best student in your class, but because you could hit a baseball farther than any kid in school; that in the seventh grade, thinking yourself something of a hotshot both on and off the playing fields, contemptuous of your parents' bohemianism and anxious to show them your superiority, you entered a statewide essay contest on "My America" and, waxing eloquently on the metaphysics of the Monterey coast, won—a thousand-dollar university scholarship to be held in trust until you finished high school and, though you did not know it then, because you were a fisherman's son and "underprivileged," an invitation to attend, without tuition and with room and board provided, a private school in the eastern U.S., where you went under false pretenses with the sons of bankers and Wall Street tycoons for a miserable six months until you were busted and fled for home. Why go through all that? The promising beginning blown to hell by adolescent neuroses. Why tell her that far from being a basket orphan, you were a mamma's boy who learned early that women could be used as a buffer against pain and suffering, against the demands of a man's world that insisted on strength and courage and quick decision, against your father; and that when she died, you were outraged, felt betrayed, deserted, as if she had done it on purpose, and you suddenly despised her for her own weakness that had allowed you to become what you were. Why bother with all that?

"I'm getting a little sleepy," Sandy said. "How about a swim?"

"No suit."

"That's just your imagination," she said, and stripping to her skin, waded out into the moon.

Before you venture forth into the cold unknown, Sandy, I will teach you the things you need to know. Indeed I will.

They dried off in the boathouse with a beachtowel that had been left there and put on their clothes, located their shoes out on the dock, gathered up plates and bottles, and walked back up toward the house. At the end of the path, just before it emerged on the lawn, Sandy turned around suddenly and Crowe nearly ran her down. Stood there a moment, hands full of garbage, and then she kissed him on the mouth. He could feel her nakedness pressing against him through their shirts.

"I like you," she said. "I like you a whole bunch."

"Well that's fine," he said. "That's dandy. You're getting an imagination all your own."

"No imagination," she said. "Feeling. That's the difference in a generation."

It rained for nearly two weeks. The storm that had approached during the picnic was followed by a dozen more like it, and they all came right over the lake and stopped. That was O.K. with Crowe. He spent most of his time in front of the fire with Sandy, reading, talking, watching the wind-chop on the lake and the way black water would fan out across gray. Hardly got off the couch except to throw another log on the fire, or when Sandy thought she probably ought to drop around her own house to let her parents know she was still in Vermont. Actually it hardly mattered. Burt was completely unconscious of his children's whereabouts and Hermina too frightened by them to ask. She knew where Sandy was spending her time, and judging from the tight-lipped little nod she would give Crowe when he'd occasionally encounter her in the village during one of his supply trips, she did not approve of him much. She had once ventured into conversation by quoting her daughter, "Sandy says you're from California," and Crowe had said "yes" and had been unsure how to proceed. He didn't know whether she expected him to editorialize or apologize, but when she gave him a tight smile utterly devoid of meaning and went on filling her basket with S. S. Pierce products, he decided she probably expected him simply to evaporate. It irritated him. "Don't you have a domestic to do this sort of thing?" he said, pointing at her shopping cart.

"Are you looking for employment?" she replied, and smiled again, rather coldly.

However unacceptable she may have found Crowe, and for whatever reasons, she did not feel herself threatened enough to bother with him. She assumed, according to Sandy, that if her daughter appeared at breakfast, the family pedigree had not been besmirched by the mongrel down the road. Her assumptions were not strictly inaccurate. Crowe, for the first time in his life, and without the faintest idea why, had decided to wait for an invitation.

It's because I'm a man of integrity, he told himself; a man of impeccable manners, of grace and style in all matters of social sensitivity, and I conduct myself with decorum in every interpersonal situation. I am, in the language of the tribe, behaviorally flexible. And I would never, ever, be so cloddish as to force myself upon a reticent maiden without . . .

You slander me, Sir.

Remember Alma.

I do not remember Alma. I remember the Alamo, but no Alma. Beside, Alma drugged herself.

She asked for aspirin. She got Frenchies Wild Party Gag Spanish Fly.

In the interests of science. And truly amazing it was that the crushed body of a lousy little dung beetle could produce such an effect. But I found, please, the antidote. That should vindicate.

Of course.

Crowe discovered, during those weeks of rain, a good deal about Sandy. She was, for all of her sophistication, a rather confused and cynical girl. Her family's money bothered her, and Crowe telling her that every rich kid he'd ever known had felt the same didn't strike her as profound or convincing. She'd heard it before.

Moreover, she had no respect at all for her father—for his opinions, his friends, his connections, his name, his way of life in general. "He hasn't got an ounce of imagination," she said. "He does what other people do, he buys what other people buy. His politics are strictly determined by his economic status and family tradition, and everything else is determined by his social status. I mean, he's just the same miserable old bastard you read about in all those J. P. Marquand novels."

"How do you know he's miserable?" Crowe asked.

"How could he be anything else?"

"What you're saying is that given *your* set of values—which incidentally are as much a cliché as the ones you accuse him of maintaining—if you lived the way he does *you'd* be miserable. Right?"

"I guess so."

"But he isn't you, and he may like the way he lives and not feel in the least bit sorry that he's deprived of the opportunity to wander around in costume muttering 'oh, wow' at the mysteries of the universe."

"That's not what I'm talking about. I'm just saying that he's a Xerox copy of a million other stuffed shirts and that he's lost any semblance of individuality or identity."

"Look, Sandy, when was the last time you were in New York, down in the East Village, say, just looking around?"

"I don't know. I don't remember that I ever was."

"Well, a few weeks ago, before I came up here, I was wandering around St. Mark's Place muttering to myself because I split from the west coast to get away from the utterly boring paraphernalia of the drug cult and here it was all around me again . . . I'm a kind of provincial westerner, I admit it. I somehow hadn't expected New York to be a 'Xerox copy,' as you put it, of California . . . anyway, it suddenly occurred to me that in two blocks walking cross town to the Intergalactic Trading Post, I had passed two Kit Carsons and a Buffalo Bill, three or four women who looked as if they were about to set out with hand carts along the Mormon trail, a couple of Indians of indeterminate sex, several members from the court of Louis Quatorze, a half-dozen African warriors, two of them white, and I don't remember what-all else. But I had to stop all of a sudden and pinch myself and look around for the real world, June 22, 1970, and I had a hard time finding it. I had to go uptown and take a look at those people you're so contemptuous of, like your father, to remind myself of where I am in history. Downtown everybody was in costume pretending he was in some other time and place."

Sandy just shook her head. "You know, what I don't get about you is how you could be in a lot of ways very hip and at the same time so *ancient* and so *dumb*. You didn't have a hard time finding the real world June 22, 1970 in the east village. It was all around you. You were just looking for it with June 22, 1870 eyes. The make believe *is* the real world."

"You know what I don't get about *you*," Crowe laughed "is how most of your perceptions could be so out of date. We were saying things like 'the make believe *is* the real world' ten years ago. I kid you not, my child, history has passed you by."

Sandy's mother was an even bigger embarrassment to her than her father because while his opinions may have been precast, Hermina didn't have any at all. As a person she did not exist, and, indeed, her physical appearance seemed to be a mirror image of her soul. She was not fat or even stout, yet she appeared to have no bones. Her face had no structure, giving the impression that it could be pushed in here, pulled out there, and it would stay where it was put. Her voice had no timbre, her hair no particular color; Crowe thought she was the most forgettable woman he had ever met. How she produced a creature like Sandy was a total mystery. "How she produced anybody is a total mystery," Sandy said. "It is absolutely impossible to imagine my mother in an act of fornication. If I didn't know better I'd swear to God we were all of us adopted."

"Left on the porch," Crowe said.

"Yeah, 'Give this kid a nice home.' " She took a cigarette out of his pack and lit it. "You know how my mother signs her letters to me when I'm away at college? Mrs. Burtrand Rinelander. No fooling. Mrs. Burtrand Rinelander. She really does it.

Not mom, or mother, or Hermina. Mrs. Burtrand Rinelander. I
suppose she thinks I might not remember who she is."

For her two little brothers Sandy had great affection. They
were always in trouble and made things hot for Burt in the village. There was nothing he hated more than a confrontation with
an irate farmer whose cow had just been peppered with birdshot
("we thought it was a cat"), or a lane of angry summer residents
whose mailboxes had been shattered by cherry bombs, or the
local pastor of the Presbyterian Church who thought condoms
ought to be filled with something other than water, and in any
case added little to the liturgy when hurled into the congregation
from the choir loft during the service. She acted as legal counsel
for the boys and, by successfully defending them in the family
court, encouraged them in even more outrageous pranks. They
were, at least, polite, kept to themselves, and existed in marked
contrast to the oldest son, Burt, Junior, who to quote Sandy was
the biggest horse's-ass on the North American continent . . . an
adenoidal, asthmatic abortion with a complexion like grape nuts
and a gum ball for a brain. Burt, Junior, was in his father's
business and would eventually take it over when the old man
retired, though Sandy didn't seem at all sure what "the business"
really was. He drove black convertibles and had lost a good deal
of his hair. At twenty-seven he was getting a pot.

Crowe heard a number of stories about the Rinelanders of
Brookline while it rained in Vermont and the logs snapped in the
fireplace. Most of them did not impress him in the way he wanted
to be impressed. He regarded Sandy's attitude toward her parents
as adolescent and not terribly interesting, and probably inaccurate. But once, while he was reading Dickens' *Christmas Carol,*
because he'd read everything else in the house and Parker hadn't
sent any money for a couple of weeks so he couldn't buy any
magazines, Sandy, stretched out on the couch and, he thought,
sleeping, all of a sudden said, "I'll tell you a Christmas carol. I
just remembered it for the first time in two years." She turned
over on her stomach and hugged a pillow under her chest. "It's
Christmas morning, see, jingle bells and deck the halls with balls,
and all the little kids tripping down the stairs to see what Santa

has left in their stockings. There's the tree and the presents under it and the egg nog and fruit cake and nativity scenes stencilled on the windows and the crèche on the mantle. It's snowing and the carillons are playing and there's a fire going on in the fireplace. We go in the living room to open stuff, and under the tree there are these pretty blue packages all wrapped up in silver ribbon, one for each kid. We get about nine million presents every year, but one special one, and this blue package with the silver ribbon is the special one."

"Spare me the details," Crowe said. "I can't stand it."

"No Sir! The details are the important part." She pushed her hair out of her face and held it against her neck. "So I take mine over to the couch and sit down to open it. Everybody is busy ripping up boxes and what-not and I take off the ribbon, the silver ribbon, and the paper, the blue paper . . . it's a kind of flat folder inside, about the size of a diploma or something . . . and guess what it is."

"A diploma."

"No."

"A something."

"Very funny. No."

"Your death certificate."

Sandy sat up and looked startled. "Did I tell you this story?" she asked.

"Come on," he said. "What was it?"

"The deed to a grave plot. *My* grave plot." Crowe started to laugh but decided that was inappropriate. Sandy got off the couch and went over and poked at the fire with a stick of kindling. "I couldn't believe it," she said. "For a minute I thought it was a joke, but it wasn't the kind of joke that would occur to my parents." She threw the stick in the fire and stood up. "A deed to your grave. On *Christmas*. I mean, what are you supposed to say? 'Thank you very much, mother and dad, for this wonderful thought?' Burtie did. He thought it was a great gas, outside himself in servility, fawned around and said he thought it was a very touching example of their concern. A couple of aunts showed up about then and I snuck upstairs in the confusion. I bet I cried for three hours." She put another log on the grate and came back to the couch. "Merry Christmas," she said. "Jesus Christ!"

Later, after she had gone, Crowe thought about it. It occurred to him that his own upbringing was so totally remote in both style and content that he couldn't begin to understand the kind of feelings that might result from the Christmas pageant she had described. In my house, he thought, Christmas was the one day you could count on the old man's humor, and that in itself was a splendid gift. Got one present from my mother, socks or a sweater that she had knitted, one from Pop. We didn't like to overdo. Hated the commerce of it all. Pop's presents were handed over at the dining table, unwrapped, and, depending on the year, varied in magnificence from a pocket knife to a .22 rifle. Once got a second-hand Evinrude that he had traded off another fisherman. The third time I used it it threw its piston clear through the casing. Old-fashioned boyhood. Dickensian.

7

Late in August one of Sandy's roommates was getting married in Greenwich, Connecticut, and Sandy had agreed to serve as a bridesmaid. She asked Crowe if he wanted to go down with her. He told her no.

"You can really see how the other half lives. We're kind of nouveau next to the Jennings," she said.

"I'm not as preoccupied with that as you are," he lied. "Hurry back."

"I don't have to hurry back. That's why I thought you might go with me. My grandmother has a house on Martha's Vineyard that sits empty all year and we could go out there for a few days and lie on the beach."

"We're lying on a beach right now. They have greener beaches on Martha's Vineyard?" They were down on a six-foot strip of sand below the Rinelanders' boat house, surrounded by cedars and hidden from the sight of everything but the lake immediately in front. Sandy had taken off the top of her suit and was lying on her stomach. Crowe had his face buried in a towel and when he raised it to speak to her, she rolled over on her back. "Much greener," she said. "I need a change of scene."

"Well, you're a brazen bitch," he told her. "What do you think I am, anyway? A eunuch? You lie around here naked as a jay bird, inviting me to empty houses on Martha's Vineyard, and think you can call in the cavalry to cut me off at the pass, huh? Well, I'm not having any. I don't want to go to Martha's Vineyard. I don't want to go anywhere. And furthermore, I hope you get sunburned on the ends."

Sandy said nothing. After a while she sat up and put her top on. "I wasn't thinking about my attire. I forgot you're such a puritan." She gathered up her towel, put on her sandals, started up toward the boat house. "Christ, that's ironic," she said. Crowe kept his face in the sand and marveled at the rottenness of his mood. "By the way," she said, coming back a few steps, "I don't know where you get this shit about *me* calling in the cavalry. I got the distinct impression that it was you, for some obscure and private reason, who was blowing the trumpet. Or maybe I was wrong. Maybe your trouble with women is not stopping but starting."

"What the hell is that supposed to mean?"

"Figure it out."

"Given its source I don't think it's worth the effort."

"Let me put it bluntly, then. Maybe you're incapable of . . . how should I say it nicely? Sexual congress. Maybe you can't get it up."

"Let me be equally blunt." Crowe rose to his feet. "You have an adolescent mind. If I ever find myself simply looking for a vacant socket to plug into I'll give you a call, though I sincerely believe that we'll find the generator broken and no current in the lines. I do not pursue sexual congress, as you so nicely put it, because I would save you the embarrassment of a mediocre performance."

Sandy whirled around, furious, and ran up the path. The afternoon wore on. Crowe lay there on the sand and mentally kicked himself in the behind so hard and so many times that eventually he had to wear a shirt every time he went swimming because people would laugh and point at the man with his bum between his shoulders. Once he forgot and a policeman came from behind the life guard's tower and arrested him, saying he was a public disgrace and a freak, and "if I were you," he said, "I'd see a plastic surgeon." Took him to the patrol car wrapped in a beach towel. Crowe, not the patrol car.

"What?" Sandy asked.

Crowe opened his eyes. "Did I say something? I thought you left."

"You said something about a patrol wagon. I came back."

"I was dreaming I guess. Look, I'm sorry about earlier. I don't know what's with me today. I'll go down to Connecticut with you. Why the hell not? I haven't anything else to do. The story of my life."

Again Sandy didn't answer, just sat on the cedar log and looked at him with a soft smile on her lips. The sun slanted down through an overhanging birch, throwing patches of shade across the narrow strip of sand. Behind the glare on the water she seemed like a piece of sculpture, anonymous, richly dark in the brightening air. Time stopped, and then suddenly she was beside him, kissing him, and he was holding her hard around the middle and burying his ancient face in the soft warmth of her neck.

Down along the Connecticut River valley the farmers were just gathering in their second crop of hay. Crowe and Sandy drove for miles past fields of perfume. Clover, alfalfa, sweet grass. Apples were ripening in the trees around the farm houses, and along the road kids too young to help with haying were selling them for a dollar a bag. It had rained during the night and the road was still wet, but the day was perfect. A few clouds floated high overhead and cast their shadows across the pasture land on the other side of the river, and there was a hint of fall in the crisp morning air.

"You know what I'd do if I had any money?" Crowe said, somewhere around Brattleboro. "I'd buy me a big farm and settle down on it and just watch things carrying on. Like things growing and birds and clouds and the pattern of wind on the river. Like the way corn silk blows and pine needles smell and the breeze in the maples sounds and all that. I'd get me a farm down by the river and I'd just lie there on the bank and look at the sun through a curtain of leaves, and I'd watch the moon come up from behind those hills over there, making everything all bright and shadowy in the middle of the night. Hot damn, what a time that'd be."

Sandy rested her head on his shoulder and hummed a few bars of a song he didn't recognize. Her daddy's Cadillac was so quiet that Crowe kept looking at the generator light on the instrument panel to make sure the engine was still running. "What a time that would be," she mused. "Would you like some company?"

"Sure," he said. "Company is O.K. if it likes what I like."

"I like what you like." She lit a cigarette and handed it to him.

"Crazy," he said, blowing smoke at the windshield and watching it curl along the glass. "We'll have a garden with all kinds of vegetables and things in it; corn, beets, beans, peas, radishes, tomatoes, potatoes, squash . . ."

"And lettuce," she said, "for salad."

"Oh, salad. Lettuce. We'll have forty-seven kinds of lettuce; red leaf lettuce, oak leaf lettuce, bibb lettuce, iceberg lettuce. What other kinds of lettuce are there?"

"Romaine," she said. "I don't know. It tells you on the package."

"Black-seeded Simpson. My mother used to plant black-seeded Simpson, I remember. And that scrinkly kind of lettuce that tastes like thistles. We'll feed that to people we don't like."

"You can feed them the beets too," Sandy said. "I don't like beets worth a damn."

"Now just hold on. Just a minute here. If you're going to put down beets I don't know if you can be on my farm. People on my farm got to like what I like because this is a no-conflict farm and if I'm entertaining beets I don't want hasslers coming on about how they don't care for the company."

"O.K.," Sandy said. "Beets are a groove."

"Sure," Crowe told her. "Beets are all right. You don't want to insult the beet."

The farther south they drove the warmer it got. No fall chill in the Massachusetts air. Went slowly through the towns of Greenfield and Holyoke, looking at all the old houses with plaques on their fronts proclaiming the dates of their births. "You can see what happens when you come to town," Sandy said. "Your logic gets gummed. Start hanging signs around to tell the world what an old crock of a house you've got. Because the older the wreck the more you paid. The more hunks, chunks, and gouges something's got the crazier you are to have it."

"I like these old places," Crowe said. "You can have the farm and I'll have a town house, but when you come to the town house you have to like what I like."

"Beets?"

"Charm. And antiquity."

"I know your trouble. You're just looking for a past."

"How else you going to tell the present and the future?"

They had a late lunch in New Haven and then drove down the Connecticut turnpike to Greenwich, found the right road, the mailbox, the drive, and motored up to the Jennings house—more like a state park than someone's residence. The house was a modest Versailles. A handyman who was tinkering with a lawn tractor came to help with the bags and Carol Jennings, bride-to-be, came running down what looked like the *scala di Spagna* but was in fact the front steps. She threw her arms around Sandy and with an excessive whoop planted a kiss on her cheek. "So *good* to *see* you, darling. You must be *ab*solutely ex*haust*ed from the drive." Crowe tried to look like a New York cab driver—stony faced, waiting for his tip. To be honest, the opulence frightened him.

"This is a friend of mine," Sandy told the bride and introduced Crowe.

"How *nice*," said Carol. "How do you *do?*"

"I do fine," he said. She turned back to Sandy, still holding her hands, and told her she looked *ravishing* and that she *wished* they had come a day earlier and weren't weddings just the most positive *pain* in the world. "Yes," Crowe said, feeling now more feisty than impressed.

"I mean I still have so much to *do*," she went on, ignoring him. "*Honestly*, people are ar*riv*ing and there was a big *mix*-up at the club about the re*cep*tion, daddy's just *fur*ious with them, anyway, I have about a *milli*on notes to write before we leave for the *is*lands, and all of Robert's friends are staying at the *True*bloods, they're in St. Thomas and mummy can't find the key. *Gawd*, I hope it's *worth* it."

"I hope so too," Crowe said pleasantly. "I sure hope it isn't a bummer."

"We're going to have the reception right out here," Carol told Sandy, pointing across a lawn the size of a football field. "Don't you think that will be better anyway? Daddy is going to have the caterer put up a big tent over there by the pool and the music will be up behind so people can dance if they want. Pray nobody falls in. Gawd! I hope it doesn't rain."

"If it rains," Crowe chirped, "it'll be a bummer." Nobody paid any attention. Carol prattled on about the trials of becoming wedded, and Crowe smoked a cigarette and ground out the butt in the drive. Picked it up and put it in his pants cuff. The sun came out and beat on his head. It made his hair hot and his scalp was sweating. A handsome woman with dyed grey hair that looked purple from a distance came out on an upper balcony and called down at them, and Carol said, "Gosh, look at me yacking away . . . with about a million things to do. Come on in everybody." She went up the stairs in a rush, leaving Sandy and Crowe to follow. He balked. "Ohno," he said. "I'm not going in that hotel. I got about a million things to do . . . all of a sudden. They can't wait because it might rain."

"You promised." Sandy said.

"Did you see that woman with the purple hair? I think she's going to have me for dinner. Listen, I don't even have a suit."

"Yes you do. I brought one of Burtie's. I also borrowed one of his ties." She looked a little sheepish.

"Burtie," Crowe said, "is about six inches shorter than me, and couldn't weigh over one-fifty soaking wet. I'd look like blue-boy in that get-up. Besides, I wouldn't wear his clothes on a bet."

"What will you do?" Sandy asked, but before he could answer Carol called from the front door. "Wait for me just one minute," Sandy begged. "I'll be right out."

Over by the corner of the lawn the handyman was under the tractor, trying to remove something with a crescent wrench. As Crowe wandered over, the sun ducked back behind the clouds and suddenly he was cold again. It seemed as if his thermostat had passed out, and he wondered if he was getting sick, or if he was about to encounter another vision. He hadn't been plagued in some time. What will you do? he asked himself. Thirty-four bucks in your pants and you can't afford a hotel. The only person you know who is still in New York is Paps and you about wore out your welcome the last time you descended. He looked under the tractor. "Trouble?" he asked.

The handyman stopped struggling with his wrench and a rusted nut, turned his head after a significant pause, and stared at Crowe for about thirty seconds. Then he put the wrench back on the nut and began trying to free it again. "Trouble?" Crowe repeated. No snotty servant is going to ignore a guest of the Jennings.

"No trouble," he said, after some delay, and with considerable irony, "Isometrics."

"Boy," Crowe said. "They sure don't screen the help like they used to around here." He went back to the car and sat in the front seat, smoked another cigarette until Sandy finally came out. As she came down the steps she waved to the grease monkey under the tractor. "Hi, Mr. Jennings," she called. "Good to see you again."

"Well," Crowe said, when she reached the car, "if there was any question of my staying it has just been erased. I'm going to take off and go into New York and I'll be back to pick you up tomorrow."

Sandy looked doubtful. "Carol says there's plenty of room at the Truebloods, if her mother can ever find the key. You can stay there."

"With Robert and the boys."

"They'll be busy. You won't have to pay any attention to them at all."

"No thanks. I'll pick you up tomorrow. Cross my heart. This is just not my cup of tea, Sandy, so let's let it go at that, O.K.?"

"O.K.," she said, and gave him a sisterly kiss on the cheek. "But come for the tail end of the reception so we can have the last waltz together. I've never danced with you, you know."

"Madam, you have missed one of the great thrills in any girl's life," he told her. "Until you have danced with me, you don't know what suffering is. Childbirth will seem no more than a gas pain alongside the swatch we'll cut on the ballroom floor. Look forward on it." He started the car. "And tell Carol I hope her nuptials are a real blast. Loved seeing her. Tell her I hope it snows."

He slept in the car on a beach near Southport; a miserable night of tossing and turning, unconscious but unable to turn off a mind whose filaments went on and on, casting light into the musty archives of the stored past—fictions, situations without resolutions, components without compositions. Thus in dreams are we transported once again to the house.

Where I sit, dozing, waiting, until on the second morning I see them coming up along the path, carrying his clothes and a canvas bag with his extra gear. The sun is high and after a night and a day of foul weather it is more than a welcome change. It makes me dance. It makes me exuberant. The pasture to the south that has been brown all summer has suddenly changed. The long dead grass has been beaten down and new shoots of green have poked through. Soon all traces of the season past will be buried by the lushness of new growth and there will be wild mustard and afterward the lupine.

A branch of the cypress brushes the canvas bag as the men come along the path to the house. Against the blueness of the sea the black, twisted trunk stands like a jagged hole in the middle of space. A child has taken a piece of bright paper, folded it, cut erratic, feathery branches along the seam, then opened his creation against the blackboard. The men, too, would seem like pasteup dolls except that they move slowly and with stiff formality across their backdrop of water and sky. It is such a crystal day that one can see the coast line as far north as Santa Cruz, and the rolling mountains behind are more beautiful than I have ever seen them.

When the men reach the house there are few words spoken. They deposit their burden and we stand a few moments gazing away from the clothes and the canvas sack on the porch, out toward the headlands where the gulls are wheeling over the beach. We sigh and shake our heads, and then they go back down the path, past the cypress, and over the hill into the blue Pacific.

Arrangements must be made, the kittens disposed of, the house retired. I will go there no more. I intend to close up that pristine chapel right now—that outworn museum of unnatural history. I am going to board the windows, padlock the doors, and I shall not look on it again, by dream or by any other form of transportation.

Make of that what you will. Analysis is not *my* job. Neither is ontology.

When Crowe woke the sun was already high and the atmosphere in the car like a green house. His head ached and his mouth was filthy; he was already bored by the prospect of a day without Sandy. Down the road, in a coffee shop, he brushed his teeth with borax and his finger, ordered a sweet roll and a cup of tea, read everything of remote interest in the *New York Times*. Went finally into a phone booth and called Parker at his office. As Crowe hoped, he was invited to lunch. "Make it informal, Park," he said. "I'm not at my most presentable."

"When were you ever?" Parker named some place on Route 104 where the drinks were big and the food acceptable.

Without Elaine around Parker was even cruder and more obnoxious than Crowe remembered. Trying to copy Milton Berle, or somebody. Loud, ass pinching, insultingly familiar with waiters he'd never seen. Can't forget that money, the club, his position in the bank, his father-in-law's position at the head of the bank, are not the most important things in the world, and does not intend to let anyone in the restaurant forget it either. Wisecrack, tell jokes, play the fool. "Didja hear this one?" Parker yells. "'Bout the guy who walked into a bar down in Louisiana with an alligator behind him on a leash. Says to the bartender 'You serve niggers in here?' Bartender says 'sure.' So the guys says, 'I'll have a double rye and ginger and my alligator'll have a nigger." Parker convulsed. Crowe *had* heard it before, but out of respect for a free meal he felt he ought to join in. People were turning their heads. Who in God's name . . . ?

But Crowe saw the other side, too. By the second round of drinks Parker began to get morose and sour about his lot. "Rotten trap I fell into, marrying Elaine," he said, suddenly, apropos of nothing. "I'm one of the walking dead. All those things everybody was going to do when we were college kids, remember? Like going down to South America to be soldiers of fortune or some such crap; that section of Canada we were going to stake out and develop. Back to the land, fishing, hunting. An' that sloop Olsen had up in the boat yard at Bodega we were all going to sail over to the islands and live on? Remember?" Crowe remembered that Parker had never been included in any of those schemes, had just been present in the room when other people plotted. "I mean," he went on, "we know that that kind of jazz is adolescent dreaming, but what the hell, we should have done it. I read where kids *are* doing it now. It's too late for us." He picked the olive out of his glass, sucked the pimento out of the middle, regarded Crowe through the hole. "You know what I finally figured out? I finally figured out that the reason people never do the things they dream about is because they get sneered out of it by their parents, by all the old farts who passed up their chance and can't stand to see somebody else pull it off. I remember when I'd bring up the desert island bit, my old man would fall off his chair, he thought it was so Goddamn amusing. Then he'd get pissed off and tell me about how he'd gone through the same silly phase when he was a kid, and somehow I was supposed to take that as a reason for not pursuing the subject further."

Big deal, Crowe thought. His old man was right. Parker would have been wiring for money inside a week.

Prince lifted a fresh drink and took a swallow. "You know, it's the old 'get serious, boy. Continue your education. Prepare yourself for life.'" His voice was getting rather strident. "Jesus Christ, the first thing you know you're all prepared and life's over. So you take your gold watch and your pension and hop off to Miami Beach with the old lady, and you croak on the second day because your heart won't take it. You've been sitting on your butt at a desk for forty-five years preparing for retirement."

"You didn't think that up, Parker," Crowe said. "You read all that somewhere."

"Ah, you book readers don't even know what the world's like. You ought to get out into business sometime and see what really happens."

"That's what I'm telling you," Crowe said. "There *have* been a few books on the subject. If you really believed that line you just gave me you wouldn't go on pushing an adding machine in a bank."

The waiter came and took the orders. Parker insisted on another drink. Crowe tried to shake his head but it was spinning so fast he didn't know where to begin. All he could think about was that the sweet roll he'd had for breakfast wasn't much of a foundation.

"You know," Parker went on, "you're probably right, you son of a bitch. I'm really barking at the wrong tree. I mean, you're *doing* what I'm talking about doing. No wife, no kids, no grab-ass job, no house that owns you, no image to keep up. Just doing what you want, going where you want, tied to nothing. Too much. I'll tell you what. I'll trade you places. The whole sheebang. My crummy house. Elaine's a lousy lay, buddy. They told her screwing was dirty when she was a kid and she still believes it, believe me. Her old man is the kind of guy who runs out and turns on the hose when the dogs are at it, but she's beautiful, right? You saw her. She's some looker, in a kind of hard-assed, up-tight way. Wooden. An' she's rich. Oh, Christ, has she got a portfolio. How 'bout it, pal. I'll try yours, if you try mine."

If I don't get some food in a minute, Crowe thought, I'm going to get sick on the table. He ate some oyster crackers and drank a glass of water. Felt a little better. "No thank you, Parker," he said. "Doesn't sound like my brand. But doing nothing, let me tell you, is not such a big time as you think. It's no time at all. Past time. Overdue." He couldn't talk anymore. Couldn't think. Didn't want to hear any more about Parker's ice-blue wife. Bad mistake to have called him. Should have just gone to the beach. Then the plates arrived and he was spared. They wolfed their lunch in silence.

Parker told a few more jokes over coffee, asked Crowe's advice on how he might persuade his wife to engage in oral sex practices, to which Crowe just shrugged and excused himself to the men's room, ordered a second serving of cheese cake, and then looked at his watch and said he had to hustle. Coming out of the gloom of the restaurant Crowe was nearly flattened by the bright sunlight. His eyes ached. His head began to throb again. He sorely wished to lie down and sleep it off. Parker, on the other hand, had reverted to backslapping oafishness. "Mighty good to see you again, old buddy, old buddy," he said. "I meant to get to Vermont but things came up and Elaine, the bitch, kept whining to go to the shore. How long you plan to stay up?"

Crowe shrugged. "Don't know yet."

"Atta babe. God*damn*, I envy that. Float along, see what comes up. Sneakin' by. Oh, incidentally, my folks are going to be sneakin' by in about ten days. Probably go to Vermont. You can stay up there and all, but you'll have them for company."

"I'll think of something," Crowe said. "If I leave what do you want me to do about the house and the car?"

"Oh shit, bring the car down; leave it up there. I don't give a fuck. Doesn't matter. Just leave the house open." They had reached Sandy's Cadillac and Crowe began fumbling with the key. Parker's eyes opened wide. "Say," he drawled, "Pretty snazzy wheels. Where you come by them?"

"They belong to Burt Rinelander," Crowe said. "I drove his daughter down to a wedding."

"Sandy?"

"You know her?" Crowe asked. It was a mistake. Obviously he knew her.

"*Know* her. Every inch, pal. She's a hot number, old Sandy." He mopped his forehead and leered at the sky. "She was about the first chick I ever laid. Fourteen years old and built like a brick shit house. I think she made the grade with half the guys on the lake one summer."

"O.K., Parker," Crowe said. "Never mind."

Parker had put a cigar in his mouth and was lighting it. He either missed Crowe's tone or didn't care. "We were on this hay ride, see, with a whole bunch of people, and I'm supposed to be the chaperon, and Sandy starts horsing around with me."

"I don't really want to hear about it, Parker."

"Well, the first thing I know we're down in this tunnel in the hay bales and I got her sweater up and her bra undone and she's hot as a fire cracker . . . man, at fourteen . . ."

"Shut up, Prince." He heard that time, eyed Crowe drunkenly, malevolently, put his stogie in the middle of his mouth, and talked with it held in his teeth.

"I'm still not too up on what's happening until she takes my hand down to the zipper on her slacks and slides it open. Never forget it. She's a regular mink. . . ." Crowe suddenly had had enough. From somewhere down around his knees he wound up like a baseball pitcher and smacked Parker right in the middle of his cigar, and Parker went down on the sidewalk as if he'd been shot. Crowe heard his skull bounce. For half a minute he lay there without moving, then slowly sat up holding his mouth. His nose was bleeding and there were pieces of cigar leaf stuck to his cheek bones; he was obviously unclear about what had happened.

"I *told* you to shut up," Crowe said, almost as surprised as Parker. He had punched him without a moment's premeditation. "You never know when to keep still about anything and you never did. The first thing comes into your gelatinous mind you blab." Parker tried to get up, reached his knees, fell back. "No wonder your wife pukes at the thought of getting into the rack with you. Big smutty game, huh, Parker. Humpty-dumpty. Here we go." A crowd was beginning to gather and Crowe realized that the police might soon be coming around. He got in and started the car, leaned out and looked at Prince, still sitting on the sidewalk. "Thanks for lunch," he said. Pulled away and drove down Route 104. The hand felt as if he had broken it, and there was an angry mark between the knuckles where he had burned it on the cigar. He licked it as he drove.

On the way back to Greenwich he tried, along with the rock singer on the radio, to see what condition his condition was in. It wasn't in at all. It had fled the country. He couldn't possibly meet Sandy, he thought, until he had thought through a few things, straightened out, and so he simply decided to leave her where she was; not to pick her up until he was ready.

It took a long time. He sat in a run-down gin mill in downtown
Greenwich and drank beer all afternoon, trying to figure out
whether he was angry, jealous, hurt, betrayed, none or all of
these. The fact that Sandy was no virgin was not particularly
upsetting. He'd never known anybody who was. What ate at him
was that she'd been had, however long ago, by a slob like Parker,
a big-mouthed ignoramus whose contempt for what he might or
might not have received was evidenced by the fact that he'd tell
stories about it. But then Parker told stories about everything,
Crowe reminded himself. In fact, he made up a good many of
thèm, and it was perfectly possible that he had never laid a finger
on Sandy, or that she had knocked him silly for an attempt, and
he was just turning bad news into good. It was also perfectly
possible that he had done as he said.

"But at fourteen," he pointed out to himself. "What the hell?
Who knows anything at fourteen. You're not supposed to know
anything at fourteen. Anyway, what is really bugging me is that I
haven't made out at all. I've been a Goddamn Prufrock debating
whether to push the moment to its crisis, and in the meantime
losing the opportunity."

That's not Sandy's fault, or even Parker's. It's yours.

"Yeah. We've been through all this before."

"You O.K., buddy?" the bartender said.

Crowe looked up, startled. "O.K.? Yes, I'm O.K."

"The way you were going on there, I thought you might be
seeing spooks."

"I do that," Crowe told him. "I forget where I am."

And so he wound up just being sad and listening to George
Jones records on the jukebox and getting drunker and drunker.

Excuse me, I think I've got a heartache,
You find a girl nowadays whose heels aren't round, and you think
you've really found something unique, something worth the
price.

And the ache's so deep inside,
That it won't be satisfied.
And then you find she's put out for a crummy bastard like Parker
Prince. On a hay ride. At the age of fourteen.

Excuse me, I think I've got a heartache,
Some of the shine, some of the glitter, some of the "you're the
only one for me," wears off. How many have there been since?
Seven years. Seven Parkers?
And I just want one more cry before I go.
Sing it George. Times have changed. Too bad for times.

In the morning, after another night in the car near the Southport
beach, he felt much better. Cured, in fact. He decided he didn't
own Sandy. Didn't have any claims on her, nor she on him. And
he had stolen her car and stood her up. He drove as fast as he
could to the Jennings estate, and when he pulled in front of the
scala di Spagna she came running down, bag in hand, and flung
herself in beside him. "What happened to you?" she asked, all in
a flurry. "I was so worried I couldn't sleep at all last night. I
thought you must have had an accident or gone to Mexico with
another girl or something, but I didn't know how to even *begin*
looking for you."

"You sound like your friend Carol," Crowe said.

Sandy looked at him for a moment with a big grin, then hugged
him so hard he almost ran onto the shoulder. She kissed him on
the cheek. "Oh, I'm so glad to see you, I don't care where you've
been."

"I'll tell you about it later," Crowe said. She put her arm
around his neck and watched the scenery roll by. He punched the
automatic selector button on the radio and picked up a country
and western station out of Hartford. *Excuse* me, sang George
Jones—really he did—*Excuse me, I think I've got a heartache,* and
Sandy wondered at the modern Quixote, tilting her father's Cadillac down the parkway at eighty miles an hour, convulsed by
crabbed and unaccountable thoughts, pursued by the apocryphal
spirits of yesterday's mind.

8

So once again they were on the road, gliding along in that big silent machine, past Saybrook and New London, up through the Hope Valley in Rhode Island toward Narragansett Bay. It might have been forever. Might just have gone on and on: Boston, Portsmouth, Bangor, into New Brunswick to the Gaspé Peninsula, Quebec and Montreal and across Canada to the Canadian Rockies, down to Seattle and along the coast, San Francisco, Monterey, San Bernardino and out across the desert, Needles (maybe pause for a chocolate Dairy Queen and a look at the Dead Mountains), Flagstaff, Albuquerque. On and on in a never ending circle, watching the whole world roll by, listening to soft sounds on the radio, dreaming the impossible. Odd to associate one's most idyllic hours with an enormous, ostentatious automobile, but that's how it goes.

They stopped in a grocery store in New Bedford and bought bread and cheese and a bottle of wine to eat in the car on the way to Woods Hole. Wandered around town, looking into the shop windows, arms around each other like high-school lovers in the heat of discovery. In the display case of a fancy men's store Sandy saw a tweed jacket, dark green, with leather buttons and side vents, and before Crowe knew what was happening she had him inside and a sniffy young man with limpid eyes and an English accent was smoothing it across his shoulders, admiring the way in which it reduced their breadth to something more in line with his notions of a popular physique. "Slimness is smartness," he quipped. "See there. Makes the brawn all gone. Ha ha."

"Ha ha," Crowe said. "I prefer something with a little more lace."

"Never mind him," Sandy told the dude. "I like it and I'll take it." She handed him one of Burt's credit cards and he went in the back to write up the ticket.

"Wait a minute," Crowe said, dragging her to the front of the store and turning his back on the other clerk. "What the hell are you doing? I don't want you buying me clothes. I don't need any clothes. I already got a jacket."

"But it's falling apart," Sandy said. "And besides, I'm not buying it, Burt is. I'm just a consultant. Burt told me he sure couldn't stand that old seersucker rag of yours, and he didn't want his daughter running around with no bowery bum, so I should get you some threads first chance I had and lay the bill on him. His very words. No kidding."

"Cut it out, will you. If you're the big consultant how about consulting me before you go saying you'll take something? How do you know I even like it? How do you know but maybe I can't stand green?"

"You said you liked my eyes."

"And listen, I'm not a welfare case yet. I can buy my own clothes, little mother."

"For God's sake," she said, "All I wanted to do was give you a present. Your gracious acceptance makes it a real joy." She turned away just as the clerk came up with the coat on his sleeve. "Could we slip into it once more?" he said. "To check the arm length for alteration."

"No," Crowe said. "We couldn't."

"Just wrap it up," Sandy told him.

"Very well." He gave her a prissy smile, put the jacket back on its hanger, and slipped a plastic protector over it.

"Merry Christmas," Sandy said when they were outside and headed for the car. "*Loved* shopping for you."

On the way to Woods Hole she made sandwiches and they drank the wine out of the bottle. A Yankee–White Sox game was on the radio and outside of Falmouth Sandy switched the station to some music. The score was tied, bottom of the eighth and the Yankees had one on. "Hey," Crowe said. "The hell with that. Put the game back on."

"We're almost there," she said, kissing his ear. "Anyway, I've an idea. Why don't we leave the car in Woods Hole? Grandmother's place is in Vineyard Haven and we can walk up from the ferry and ride bikes while we're there. I haven't ridden a bike around the island since I was a little girl. O.K.?"

Crowe muttered something, agreed.

"Goody," she squealed, sounding like she was still a little girl, a six-foot little girl with green eyes and soft, warm lips against his ear. Green *is* the favorite color.

"O.K., if we make it," Crowe told her. "You put your tongue in my ear once more and we won't."

"We'll make it," she said. "We'll make it and make it and make it."

Which, as it happened, they did. It seemed as if once across the sound Sandy departed from ordinary, everyday reality into a world without limitation or consequence. It was as if nothing she did on the Vineyard had any extension beyond that time and place; as if there she could submit without conscience or regret to anything and everything. Submit is not quite accurate. As usual, Crowe was two steps behind.

Perhaps it was simply a question of age, he thought. Being ten years older than Sandy he was constantly aware of his intrusion into her life; constantly stepping back and looking at the situation from the disadvantaged point of a third person, a moral voice, an intruding author come to qualify his fictional creations and judge them from some external and artificial stance. Had she and Crowe been contemporaries nothing about their relationship would have surprised him. As it turned out he was stunned to discover, when he brought up the mundane subject of contraception, that Sandy had been on the Pill ever since they had left Vermont.

"You planned this," Crowe said, as they lay on her grandmother's ancient, canopied bed. Dawn was breaking, and turning his head he could see down to the water through the French windows that faced the harbor. "You had it in mind all the time. My, my."

She put her fingers on his lips and looked down into his face. It was still dark in the room, but he could see the light glint off her eyes. Her hair brushed against his face, tickling his cheek. "You're really a funny guy," she said.

"Why here? Why not in Vermont?" Crowe asked.

She lowered her head and spoke into the curve of his neck. "It could have been arranged. But to tell you the truth, Capt'n, I ran out of pills, and it's kind of a close community to go around buying contraceptives when you don't have a husband. Had to write away."

She yawned and snuggled against him, and he thought, with a kind of cold detachment, so Parker wasn't lying after all. I've been a jerk all summer long. I should have been balling her up one wall and down the other, giving her her money's worth, Burt's money's worth. Should have been blasting away so often and so fast she'd stagger off with her eyes crossed and her legs bowed. Should have . . ."

"But there were a few other reasons," she went on, unaware of the sudden blackness of his mood. "Like it was enough to just be with you, to just look at you and touch you and listen to you talk about things, just sort of feel your presence all around me, inside me in a different way. So I didn't really want to risk spoiling it all. I can't explain it exactly. With some people, you know, there isn't anything *but* sex. I mean, that's all you can do with them, and they aren't anything, just a kind of animated dildo. But with you it was all different." They lay there for a while without speaking, Sandy on her side with her leg over Crowe's. He began to see a little glow in the corner of his mood. "I guess what I'm trying to say," she finally murmured, "is that I knew I was going to love you if I gave it a chance. And that made all the difference."

Dawn came on slowly, tick by tick. Crowe ran his tongue down her throat to her breast, put his mouth over the nipple, felt it rise. Felt her hands in his hair and her hips stirring slowly beneath him. Thought shall I bite this luscious fruit? with its pale pink flower, so smooth even when aroused, so perfectly round and tapered. Not like the coarse buds of other women whose breasts have known the scrape of my beard, the flick of my tongue. Not the giant raspberries of unlovely Alma, the sad and drooping thumbs of horrible Suzie, the slyly peeping eyeslits of fat Pat the sack rat. Not like any I have seen except on marble statues in the palace gardens, Amazon mountains of icy stone gleaming in the dusky recess of some ancient museum. Shall I bite? A playful nip? There. But this is not in jest, no "ouch," no "stop that," only fingers weaving in my hair and the pressure of thighs around my middle. And you are warm, Sandy, inside, and smooth there like silk. Would have found that my tongue, too, but we have come a long road and are in a hurry to be home. There will be time to stroll in the garden later, hours, days, maybe forever. The torso of a goddess, you have, long yet full, and strong legs from summers of tennis and the water. Should be a dancer, a belly dancer, a strip artist reviving the dying dead world of burlesque. Wonder will you forever moan so freely, your legs over my shoulders, hands squeezing my arms, my chest, and I wonder how long is forever in this tangle of limbs and mingled sweat—can we ride it through time and never wake to the morning of discontent, sour mouths, tired skin, the tedious labor of simply being alive. I know the answer in the quickening thrust of your hips, the heave of your belly. Time is running out. For thee. And for me.

The air is cold on one who has been warm, but no matter, I am just now your object, your pupil; lead and I follow. The bed is hot on my back where you have been, enough warmth, and your hair trails fire down my stomach and tickles me with light as you tease, enjoying the delay, the anticipation, the tenseness in my body. To watch your burning hair sink like the sun below the horizon and take me into the heat of your mouth. I will come apart and flow across the bed. Do not bite, no playful nips. This is not in jest. Be ever watchful. I am no watermelon rind, but I have seeds to spit on the shallow waters of the lake. And time is running out for me once more.

Mid-afternoon before Crowe was conscious enough to fumble for Sandy and realize she wasn't there. Rolled out of bed, took a shower in a bathroom the size of a barn, went wandering around

with only a towel around his middle. The house had parlors and
sitting rooms and living rooms and drawing rooms and about
ninety-seven bedrooms, a library, an enormous kitchen with three
pantries, a dining room where Beowulf and all his thanes could
have been comfortable. Another hotel, that place. Once upon a
time a gay spot for a multitude of young ladies and gentlemen
around the turn of the century. Crowe could almost see them
waltzing in the ballroom and strolling around the gardens of a
summer's evening, admiring the lights of East Chop across the
harbor. Most impressive. Awe inspiring, in fact, all those traditions and roots going back so far. Envied those ladies and gentlemen. They knew the rules and regulations and played the game
accordingly. Thank you Henry, thank you Edith, he thought. My
sense of history is all your make believe.

Two staircases leading to the upstairs, one of them lined in
leather, and stained glass in the windows on the landings. At the
end of one long hallway Crowe found more stairs that led up to a
circular room with curved glass facing the harbor and a magnificent view of the sound. Below him the lawn sloped down to a
thick hedge of boxwood, a path led from there to a little gazebo,
and beyond that through an open field to the sea. Or perhaps
memory is playing tricks and two places have become confused.
No matter. Sandy came back with an armful of groceries and a
pasteboard box with seaweed and two live lobsters in it, and
Crowe went down to meet her. "We have to keep your strength
up," she said. "Eggs and oysters four times a day."

"My strength, huh? That's all you want to keep up?"

"Don't get smutty."

"If I'd known what was required of me," he said, "I'd have
charged a fee."

Sandy handed him the box of seaweed and he scrutinized the
beady eye of his dinner. "Looks like somebody I know," he
said.

"Looks like Burt," Sandy answered. "That's what first at-
tracted me. The thought of dropping him in the boiling water."
She did a little pirouette and clapped her hands. "We have a
bottle of Pouilly Fuissé, artichokes from your native state, and
strawberries from mine. What did I forget?"

"The appetizer," Crowe said, dropping his towel, picking her up and carrying her into the drawing room. Where they ruined the plush on a very fuzzy divan.

After dinner they sat on the lawn and watched the boats come in to anchor at their moorings in the Vineyard Haven marina. The ferry from Woods Hole pulled up, disgorged a load of people and cars, went back with a load of people and cars. In a few hours it would repeat the process. From somewhere behind a line of white pine to the left of where they were sitting there was music and the sound of cocktail voices, but they couldn't see anyone through the barrier of trees. The sky empty and no breeze. Promise of a good tomorrow. Crowe smoked a cigar Sandy had bought him and they finished off the last of the Pouilly Fuissé, and then while she went in to make coffee Crowe walked down through the hedge, past the gazebo, and on to the beach. Lights winked on, one by one, over on East Chop, just as they had probably done for a hundred years, and Crowe suddenly felt empty, isolated, dislocated, reminded of his own mortality. Sitting there on the coarse grass just above the water he was conscious of the steady thump of his pulse and of its temporary principle; of the deciduousness of his recent complacency; of the fact that he was about to wake up and find that he had indeed been waiting for Godot all his life and that he might well go on waiting forever. Perhaps that realization is cathartic, he thought, but it is also frightening. Out over the sound a single gull slid off into the wake of the sun.

Three days on the Vineyard. On the second morning they took the bikes and rode out to Gay Head, fourteen or fifteen miles on the southwestern tip of the island. Climbed around on cliffs of various colored clay, ate sandwiches in a secluded little notch, rode back to Menemsha Pond and swam in the cold green water. The horse-shoe crabs were mating and they were everywhere a few feet beneath the surface. Crowe and Sandy walked far down the deserted beach toward the mouth of the pond, and while their underclothes dried on a rock they lay naked on the sand and shut their eyes against the sun. Hot afternoon and quiet except for the gentle wash of water on the pebbles and the cries of the sea birds."

"I tell you what," Sandy said, after a drowsy hour. "Let's stay right here and make a hut out of driftwood, live on clams and berries and things. Like the Gay Head Indians. Jellyfish on your morning toast, Sir? Seaweed or marsh grass with your plankton? I'm having mussel pie myself."

"Where you going to get toast?" Crowe said. "Anyway, I've been that route. No thanks. I think your granny's place is more the style to which I've become accustomed. But I'll come out and visit you during the mating season." He tossed a rock at two crabs on the wet sand.

"When is that?" Sandy asked.

"Daily, from dawn to dusk," Crowe said.

"Pretty short hours. I think I'll move back to town where folks have a more liberal sex life. Speaking of which, you're going to get something sunburned if we don't go. Be no use to anybody."

On the way home they stopped by an old graveyard full of monuments to fishermen who had died at sea. A thick fog had come in and they were both startled when a horse who had been grazing around the tombstones suddenly materialized out of nowhere, snorted in his own surprise, and shied back into the mist. There was considerable evidence that somebody's cows had paid frequent visits to the site. "You have to admit," Sandy said "the grass is horribly lush." On one large, granite marking crossed harpoons had been carved, with heavy lines descending into stone tubs at the pedestal, and between the lines twelve names of whalers lost at sea. "There is a similar monument in Monterey," Crowe said to Sandy, "without the harpoons and with only one name."

"Someone you know?"

"My father," Crowe said.

They pedaled back slowly, coasting along miles of empty, tree-lined road, and down the last hill into Vineyard Haven. On the way Crowe thought about all the things he had not told Sandy—who he was and who he was not, what he was trying to find and how he wasn't finding it because he wasn't sure what it was or where to look, how many girls not quite like herself he had not quite loved enough and had dumped here and there along the way, without bothering to tell them they had been dumped because he lacked the courage to face their outraged suffering, how many times he had set out to straighten up and how many times he had lapsed back into indifferent drifting. She would have said his problems were everybody's problems in this world. He was aware of that and misery is bored by company. He wasn't eighteen anymore. Somewhere along those last few miles he decided once again that the joy ride had to come to a halt. The search for something to latch onto was fast becoming an end in itself, or the *idea* of something to search for was becoming an end, since he had done precious little searching, and time, blessed, inconsiderate time, was running out. If you don't find where you're at right now, he told himself, you're never going to find out at all. Maybe the run-in with Parker was a good thing, since it put an end to a convenient way to avoid finding a job. The time is at hand. Either stop moving or go home and sit around a town full of bad memories. Tempting, that town, that coast, in spite of those memories. Easy to lie in the sun and become uninvolved. Easy to lie, easy to die. And go on looking. Easier there than anywhere else.

On their last day they shuffled from bed to beach and back again. Bought tickets for the early morning ferry, ate supper in a restaurant in the village, walked back to the house by moonlight. They took a couple of blankets and sat out on the lawn finishing up the last of a bottle of Scotch. After a ten minute study of the north star, Crowe said he had something to say. Sandy waited, finally prodded him. "So say something."

"I guess we had to get around to it eventually."

"Get around to what?"

"Get around to tomorrow. What I have to say is that I'm not going back to Vermont with you. I'm going into New York. Lemuel Pitkin is about to launch his career."

Sandy rolled over on her back. "In New York? I thought when the summer was over you'd go back to California."

"No," Crowe said. "Not a chance. No money, for one thing,

and for another I left California to get out from under it. Too
many people, places, and things I can't seem to resist." He took a
swallow from the bottle. "I don't know that I can explain it; you
have to grow up there to know what I'm talking about. And
maybe you have to grow up in a *particular* place there, I don't
know, but California becomes a state of mind, a mystique, a
whole set of attitudes and pressures, rather than just a piece of
geography, and after a while you begin to find out that a lot of
that mystique isn't very good for you psychologically, because it
produces more conflicts than resolution. You get like a half-
enchanted lotus eater who is really stoked by his island out of
time but who can't quite forget that Ulysses is out there beating
the drum." He put the bottle down, lit a cigarette, looked out over
the bay. "You don't know what I'm talking about, do you."

"I'm not sure."

"I'm not sure either."

A small ragged cloud slipped over the moon and the shadows
dimmed. Sandy lay back on the blanket with her arms behind her
head. "I was going to tell you . . . I started to tell you once . . .
that I've been accepted as a transfer student at Berkeley . . . it
finally came through . . . and planned to go this fall. I go in about
a week. It was kind of dumb of me, but I just assumed you'd be
out there, that maybe we could get a place together or something.
Boy, talk about fantasy and reality. I was so convinced they were
the same I never even asked you what you were going to do."

Crowe decided there would not be a better time to negotiate.

"You don't have to go," he said. "You could come to New
York with me and we'll get a place there."

For a few moments she didn't answer as if she were thinking it
over.

"And what would I tell my parents?"

"Tell them you're working."

"And living?"

Crowe shrugged. "With friends."

It was Sandy's turn to light a cigarette and stare at the bay.
Preamble to thought. I wonder why we always strike a pose,
Crowe thought, when we are about to pontificate. "No," she fi-

nally said. "I do have to go. I think. I'm not sure I can explain myself either, but maybe it's something like why you think you have to stay away, only reversed. I need to get into what you need to get out of. I need to see some other part of the landscape, some other way of life; to get away from New England, New York, my parents; from the same old thing year in, year out. You know, most of my friends think anything west of the Great Lakes is the wilderness. Maybe you don't know." She crossed her legs underneath her and looked at Crowe. "It's getting windy and it's going to rain. Let's go in and build a fire."

Crowe brought kindling and logs from the basement, laid them on some paper and struck a match. Lay down on the couch and put an embroidered pillow under his head. Sandy walked around the room.

"All my life," she said, "I've lived in this community of affluence where I've had everything I've wanted, and a lot that I didn't want, and nobody in that community has ever once thought about anything but *things* and how to acquire more, and how to protect what they already have. Oh, I know I'm always handing them a clichéd rap, but it's true. I mean, they're not bad people, they work hard and they pay their way, and some of them are even honest, but there is just a whole aspect to being alive that they aren't aware of. Like Burt, with all his boats, has never, I bet, sat back and looked up at a sail full of air beating to windward and said 'That's pretty. That's a beautiful shape.' It's just a boat to him, and it cost so much money, and it goes so fast, and sailing it kills an afternoon that would otherwise be total boredom."

She walked to the french windows and looked out over the garden toward the sea. Squalls on the water now, from the wind-chop. The sky growing darker and moving swiftly to the south-east. Now and then a blast of rain like pebbles on the glass.

"I'm not opposed to *things*, you know, but in my house you only talk about what you're going to get or what you just got or what somebody else is going to get that you want one of too, and how much it cost, how much it used to cost, and how much it will cost if the damn Democrats or the damn Republicans don't stop inflation. We never talk about a book or a play or an exhibition.

Burt looks at a painting by Paul Klee or Kandinsky or somebody, and all he can say is, 'I could do that. A kid could do that.' He took us all to Expo a couple of years ago and you know what we did? We rode around the monorail twice and then went and sat in some phony Jamaican bistro and drank rum drinks for three hours. We never saw *anything*. 'The lines are too Goddamn long,' Burt says."

Raining hard now, beating against the house in gusts. Like to sit inside by a fire and listen to the sound of water running in the gutter, off the eaves. Cozy and warm. Takes money to be cozy and warm. And things. A house is a thing, and drain pipes, and even rain. But she's right. It's not the house or the rain, it's the sounds they produce and the feeling of quiet and peace when the drops are pattering on the shingles and the fire crackles. The firelight throwing shadows on the low beamed ceiling of the den. Nothing can touch you here, and you can always come back because it isn't the things, it's the idea of them in the head, all in a particular combination, that matters, and they can't be burned down or sold or blown away or forgotten. Ever.

"And on days like this," Sandy said, "you should see them all sitting around the house. Suffering. It's raining and what can you do when it rains? Nothing. They won't read a book, or write a letter, or work a puzzle, and the TV's on the bum, so there's nothing to do but sit and look glumly out at all the wet, miserable, stinking weather and curse because the golf course is going to be a swamp and Burtie's going to get his feet sopping when he streaks out there the minute the sun pokes through.

"What's worse is they infect me, my family. I become absolutely catatonic. They do that. They're so Goddamn miserable unless they are being entertained in some way that they poison everybody in their path." She went over and sat beside Crowe, hands in her lap and her face to the fire. "So to wrap up a long, boring diatribe, I've got to get away. I *want* to get away. And I mean really away. If I don't go clear across the country they'll be saying 'Why don't you come home for the weekend,' or 'We thought we'd drive over and see you. We'll stay in a motel.' For about five months."

"I thought you implied," Crowe said, "that they were indifferent to you. Your hostility seems a mite confused."

"Hermina doesn't know what she is. She's just vaguely worried that one of us will besmirch the family name. Like when I once spent four months in Bermuda with a girl friend and her family, Hermina wanted me to walk around downtown in a pair of tight Levis so people would know I hadn't had to leave because I was pregnant. She's just crazy as a bed bug, but Burt, in his own curious and not very endearing way, cares about us, our welfare. The family provider bit. Make sure everybody gets the right start. The impulse is okay, it's just that his idea of a right start is somewhat limited." She lay down beside Crowe with her head on his chest.

"Oh, Crowe, don't you see. If you'd just come back with me to California we could have it both ways. I'll live with you in a cave if you want. I'll even give up the idea of going to school and work so you can get started at something. Like writing again or something. Only don't make me do it where I'd have to lie and hide all the time. New York is just too close to home."

"You don't have to lie. Just tell them you're working in the city and it's easier to live there."

"And when they come in and want to see my apartment?"

"I'll hide under the bed."

"That would be a lie. You know it would never work. And anyway, it's just what I said I couldn't do. I'd wind up lying about everything."

"Well then, don't lie. Tell them you're living with me, and just lay it on the line. Let 'em lump it. What are you, their vassal?"

"No. But I'm their daughter, and I guess I'm not as emancipated as I like to think, because I couldn't do that either. I just don't have the guts."

"Are you going to tell them about this little vacation?"

"No."

"Then you're already lying."

"If I am, compounding the felony doesn't make it any better."

Shrug. Silence. Leave the rest unsaid. No tickee, no laundry. Can't solve my own problems, so I can't take on yours. But I won't follow you to California either, because that would reverse the proper order, and we must, above all, maintain the tradition. And the male ego. The lady follows the gent. "Okay, then let me rephrase the question and see if we come up with the same answers. If we got married, you wouldn't have to lie." What sort of reaction he had expected to his backhanded proposal he wasn't quite sure but it probably had Doris Day directing and Roger Somebody's choral singing and maybe some dialogue lifted from "As the World Turns." Whatever he may have expected it wasn't what he got.

"If we got married that would be the biggest lie of all." She didn't look at him and he said nothing. The squall was passing and he could see the moonlight picking a sail up out of the dark water. A cat crept across the yard and disappeared beneath the hedge.

"You'd live with me but not marry me?" Crowe finally said, "I don't follow."

"I wouldn't marry anybody I hadn't lived with. My God, how would you know it was going to last? Why would you want to tie yourself down with a lot of legal stuff if you decided it was no go after a year or two, or however long it takes to find out?"

"I'm just a little confused here, Miss Rinelander," Crowe said. "I am assuming that since you are cohabiting with me at this moment you are not completely indifferent to my many charms and are willing to take me on spec, so to speak. Now I asked you first to come and live with me and you gave me some smoke-screen about lies and family pressures, and then I ask you to marry me and you tell me that you'd never buy a hat without trying it on first. I find this line of reasoning somewhat circuitous."

"All I said was I didn't want to have to tell lies to my family. If I'm far enough away, I don't have to tell lies. I said I'd live with you in California."

"So we're back to that," he said, irritation now clearly evident in his tone. "If I'll just trot along behind you and carry your bags you'll permit me to service you now and then, but only on location in California."

Sandy grew sullen herself and picked at her nails. "This is a stupid conversation," she said. "Let's go out and walk, or something."

"Why is it stupid?" Crowe said a little too loudly. "I don't think it's stupid, Goddamn it. I happen to be in love with you and want you to stay around on any terms that suit you, but you keep giving me a lot of adolescent crap that simply evades the issue."

"You are?" she said.

"Are what?"

"In love with me?"

"Sure" Crowe said, realizing for the first time that he probably was. "What do you think I'm doing here anyway? Taking the water?"

"You never said that before." She sat back in a chair and looked at him until he became uncomfortable and got up and walked to the window. For some reason he was not thinking about their relationship but of Parker Prince.

"Well now that I've said it," he asked, "does that change anything for you?"

She stirred in her chair. "I don't know," she said. "It does, but not the way you want it to. I still wouldn't marry you now, and I'm still going to go out west. You *could* go with me if you weren't so stubborn."

"You mean, I obviously don't have much else to do," paranoid Crowe said. He felt as if he wanted to hurt her for insisting on her dreams and ignoring his, but she seemed invulnerable. He was the one who kept getting hurt.

"Well . . . yeah, I guess. Your schedule doesn't seem too crowded. I don't see why it would make any difference."

"You haven't heard a word I've said, have you? Not today, or yesterday, or the past month. What I am or am not doing has little to do with it." He thought again of Parker and "half the guys" on the lake, and it suddenly occurred to him that he was probably no more than they were, that he undoubtedly *was* just an animated dildo when it came right down to the put up or shut up stage; or if that was unfair, if she really did love him, it was probably for unsubstantial reasons like his age and his freedom from obligations and the place he was from. He could not imagine why she was so obsessed with California, but it was clear that whatever pulled her in that direction was stronger than what pulled her toward him, and he decided right then in a kind of self-righteous moment of self-abrogation that he would not argue. What he really wanted more than anything, he told himself, was to put an end to this endless vacation and get a job and a decent apartment and enough money in the bank to dine at Pavillion whenever he felt like it. Maybe it was just as well that she preserve her illusions so that he could get on with his practical efforts, and, in fact, the more he thought about it as he sat there listening to the dripping eaves, the more he thought that he was right to retire from the field. To grub together in some flea trap in New York without much money (he knew she would never accept Burt's charity under such an arrangement) would be squalid and dreary, and not at all in the style that he had in mind for himself. They would fight and tear each other apart, and out of sheer perversity he would spend his days thinking of newer and better ways to torture her—and through her, himself. He'd done it before with other women, and had come away from those broken affairs hating himself more and more each time until eventually he'd begun wondering if he was capable of really loving anybody. It always seemed so at first.

"Well," he told her sadly, "it makes a difference to me. That's all. You take your trip, I'll take mine."

She nodded, as if she understood his meaning, and then, surprisingly, left him in a state of confusion once again by walking over and kissing him and saying, "Let's go upstairs. I do love you. I don't *want* to go away from you ever."

The island is gray and still. On the pine needles the fog condenses, falls in random droplets to the spongy turf, seeps away into the ground. Sounds carry a few feet and die suddenly on the moist air. Only the strident honk of the ferry approaching the harbor breaks the illusion that all forms and shapes behind the mist are chimerical. On a piling near where they are waiting with their bags, a white gull stands like a carved decoy, orange-footed, red-eyed, hook-beaked, motionless, indifferent. A scavenger, he is, devoted to the garbage pail.

The ferry pulls into its slip, backs its engines, churns the water green and boiling. The wharf creaks and resists, bells ring up in the pilot's house, and then the lines are secured and the ramp lowered. As the bread trucks move off, Sandy and Crowe move on, up the iron stairway to the deck. It is cold. The benches are wet, and they stand shivering at the rail, looking down into the opalescent water and wondering what today they are going to say to each other. The smell of her perfume is on his skin and his neck still hurts where in last night's last-time love making she bit it and left the mark of the farewell blues. He looks frustrated by their wasting silence, and yet he does not seem to know where to begin. Below, the gull is still on the piling, stiff, formal. Perhaps he too is in pain.

A boy and his little sister come out on deck and stand at the railing between two life boats. The girl starts to climb on the heavy wire fencing and is hauled down by her brother. The whistle blows above their heads and they both jump with shock. The little girl begins to cry.

The process is reversed. A half-dozen cars that have been waiting outside the gate drive up the ramp and into the ship's mouth. The ramp is drawn up, the lines freed, the water boils a moment, and then the gull begins to slip away beneath the boat and the shore fades, blurs, evaporates in smoke.

Sandy took Crowe's arm. "Let's get some coffee," she said, and they went into the lunch room to sit for the entire trip on a wooden bench and warm their hands with the hot paper cups.

In Woods Hole they ate a box of cookies while they watched a dredge working in one of the slips, then reluctantly got in the car and started for Providence where Crowe could catch a train to New York. Sandy drove and Crowe sat fiddling with the power equipment on Burt's Cadillac, punching the radio button, opening and closing the air-conditioning vents. He clearly made Sandy nervous, but for once she said nothing.

"Well," Crowe remarked, after a while. "This is sort of where I came in."

"I was thinking the same thing. I was thinking how mad you made me the first time I really met you . . . going to get Parker's car." She took her foot off the gas. "What are you going to do about the car?"

"I'm supposed to leave it there. Parker's parents are coming back from Europe in a week or ten days and going up to the lake."

"I didn't know you had heard from him," she said.

"Oh, I heard from him all right. In fact I saw him while you were at the wedding. Had a minor altercation with him . . . over you. That's why I was so late getting back."

Sandy again said nothing. Her eyes did not leave the road. "I gather from your silence that you can guess what that little tiff was about," Crowe said. Wondering why bring it up now? Why do you always have to try to vindicate your own cop-outs by putting someone else down?

She gave him a long glance and shrugged. "Maybe."

"Started pretty young, didn't you?"

She took a cigarette from the pack on the dash. "I never implied that you were going to have to weep for my innocence."

"That's right, you didn't."

"Shall we weep for yours?"

"Touché. It's what I deserve. Anyway, that's why I was late, in case you wondered. It took me a while to figure out that I really didn't care."

"I don't know if that's supposed to be good or bad," Sandy said. "But I'm glad you didn't care, because I certainly don't." She gave a nervous laugh. "Oh lover, you're such a bird sometimes."

Providence is thirty miles. He sat back and lit his twenty-first cigarette and said, more to himself than to Sandy, "Full circle. You think that's symbolic of a completed action? End of song? Ring down the curtain? Not responsible for articles left in the theater? Everybody back into the loneliness of two A.M. and nowhere to go and nobody to go there with, back to the rented flat where the air is heavy with soot and the wall-flowers are peeling off the plaster. You think that?"

"I don't know," Sandy said. "But it's a crummy enough day without your talking like that." When he looked at her he saw there were actual tears in the corners of her eyes, and he was surprised.

And then it was over, the thirty miles behind them, and the depot looming in front. Crowe took his rucksack out of the trunk and set it on the curb, feeling as if he were about to vanish behind prison walls and never look on the sunshine again. Neither of them wanted to drag it out. Sandy stayed in the car, and Crowe walked around to her window, bent down. "I lost the script," he told her. "I don't know my lines." He began to think the whole New York idea was a bad mistake, but it was too late to back down.

"It doesn't matter. They're just full of promises that nobody would ever keep." She twisted a hair ribbon around and around her fingers. "Write me. Tell me where you are."

"I'll be here for a while," he said, giving her Paps's address on a torn envelope. "I'll give you a full report as soon as I get settled." She smiled a little but her eyes were distant. She seemed primarily concerned to maintain her poise.

"If you'd call me at the lake I could tell you my flight number. I leave from Kennedy. We could see each other for a few minutes."

"I will," Crowe lied. "Good-bye, Kiddo. Take care." He leaned in and kissed her. Her mouth trembled and when he put his cheek against hers it was damp. "You certainly have green eyes," he whispered.

She squeezed his hand. "They come with the car."

Part 2

LAND OF THE CIMMERIANS

1 On the train. Crowe sat for three, four hours in righteous discomfort while seven million clicks and five million clacks wound off the computer, and he wondered what happened to the missing two million clacks. Arrived at his destination and gathered up his pack, hurried along with the crowd toward the subway entrance, and passed himself going the other way on the escalator —headed for the train, the station in Rhode Island, the Connecticut River Valley. Smell of clover and alfalfa in the air, and the kids are selling apples along the roadside.

He put his token in the slot, rode across town, downtown, to emerge from darkness into darkness, to stand for a moment at the point of his departure, to shake hands with his reflection in the drugstore glass. Half a block to Morton. Or is it two and a half, or perhaps three. And good old Francis to greet me with a churlish grunt and a groan or two of feigned discontent. All paths to here and now seem merely circular tracing superimposed upon then.

Faded red carpet on the foyer floor, color-matched wallpaper with embossed fleurs-de-lis on the walls, plastic table under the useless and now cracked mirror. At Grand Central Station he bought two chocolate bars and ate them in the shuttle. Caught the Seventh Avenue to Sheridan Square and walked the rest of the way to Morton where he stepped straight into a batter of dogshit outside the apartment. Cleaned his shoe on the rug, and thought to tell the truth it looks rather better. Dull but unscuffed.

Pushed the button under PAPANIKOLAS, A.F., but nothing happened. Pushed it again, and still nothing. Tried SIMKES, AL, and after a moment the door gave its static sputter. Pushed the button for the elevator and again nothing happened, so he walked up the dark stairway, past a hundred years of unwashed clothes and fried foods. Linoleum runners in the halls worn away in the middle and the black bannister smooth as metal. On the fourth floor he encountered Simkes, Al, in a terrycloth robe and carpet slippers. Smile pleasantly. Why are you standing there, my good man?

"You ring my bell?"

"I beg your pardon?"

"Who you want?"

Pugnacious, nasty. Typical New Yorker. No manners whatsoever. "Are you the manager? Who I want is perhaps none of your business."

"I'm the bell you rang."

Then you're not the manager. Out of my way Simkes, Al, before I break your heart. Push on by, and the slippers and robe fade through the door, gone to call the Super, the cops, the Feds. Christ, New Yorkers are a miserable breed, a shabby, contemptible, abject, puerile sub-genus with no dignity and no style whatsoever. Apartment 7. Prepare for the assault. I know you're in there Franny, because I saw your light from the street.

"Whodyawant?"

"I come for the merkins."

"*What?* Who is it?"

"The man in the poster. The man with the Scythe. Uncle Sam. Death. Open up, Faustus, it's time."

Paps fumbling with the chain. "Aw naw! Crowe?" Pulling the bolt lock. "Tell me it's a dream, God. Twice in one summer." Opening the door. From under a derangement of curly, black-gray hair two eye sacks peer out. Prickly chin under the sacks with an off-center mouth in it, and below, a revolting pair of pajamas stretched and bursting from his powerful frame. "No kidding around, man," Francis said, "What did I do to you anyway, that you should be doing *this*?"

"This is my autumn visit," Crowe said. "Summer was last time."

"Of course," Paps said. "I should have known. Really, I've not been myself since you left. Just a note, a 'Dear John,' and away with no good-bye, nothing."

"You look terrible, Paps," Crowe told him. "Failing badly. Your place looks terrible too. Disorder and early sorrow."

Books and drawings all over the room. A half-finished clay bust in the armchair. Stacks of five-by-eight photographs, mostly weddings and babies, on all the tables. Negatives on a wire across one end of the sitting room, interspersed with socks and several pairs of hideous jockey shorts. "I've had the flu," Paps said. "Clear yourself a chair. Don't sit on the bust." He shuffled around the room, rubbed his eyes, picked up a cold cigar butt and lit it. "You might have had the finesse to come in the morning. What time is it anyway?"

"The sun is over the yardarm, Francis."

"I suppose that's supposed to mean you want a drink. Sure it does. You always want a drink. Drinks for everybody at Papanikolas's. Free eats. Three hots and a cot. Good old Paps. Bend over Paps." He brought a half bottle of brandy from the kitchen and two glasses. Backed over to his armchair and sat on the clay bust. "What is that I *smell*?"

"Something you left on the stoop. I stepped on it."

"Don't you clean it off?"

"I tried, but it got in around the edges. I got a hole in my shoe."

"New York. You can't even live here anymore," Papanikolas grumbled. "Festooned in dogshit. It storms dogshit. Guys go to work along here in the morning before the cleaner's been around, and it looks like home leave from Bellvue. Jumping this way and that, slipping and sliding, scraping their shoes on the car bumpers, freaked out mad and the day hasn't started. You just can't live here anymore. It's an open sewer."

Crowe was only half listening. A tiny muscle near his eye began to jerk convulsively and he was reminded of how tired he was. Only this morning it was the Vineyard. The ferry ride through the fog seemed ten years in the past, Sandy an ache recollected through broken snatches of time. He tried to picture her face the way he had left her. Could not. Tried to recreate the points of the argument for living east, living west, living together, living apart. Could not make sense of it. Smells of rancid butter in here, he thought. Needs a cleaning, this place, a woman's touch. "An Afghan around the corner on Eighth Avenue that I don't know what it eats but it dumps orange, ten pounds to the block. Mangos. Pumpkins. Imagine that." Francis stood up, peeled the clay off his behind, stared at it blankly. He went into the kitchen and returned with two cans of beer, pulled the caps and cut his finger. Watched it bleed onto his pajamas. May not want to stay after all. But not much choice when you think about it. Get a job and a little coin in the bank and move into something more elegant, something with a view of the river, maybe, with a few tasteful antiques in the hall and a glass apothecary jar of lemon soap in the bathroom.

"Next door there's a couple of poodles. Drizzlers. Wet farters. Like they're laying lines down the sidewalk for three, four blocks. It's amazing."

"You better put something on your finger," Crowe said. Small fireplace, perhaps, for the wet nights. The cozy supper for two laid on a small walnut dropleaf table, candles, and the blood-red shadow of the wine cast on the linen, the fire flickering against the dark wainscot of the den.

"Two faggots on Jane Street got a wolfhound they walk way down here, an absolute behemoth. Unloads like . . . I don't know what."

We sit face-to-face across the table talking softly over softer music, of love, of peace, of the children we will have, of the farmhouse we will have in the country, of walks in the woods and a moonlight swim in the brook where the rocks have formed a natural pool, and the way the light shimmers away on the water down through the trees. And the trips we will take in the spring, to Europe, to Spain, to the rain forests of Latin America, with a month here and there in a rented house, a chateau in southern France, a cottage in the Alps, a hacienda in Mexico. He ached for Sandy.

"Stretches out, smiles one time, and *ka-blawee*, butters the street, the cars, the buildings, the Hudson River. Thunderous. A shit storm. You just can't live in the midst of all that."

After the fruit and cheese a bit of sweet, a brandy in the living room looking out over the river, something of Beethoven's, and a look from those deep green eyes that says now, the best is yet to come, and we go with arms around one another to the bedroom with its four poster and its New England furnishings to lie in almost dark on quilts and pillows and love until the sky begins to lighten and the rim of the sea emerges out of the fading night.

"Well, give me the bad news," Paps said, stretching his legs over the arm of the chair. "How long are you staying this time?"

"Staying? Oh, well . . . most generous of you, Francis, to offer. Briefly. Briefly. Just until I get a job."

"Just until I get a job," he repeated at breakfast on the morning of the eighth day. Papanikolas was scrambling eggs with one hand and stirring the frozen orange juice with the other while Crowe made coffee. In the tiny kitchen they confused more than assisted each other. "I needed this week to adjust to a bleeding heart."

"A job," Paps said. "You'll never get a job. Last time you were going to get a job and what happened? A vacation in Vermont. But hell, I don't care. I'm out all day now anyway, and I might as well drink with you at night as with myself." The toaster let go its load and fired both pieces on the floor. Crowe picked them up and put them on the plates. "I might give you a job myself. I've been thinking about a partner. You know anything about photography?"

"I was a sign painter once," Crowe said. Francis covered his eyes in a gesture of weariness. "I mention it only to indicate I've had artistic training."

"I suppose I could teach you to develop negatives. I rent the custodian's storeroom down the hall for my office and dark room."

"I thought you worked for a printing firm."

"Got a new racket now," Paps said, ladling the eggs onto the plates and sitting down. "Currently making it in the photo game. My card, Sir." He picked an advertisement for himself off the windowsill and handed it to Crowe. ARISTOTLE F. PAPANIKOLAS, PHOTOGRAPHER. ALL FORMAL OCCASIONS. "I don't mind telling you it pays off damn well. I go to weddings, you know, and shoot the mommies and daddies and uncles and aunties and, of course, the sacrificial lambs. First moments of nuptial bliss, cutting the cake, throwing the rice, gaiety, song and dance, off we go into the sunset dragging our cans behind us. Smiling smugly. Goo'bye little girl. We know where you're going, and we know you been there before. Great event, the wedding. Everybody should have three or four." He began inhaling his eggs.

"I don't know, Francis," Crowe said. "I sort of had in mind a job with a little more future, a little more room to grow."

"Growth is the name of the game." Paps poured himself some coffee. "I've had a sideline going here for a little while that promises to render obsolete all other forms of photographic inquiry. Babies. Babies are where the real bread is located. Hundreds and thousands of little shoats who will all grow up to be delinquents and drug freaks but who now need, thanks to their doting parents, to be recorded for posterity. The twelve shot, five-by-eight photo album of your kid is fast replacing the copper dipped shoe syndrome so popular in our generation. Babies, man. Grinning, burping, farting little babies. With colic, bucolic, melancholic, gas pains and soggy diapers. With snot in their hair and pablum on their jib. It's staggering, Jack, frightening even, how many babies there are in this world. In this *city*."

"I don't like babies," Crowe said.

"I don't like 'em either. They ought to be kept in cages. But they are money in the bank." He buttered a piece of toast, tore it in two, put half in his mouth. "Listen," he said through the crumbs, "How much I don't like babies is this. They give me nightmares. Like I'm lying here in bed, and out there, out there are seven or nine or eleven million people all humping like crazy . . . except me, which is the nightmare part of it . . . and the whole New York area, Brooklyn, Queens, Long Island, Manhattan, all of it, before my very eyes, turns into this great big uterus out of which are popping babies at the rate of two per second, per second, and I'm standing there with my camera and my photo album kit tearing out fistfulls of hair because it's Sunday and I'm out of film and all the stores are closed. I have that dream a lot."

Crowe got up from the table and walked to the window, looked down into the street where two kids were racing each other up and down on homemade boxcars. Funny, he thought, that in the daytime it's not so bad. It's at night, when you begin to doubt, when you feel your own mortality most intensely, that you long for what is denied you, what you have denied yourself. But in the morning everything seems possible. In the morning nobody is lonely. At night you tell yourself that you have been almost four months trying to straighten out your life, your head, and you haven't made one step forward. In fact, you may have taken two back. But in the morning you think this might be your day.

"Babies," Paps said. "You do the darkroom work and I'll cut you in. It's my finest offer."

"Not babies. I'm not kidding around, Francis. I'm over thirty, and here I am doing nothing still, like I was eighteen and had the world by the short hairs. I've got to get going. I need a placement bureau or something to find me a career. Really, I'm that desperate."

"A *career*? Is this really you talking? A career? Wow. What ho, the rake's progress. It's a sad day, a sad day."

"I don't think it's funny."

"A placement bureau. A career," Papanikolas was overcome. "How about a business career? Law career? Medicine? Teaching? Why don't you be a famous physicist and go to work for NASA? Or how about a philanthropist? Be a Carnegie, a Guggenheim, a Rockefeller. I got it. You could get some dark glasses and a tin cup. Work a hype." He broke into song. *Don't cry lady, I'll buy your Goddamn violets, Don't cry lady, I'll buy your pencils too. Come on lady, take off those colored glasses. Hello mother, I knew it was you.*

"I'm not screwing around, Franny."

"Bullshit. You're always screwing around. You're one of the last of the big time screw-arounds in the western world. A career my soggy arse. What can you do? What are your skills? Your training? Oh sure, I know, lots of people have little skill and no training, but they don't have many brains either and they haven't acquired a taste for the good life the way you have. The only things you're probably equipped to do right now you won't do because they are beneath your dignity, your image of yourself as clever, gifted, tasteful, and faintly aristocratic. You won't do any of those things because the guys who do those things don't ride around in expensive cars wearing three-hundred-dollar Morty Sills suits and eating at Lutece three nights a week. They ride the subway and they buy their clothes at Barney's and maybe once a month they take their wife out for a big time at some local hash house and a two dollar movie uptown afterward. So you'd rather do nothing than that. If I can't be vice-president, fuck it, I'll be Henry Miller instead."

"You finished?"

"No there's more. I just want to say, now that the opportunity has arisen, that in one week this here spiggot is getting turned off. Pension Papanikolas is evicting your ass in one week, not because you're an economic drag, but because I can't afford you spiritually."

"Come off it," Crowe protested.

"I'm serious. Whenever you fall in on me for one of your tours of duty . . . Chicago, San Francisco, and now here, I become your Sancho Panza, your straight man, or whatever you want to call it, for some immensely entertaining, private joke that has something to do with your imagined wit and my supposed buffoonery, and when you blow out of town each time leaving your dirty laundry and your unpaid bills, I find I despise myself for quite a while for being what I suppose I am, an indiscriminate lover of all humanity, a shelter for all strays, no taste in people at all. I like being that way, frankly, but you happen to be the one person on earth who reminds me that a guy who puts welcome on his doormat is probably going to get taken to the cleaners by most of those souls he's so warmly embracing. I prefer not to be reminded. I prefer to share the goods without the nagging suspicion that I'm somehow paying my dues to Beelzebub. So one more week, mother fucker, and if you haven't found a job by then it's just rough apples. Out."

Crowe was somewhat stunned and couldn't think of a retort, so he just let it drop. There was an embarrassed pause, then Paps broke into a grin. "Aw, what the hell," he said. "Tell you the truth

I don't know how long I'm going to stay in New York anyway. You remember that piece of land I bought outside Monterey when I was living in San Francisco? Well, my current dream is to retire out there, do some farming, do the Ansel Adams kind of photography I really like instead of this weddings and babies crap, and I just don't want you to get too entrenched here, Jackson. I wouldn't want to feel when I split for the coast that I'm deserting my obligations."

"Jesus," Crowe said, "Can't anybody stay away from out there?"

The whole problem is, he told himself as he thumbed for the third go around through the Sunday *Times* "business opportunities" section, you either have to know some*thing* or some*one*. A liberal education isn't worth a good Goddamn when you're looking for a job. Lots of slots for senior systems analysts and sales administrators, and product managers and group controllers with operations background, but Crowe didn't even know what the titles meant much less have any qualifications for applying. The things he could actually do (Baskin-Robbins needed a soda jerk, Shields and Company needed a runner, Laundra-matic needed a manager in Baldwin, Long Island) he wouldn't. As Paps had said, it was beneath him.

For one week he canvased all the publishing houses he could contact, and for another he made the magazine tour, but what was always needed, if anything, was a secretary not an editor-in-chief. One personnel director told him that there were so many experienced people floating around in publishing now that nobody had to look for fresh blood anymore.

Eventually he gave up on the literary racket. In desperation he took a part-time night job with an air freight company that employed, among other things, used onion sacks as packing, and his job for six hours a day was to turn the onion sacks right side out and stack them in bundles. After the fifth night of shrieking boredom he collected his fifty-two seventy from payroll and quit. Then he bought a quart of Old Overalls and went home to Paps's to drink it.

Another half-week went by and Crowe did very little besides sit in the apartment and think about Sandy. He read a few magazines, searched again the help wanted ads in the *Times* but made no calls, asked himself repeatedly what he ought to do. He came reluctantly to agree with Paps that maybe he was just screwing around, that the idea of a career and its rewards was a great deal more entertaining than actually doing anything about it—anything, for instance, like starting at the bottom and working up. The phrase itself nauseated him. It was, he thought, rather like writing. Stories in the head were so much better than stories on paper. And easier to do. He could remember a great many nights, lying in bed thinking up plots, characters, situations, deliciously anticipating the morning when he would get up and get to work. But five mornings out of seven the work got preempted by something and the stories dissolved, were forgotten, lost their interest. At least I admit it, he told himself. It's a start. That ought to be worth something.

On Saturday night Paps suggested they go bar hopping. "Big score today. It's on me," he said. Crowe had half expected a letter from Sandy, though he had not written himself, but nothing had come and he was too depressed to care whether he went out or not. Paps noticed the lack of enthusiasm. "What's with you? Some free sauce doesn't turn you on anymore?"

"I don't know, Franny," Crowe said, as tragically as he could. "I guess maybe it's this girl that I told you I spent the summer with. She's got me rather twisted."

"I should think a half-dozen boilermakers could iron out the kinks. Why has she got you twisted?"

"I love her."

"I find that hard to take seriously."

"I'm not above it."

"So, go see her."

"She's in California."

"Ah, the fog lifts. I begin to see the horizon. You want to bum the plane fare to San Francisco, which of course you will pay back as soon as you get that job we've been discussing, and you are now softening my heart with a long face and a tragic tale of romance that you have spent all day preparing. Are you going to use notes, or talk off the cuff?"

"On the contrary, I have no intention of going to San Francisco. I was simply answering your question about why I wasn't so jolly."

"Is she of age?"

"Of age? Sure. She's over eighteen, if that's what you mean."

"Does she love you?"

"I believe she does."

"Is she rich?"

"Her father gets by."

"Why didn't you get married then?"

"It's a long story that I would rather not go into. Suffice to say that I lack the wherewithal to support a wife."

Paps took an overcoat from the closet and flung it at Crowe. He put on his own duffle coat and started doing up its peg buttons. "Suffice to say that that is more of your bullshit," he said. "Everybody I know like you lives off his woman. The real reason is that a wife wants attention, she wants fidelity, she wants appreciation. She wants you to keep cleaner, she doesn't like your friends, she wants, above all, a ceremony to confirm things and give her legal recourse in the event you turn out to be the prick she suspects you might be, she wants you to stop smoking, she wants less drinking and more thinking, she does not regard herself as your whore but as your intellectual companion and would like you to talk to her now and then. Marriage is an endless accommodation, and you know it only too well. Accommodation has never been one of your strong points. That's the reason you didn't get married to this girl you 'love' so much you can't go out for a drink, you ache too good."

"You know, Francis," Crowe said, putting on the overcoat. "You're becoming a thorough pain in the ass. What are you anyway? My conscience? My analyst? Ever since I came through that door it's been a put down. Just lay off, will you, or I'll cut you off. I won't even give you the full week. If you want to know the real reason I didn't get married it's because I got turned down."

"Ah" Paps said, raising his eyebrows. "A wise girl. I would like to meet this girl. Only let's go, huh? The windmills are waiting."

They went out onto Morton Street and walked east to Seventh Avenue, angling through side streets to Third, MacDougal, and then across Washington Square and along until they hit Fourth Avenue where the bookshop windows are dark and piled with twenty-cent losers, purple and black, faded and the pages yellowing to brown along the brittle edge. Can't see in the dark, but that's how they are, and I know the musty smell of old books in old stores never swept, where the old men sit and ruffle papers in the gloom; accounts, ledgers, a semblance of labor.

It started to rain lightly, just enough to wet the street and make the occasional taxi tire hiss. In the window of a cafe Crowe saw a girl. Dark copper hair around her face, and when she raised her head to meet his gaze he saw the eyebrows black and the dark roots along the part. Face scarred from acne. Not like my Sandy. And where are you tonight, my Sandy? On a plane for the coast? Sitting in some college hangout along Telegraph while the bombs burst in air and by the rocket's red glare the boys are marching in their Goodwill uniforms to the picket lines to protest the latest inanity of a backward and confused local, state, national administration? Or are you in your room, bent over a book while the study lamp shines down on your burnished head, on the page, on the print reflected in your eyes? Noble ideas. The best thoughts of the best men who know what they mean and can say it.

They went into a neighborhood bar on Avenue A. Two fingers and a vote for Miss Rheingold. Allow me, please, it's my round. But if you could lend me a fiver until payday. . . . Payday? There will someday be a payday.

Paps brought the drinks from the bar, poured the beer and put a dash of salt into his glass. In Mexico we used to salt our beer, Crowe remembered. Hiding in the dark corner of some cantina from the proctors who led our Southwestern prep school, my second, Pap's first, on its annual culture break south of the border, putting salt in our beer the way we saw the patron do it. In Mexico where I tried on my first piece of tail and failed because I felt foolish standing there age fourteen with my pants around my ankles and my boots still on while the good mama, old enough to be *my* mama, washed my shrinking joint with soap and water and said, *"Tu tienes frío."* and Paps later confessed the same affliction.

"Personally, I don't see much difference between the moral order of one generation and another. All a question of semantics, right?"

"Right," Crowe said. What are we talking about. Must have missed the first act.

"The terms change and the equipment changes, that's the big thing, but the impulse is the same, and nobody digs this. I mean, Jackson, that what turns kids all on is they think they're different because they pop a few new pills and take a few new trips and go a little farther. But I don't give them too much credit. They're just better equipped. We would have done it too."

"I think you're getting dated, Francis. It's brown rice and mu tea these days. The organic life. No equipment at all."

"There's just more of them."

"Sixty million."

"And you know whose fault it is? As your local representative of the National Association of Natal, Prenatal, and Postnatal drips, I am here to tell you who is responsible for this sad state of affairs. All the ding-dong daddies out there in my dream, fornicating like mad and over-populating the world. They ought to pass a law. Everybody with over two kids gets nutted. Do you know that in fifty or sixty years they say we'll all be standing two deep all over the world, just able to keep our noses above our own crap, which won't be any comfort because there won't be enough air to breathe anyway. You know the more I think about it the more I think I'm going to split in the next few months. Go out and fix that farm up."

"I have a theory," Crowe said, "a Darwinian extension, that evolution has reached its apex, biologically, morally, spiritually, and that we are now on the journey back, to the cave, to the trees, to the jungle floor, to the slime, to the water, and then one day, poof, the last cell is going to squeeze off one last fart and candle's gonna go out. There will be silence on the face of the earth. I'd kind of like to be there."

"Well, it sounds rather empiric to me, but I'll buy it. I'll also buy another round."

"Two more for Miss Rheingold."

When the bar closed they went out into what had turned into a light but steady rain. Half drunk, they walked in the middle of the street with their heads tilted toward the sky.

"Feels good," Paps said.

"Feels like the mountains," Crowe said.

"Yipee," Paps yelled, hopping up on the curb. "We're in the mountains, in the high ridges of the terrible mountains of the north, on the plateau of the world where the Tenzing Norkeys and the Edmund Hillarys fear to go. Walking above the tree line, the oxygen level, the very atmosphere itself, where only the Gods sport in their cloudlined bowers of unearthly delight." He stopped and peered down into the gutter, pushed his glasses back on his nose. "Hey," he said, "what's all this fucking garbage?"

"That's not garbage," Crowe told him. "That's the world, man. Down there." He pointed at the broken sack on the drain hole. Lettuce leaves, chop bones, coffee grounds, melon rind, dog food cans, soup cans, a soap bottle. "That's where the people live."

"Thank God," Paps said, wiping his forehead. "For a minute I thought some clutz had thrown his stinking garbage into the bower of unearthly delights."

It began to rain harder and they jogged all the way to Mac-Dougal, pacing each other stride for stride, punching one another in the arm now and then out of sheer exuberance. They stopped under an awning on Third to catch their breath, and Paps, when the puffing and blowing subsided, said, "Say, I wasn't kidding the other night about that job. I got more work than I can do, and I really am going to have to get somebody to help out with the darkroom stuff."

"I thought you were turning off the tap in one week."

"Well, yeah. But you know me. I talk a lot and forget easy."

"I thought you were pulling out for California."

"Now that, baby, is so. Soon. But not yet. Fixing the place up is going to take some people and so far I haven't found anyone I want to do it with. Say, you wouldn't . . ."

"Lord no. What are you paying that darkroom assistant?"

Paps thought a minute. "It's no eight hours a day trip, but I can give you a sixty-five a week and an even split on the baby albums. We do more business, I'll raise it."

"There's just one problem, Franny. I don't know a camera from a hot rock."

"You don't need to know that. The darkroom stuff I can teach you."

Crowe looked out into the rain and thought about the isolation of the single bill in his wallet. "Well," he said, "It's a step up from onion sack inverter. I'll give it a go. Let's get out of this swamp before I sober up and change my mind." The rest of the way home, he ran like a crazy man, whooping and hollering, now and then ducking into an apartment building to run his finger up and down the rows of black and white buzzers, and singing at the top of his lungs *"Cats on the rooftops, cats on the tiles, cats with their assholes wrapped in smiles, cats with syphilis, cats with piles, reveling in the joys of fornication."*

2 He went to work for Paps, learned how to mix chemicals, develop film, run the dryer, make prints and use the enlarger, mount and frame. He found he rather liked what he was doing; that there was a certain satisfaction in taking a piece of gray celluloid and turning it into a picture, five, eight, ten times larger than it had started out on the negative. He began fooling with his prints, making them darker, lighter, shading the tones; began composing on the light table. It was more satisfying, in a way, he thought, than trying to write. More like painting. You could always see where you were and where you had been. You didn't have to wait five years for the finished product. If it didn't work out you could redo it in an hour.

By the end of September he was reasonably competent in the darkroom and hankering to do some camera work himself. Paps lent him an old Agfa with a built-in light meter and he began wandering the streets for an hour or so each day, shooting up rolls of film, plotting in his mind a book on New York. Since he was still living with Paps (the deadline had come and gone with nothing more said), his beat became the Village, Eighth Avenue and across town to the Bowery and as far up as Fifteenth, and he began to focus his ideas on that part of town. "You could do a then and now thing," he told Francis. "You know, get a bunch of old pictures circa the exiles' return, and shoot a lot more of the village now. Bohemian to hippies. Call it *Downtown, Downhill.*" He even went so far as to call a publishing house and spoke to a young editor he'd met while job hunting who told him it sounded vaguely interesting. The editor would, of course, have to see the pictures, read an outline of the text. Crowe asked for a month; said he would come in.

The idea of a book helped assuage his preoccupation with Sandy. She was always there, a face on the subway, a tall girl moving before him down Lexington Avenue, the green eyes of an advertisement staring at him out of an oculist's window, the unconfined breasts of a girl on Bleecker Street bouncing beneath her peasant blouse as she skipped along, but he no longer spent the better part of each day with her on his mind. She had not written. He had not written himself. He did not, he said, know her address. Besides, there were other girls cropping up. In particular a tiny Japanese doll named Shira whom he had met at a party thrown by a commercial artist friend of Paps's. Shira had the longest hair and the shortest skirts he could remember seeing. They danced most of the evening together, smoked some Acapulco Gold that turned out to be oregano, and talked about Zen orgasm until Crowe thought he would either die of anticipation or boredom. He had gone home with her that same night. Found she talked a better game than she played. During a period of controlled breathing she fell asleep or passed out, but Crowe had gone on alone in his old fashioned, uninspired, Aristotelian way, and didn't mind at all. He saw her now and then. Thought she was, if not particularly bright, delightful to look at.

And there was the wife of the computer scientist, George Rao. Stephane. Paps had introduced them. "We've all got to get together," he had said. "George owns a piece of a ranch in Oregon. He does something with computers that not too many people know how to do. In New York for like a year and he's going to make a big enough bundle that he can retire to his spread, and be Rancher Rao for the rest of his days. In fact, *he's* looking for people to go in on it with *him*, if you're interested in that part of the country."

"No," Crowe said. "I'm not."

"Didn't think so. Anyway, his wife, Stephane, a tasty little number if I ever saw one, went to the Verde Valley School. Only six years later than us. Small world, huh?"

"Too small," Crowe said.

Paps arranged a dinner at a nearby Spanish restaurant he admired, invited the Raos and about a dozen other people. Stephane started to make her pitch ten minutes after Crowe met her. "You're from the coast, too," she said, full of bubbles and bounce. "You belong to the sexual freedom league?"

"I don't think so," Crowe said.

Stephane was attractive in a sullen sort of way, short, with a pouty mouth and amazing buttocks. They moved under her knit skirt as if they had a mind of their own. Either that, or she kept flexing them to the beat of some internal and mysterious drum. She wore no makeup and no underwear, the first obvious, the other a whispered confession. "I can't stand New York," she said, "I want to get back to California and take my clothes off. You like to take your clothes off?" She pinned her eyes on Crowe.

"When I swim," he said. "When I sleep."

"How about when you make love?"

"God made the zipper for that."

Her husband, George Rao, was a small, dark number who spoke quietly and infrequently and looked as if he might have quite a lot in his head. Crowe wasn't sure. When dinner was over and they all went back to the apartment, he and Crowe walked together and talked a little about the city. "All I've done here in six months, besides make money," George said, "is reaffirm my conviction that an urban existence is less and less possible as the years go by. The kind of life we all live in New York now just doesn't make it, even if you're rich. Too bloody many people. No time to think, to contemplate, to enjoy, to look around you and absorb the environment. You just shuttle in and lock the door. The only time I ever like New York is on Sunday mornings." They stopped to wait for a traffic light. "You ever go out on Sunday mornings? It's quiet. Nobody around. You can walk about without having to keep one eye out for the insane taxi drivers, one eye out for the circus lady with her arms full of packages, one eye out for the dog manure, and the other eye out for falling bricks. In a way it's spooky, but it's nice, and you begin to notice things, buildings, trees, birds, that you never see during the week." He stretched his arms and let out his breath in a rush.

"A few more months and I'll have a big enough stake to lay low for awhile, read, grow things, sit around and enjoy the weather. I understand you're from Monterey. You know where the Tarsajara Hot Springs are?"

"Sure," Crowe said. "Great country, that."

"Paps tells me he has a place near there. I prefer it farther north where it stays green all year, but I hear Monterey country is nice. You ever think about retreating from the madhouse and just cultivating your own garden?"

"Most of the time," Crowe said. "Only I've been retreating for some years now, and I'm trying to reacquaint myself with its horrors. I don't find them all that bad. At the moment."

"Wait six months. You'll be nuts or numb."

"Say, George," Crowe said, walking a little slower so that they might fall back from the group, "this thing you do with computers, how do you learn to do that? I mean, are there special schools where you go? Or what?"

Any college. Courses in computer programing. Nothing very esoteric about it. I took a degree in computer science at Oregon State."

"Oh. That's the only way."

"It's the easiest."

The others had gotten ahead. Crowe and George had to wait for the elevator to rise six floors and descend seven. As they got in George said, as if he'd just remembered it, "Oh, listen, about Stephane. She'll probably ask you if you'd like to make it with her, and I just wanted to say don't be embarrassed or anything. I mean, it's obviously up to you whether you're tempted, but I, frankly, have no interest one way or another so don't worry about me. One of the ways we get along is by letting the other person be and do what he wants. We believe in that kind of freedom."

"Hunnn," Crowe said. The elevator reached the top floor and they got out. The party was already shaping up in Pap's apartment, and Crowe went through the door wondering if he had gotten himself mixed up with another nut. He still wasn't sure.

The party got louder and a neighbor came by to complain about the music. Stayed to drink more than his share and eventually threw up in the hall. Two girls that somebody knew came by with their dates, looked around, had some peanuts and left. Someone pushed the flower pots off the window box and they smashed seven floors below in the alley. The super called and said to tone it down or he would throw them all out. Around midnight, Crowe, sober and tired, went into the bedroom, pulled the mattress off the bed, and started to drag it down to the darkroom where he could go to sleep. A book fell off the dresser as he went by, and he bent over to pick it up; saw a letter addressed to him. It was from Sandy. Paps had been using it as a bookmark.

He put the letter in his teeth and continued on to the front door with the mattress. Rao was there with Francis, saying goodnight. "Just throw her out when you close up shop," he said to Paps. "I'll grab a cab home. Work tomorrow. I've got to get some sack time."

"Where are *you* going?" Paps asked Crowe as he shouldered by.

"Mail must go through," Crowe said, the letter still in his teeth. He trailed his mattress down the hall, put his key in the darkroom door, and opened it. Went back for a pillow and a blanket. Put the blanket over his head when he saw Stephane approach. Stood up against the wall. "I know you're in there," she said, lifting a fold and ducking into his darkness. "Thought you were going to sneak out, huh? Mama saw you." She did a drunken bump and grind against him and tried to kiss his mouth but she was too short. Got him on the neck and banged her nose on his chin. "Excuse me," Crowe said.

"What are you doing under this blanket?"

"I'm a root," he told her.

"Are you an edible root?"

"I'm a poison ivy root."

"Yuk." She smelled like a cigarette butt in the dregs of a bourbon and water. Crowe began to wish he weren't a root. "Don't you like me?"

"Absolutely," Crowe said.

"What does that mean?"

"Yes," Crowe told her.

"I don't think you do. I think you've been avoiding little ol' Stevey. Does Stevey scare you, honey?"

"Somebody put chlordan on my bush," he said.

"Oh brother," she laughed, "I bet that plays hell with the root." She put her leg between his and pushed her hip into his crotch. "Oh, honey, it's on its last legs. Maybe we ought to revive it."

Crowe felt a wave of exhaustion wash over him, almost taking his breath away. He wanted nothing more in the world than to lie down. Alone. "Another time," he said removing the blanket, picking up his pillow. He started to move toward the door.

"Don't you want Stevey to tuck you in?" Still trying to be coy.

"No, Stevey," Crowe said. "I don't. But when I do, you'll be the first to know." No humor in his voice, and she backed off.

In the darkroom he put the pillow against the wall, lay down and opened his letter. A picture fell out on his chest and when he looked at it he nearly cried. It was of Sandy, lying on the dock in Vermont, the lake and distant shore line in the background. She was on her side with her head propped on her hand, her hair falling behind her arm and touching the dock. He had forgotten how beautiful she was, forgotten the slight cleft in her chin, the clear line of her cheek and forehead. Her eyes and her hair. They dominate memory.

He unfolded the sheets of paper. *I tried for a long time not to write this*, it began, Not dear Jack, or my darling Crowe, or hi there, just

> I tried for a long time not to write this. I knew the minute I left you in Providence that to try to see you in New York before I left, or to try to call you, would be my undoing. Even to start up a correspondence would be stupid and emotionally destructive, so I decided to let the world end in a bang, not a whimper. It should end in a bang. Pow. So you can write it off and go on to other worlds. That's what you were trying to do when you brought up my teenaged transgressions during our last ride

together, wasn't it? Trying to end everything with a fight
so that it wouldn't hurt too much? But for me, it hurt.
I know you didn't really have the heart for it, and I thank
you for that, Crowe, even though it might have been
better in the long run. Now I'm not quite sure of myself,
but I can't just let go unsaid all the things I've been
thinking for the last month and so this letter.

Did I ever tell you how I'm scared of flying? When I
fly I have to work very hard at not thinking about the
plane crashing because I have this idea that the mind may
somehow affect reality, and if I concentrate on the plane
exploding in mid-air, it *will* explode. It's hard work because
there's always a struggle going on—a desire to test the
theory vs. a conviction that the theory will prove out. But
on the flight to San Francisco I was spared, for once, that
battle because I couldn't get my mind off how sad I was
and how tragic to be torn between love and duty, and
various other soap opera sentiments with which my
emotional control center seems to be constantly clogged.
The man next to me began a conversation but he gave up
when I didn't respond. I spent five hours and twenty
minutes staring out the window and trying to capture
your face in my mind. I wore out the negative, and by the
time the pilot came on to announce a thirty-thousand-
foot view of the Rocky Mountains I couldn't remember
what you looked like at all. I actually cried when I
realized I didn't even have a photograph. But I kept telling
myself, Sandy, you're an ass. What's past is past. If you
don't let go of it you're going to screw up whatever is
ahead—assuming this damn plane doesn't fall apart and
dump you in the middle of the Great Salt Lake, and it's
what is ahead, your whole life really, that matters. And
then we landed and for three hours, from the time I
picked up my bags to the time I set them down in the
hotel room in Berkeley, I managed to get you out of my
head. Around dark I lay down on the bed and looked at
the spots on the ceiling and asked myself what in God's

name I was doing three thousand miles from anything
I knew, and when I couldn't think of the answer I really
started to bawl. I cried until I fell asleep. That's sort of
how it went for three weeks. I was really turned around. I'd
think about you and it was like somebody shouting and
I couldn't hear, and I'd keep telling them 'louder, louder,
louder' and they would shout louder but they still weren't
making it, like they had a monaural pre-amp plugged into
a stereo post-amp, or whatever those things are called,
and somehow the leads are all fucked up so that there
was nothing but hum and distortion coming through the
speakers, and I'd think there's only so many ways to listen
to feedback, your set's a bummer, Jack, it gives me the
bends trying to filter sense through a hundred and
twenty watts of whistle, groan, and ack-ack, so when I
find the right knob I'm going to turn you off. Click.
Only you wouldn't go off.

Crowe rolled over and laid the letter on the mattress. He lit a
cigarette and looked around the darkroom at the light table, the
enlarger, the shelves with chemicals, paper, film. Never knew her
head was like that, he thought. Whistle, groan, and ack-ack. I
never knew she knew that stuff, never looked much beneath the
surface. As usual. He suddenly felt miserable at the lost opportunity, cursed himself for being a solipsist, a monomaniacal pig, a
sententious fool. He crushed the cigarette out on the floor and
picked up the letter again.

It wasn't always like that. Sometimes when I'd think
about you it was like snow falling in the woods, soft,
drifting down easy through the branches and in around the
trunks, building out a big white collar, and spreading
off into a blanket of silence under the trees. I'd lie
listening, straining for a whisper of wind among the
needles. It was O.K., then, but I'd wait for a sound, and
nothing. It was like drowning in honey, sinking slowly
down like a tiny pearl in a bottle of yellow goo and yet

I wasn't like a pearl because I had no substance. I was
just an idea, really, all rolled up in a ball, and looking
for a companion. Pylades cut off from Orestes, a celibate
conceit crying to get laid. That's English Literature 143.
So you see I'm learning something. Anyway, that's how
it was other times, when I needed you. I told you I was
twisted around. Sometimes I thought I was going crazy,
that if I could find the right knob I could turn myself off.

But what all this rambling is leading to is that I think
maybe I finally found that knob and it was under my nose
all the time. You. Click. It isn't as easy as it sounds put
down on paper because I loved you, I really did, and I put
it in the past tense because that's part of the click. In
order to just stay on top of the minutes of the day and
function, I have to turn the amplifier off. To just get up
and eat and go to class and study and go to bed I have to
shut out the echoes, the reverberations. It's cold turkey,
Crowe. It's like not having that cigarette with your coffee
in the morning (by the way I quit smoking)—hard for a
while, but then you get used to filling a lack and it's not
so hard anymore, it gets to be one of those tastes that you
can't quite locate, can't quite remember where you had
it before. And before you throw this down in disgust
wondering why the dumb bitch is taking so long to say
farewell to something that I guess for you must have been
long gone and buried, let me announce that, numero uno,
I didn't want you to have a bad conscience thinking you
had maybe gotten me into an emotional situation I couldn't
handle and that you ought to do something about it (I
know that's presumptuous, but I can't help worrying about
it), and numero dos, I needed to write it down to get rid
of it. Writing it down is a kind of emetic for me. And
so having written it, I'll quit. Only I don't know how one
ends a letter like this. It's been nice knowing you? It has,
Crowe. Nothing in my life has ever been nicer.

                                                             Sandy

Crowe leaned back on the pillow and stared at the pages in his hand, his mind as smooth as a billiard ball. He tried to think about what she had said, about what she meant, but nothing would crack that hard ivory surface. He felt anesthetized, and wearily he reached up and snapped off the light. In the dark he could still see the bulb's filament burning, a hypnotic memory before his eyes, and he lay there feeling rotten and lonely wondering why it would not turn off. "If I could do it all over again," he said out loud to the darkness, "I'd do it all different. All of it." After a while he thought, that's the saddest thing I ever said, and in order to keep himself from becoming utterly maudlin he got up, went down the hall, and stuck his head back in the party. When he saw her coming out of the bathroom he went over and said, "Hey, listen, I think there's a boogy man under my bed, ma, and I want you to make it go away."

"A boogy man?"

"Yeah. It's only got one eye. It's a terrible thing to look on." He backed toward the door. "You coming?"

Stephane smiled and threw him the world's stalest return, "Only breathing hard," she said. "Only breathing hard."

He woke with a headache and a bad taste in his mouth. When he sat up and turned on the light he saw that Stephane was gone. His letter was on the floor, and he refolded it and put it back in the envelope. So be it, he thought. What can you do? He got to his knees. On the mattress Sandy looked up at him from the dock, face and body creased from the weight of an uneasy sleep. So be it. You can't win them all. It does seem, though, that you ought to win a few.

Crowe's second and last encounter with Stephane took place four nights later when he and Paps and the Raos had all gone in the Rao's car to Englewood Cliffs to meet some young and coming artist friend of George's who was doing computer drawings on fiber glass or polyglas or Plexiglas. Crowe never did quite find out. It was a private showing at his home and there was a great deal to eat and drink and a great many people milling around. George was busy explaining the patterns of culture that could be programmed into the mind of a machine. Paps, with his usual generosity, was trying to entertain a one-legged girl. Stephane glued herself to Crowe and rubbed her buttocks against him at every opportunity. He went around most of the time with his hands folded on his head. Actually he had come largely in the hope that he might meet somebody important who would change his luck, and the only reason he hung around Stephane at all was because she seemed to know a great many people and to be socially at ease with everybody from hip artists to suited columnists and art critics. His luck had to change before too long. She pointed out various people, a few of whom Crowe had heard of because he'd seen their names occasionally in *Commentary* or *The New Leader*, incestuous little magazines he did not deign to read but occasionally thumbed through on the periodical rack at the public library. One man at the party was a columnist for the *National Observer* and Crowe, after Stephane's fifth proposal that they slip into the bathroom, made her a deal. "You introduce me to Charles Goodell," he said, "and I'll take you wherever you want and screw you backside to breakfast."

"Crude boy," she said, snickering. "Why do you want to meet that fool?"

"Never mind. You got five seconds or I retract the offer."

"I accept, I accept," Stephane squeaked. "Jesus, I'll introduce you to the cook if that's what it takes. Come on."

Charles Goodell was pleasant but noncommittal. He listened to Crowe's vagarious allusions to a "communications" background and they chatted a bit about Gay Talese's book on *The New York Times*, which Crowe knew nothing whatever about, and he responded to a direct inquiry about a job by pointing out that he only wrote a weekly column and didn't do the hiring, but that he would be happy to put in a word on Crowe's behalf. It was clear, however, that he was making polite cocktail talk and that in any case he had little power, so, disappointed, Crowe picked an early opportunity to escape. "Gotcha," Stephane said, coming up behind him and taking his arm. "Now I want my pound of flesh."

He groaned. "I'll give you a rain check. We ought to get going. Everybody's clearing out."

Stephane opened her mouth to protest but at that moment the
rest of their entourage appeared with hats and coats and "come
on's," and her chance, for the moment, was lost. He had, he
thought, pausing to thank God, successfully parried all of her
suggestive thrusts at (as she liked to put it) his dangling participle. He'd had enough of the Raos. It was by now pretty obvious
that they weren't going to be of much use to him.

Because he had had the least to drink, Crowe drove home.
Stephane sat between him and George in the front seat. Paps and
the one-legged girl took the back seat. It was late but the traffic
was still heavy, and driving was difficult. He was not as clear-
headed as he had thought. The white lines kept eluding him and
slipping between his tires. Something else was slipping between . . .
he nearly missed the turn for the George Washington Bridge,
nearly sideswiped a truck, nearly took out the concrete pillar of
an overpass . . . because Stephane, nearly beside herself with
amusement, had reached under his right arm, unzipped his pants,
and taken out his . . . dangling participle. It became, in spite of
his attempts to restrain it, an exclamation mark. He tried to push
her arm away with his elbow, but she would not be denied. He
stole a glance at George, who didn't seem to notice, hissed "quit
it" at her, to which she simply snorted and began to manipulate
him. He shoved out his stomach and tried to hunch his legs.
Nothing doing. He took one hand off the wheel and tried to shove
her away while negotiating the bridge approach with the other, on
a curve, between two roaring Kenworth diesels. Too dangerous.
Well, he thought, what the hell. As long as I can keep her husband from seeing. He was hunched over toward the passenger
seat in a most grotesque manner, elbow clenched in a shield, hand
clutching the wheel near the bottom of its circle. Christ, what if
that truck driver looks down. A horrible realization struck him.
The tollgate. He was approaching the end of the bridge. Fifty
cents please, and he has no change. Are you ill, Sir? Why do you
cramp like that? Hiding something? How in the hell was he going
to cover himself on both sides, drive, and fish out a bill all at the
same time? Blinking orange lights approaching, slow to fifteen, all
cars left lanes, sweating now, in a real panic, don't care what Rao

says about don't mind me, that's an old line that sags the minute
you take up on it. Horn blast behind. Move up buddy. And then
from the back seat, oh the sweetness of his voice, the goodness of
his soul, "I got it from here, Crowe," and the cool air blowing
through as Paps rolls down the window, hands out a bill and
takes his change. The light flicks. Green for go. We made it.
"You're a lucky bastard," Stephane whispered.

They dropped the one-legged girl at her place on 119th and
Amsterdam and continued on downtown, Crowe zipped and grinning.

"You all want to stop at the White Horse for a nightcap?"
Stephane said.

"I'm pretty bushed," Paps said. "Think I'll make it on home.
You go ahead if you want, Crowe." George was sound asleep and
snoring.

"Naw," Crowe said. "I've had it. I'm going to stop at Sheridan
Square and get some butts. We can walk from there, okay, Francis?"

"Sure," Paps said. "I got just about that much poop."

They said their good nights. Stephane slid over into the driver's
seat and looked up at Crowe, hugely amused. He grinned back. "I
had you there, didn't I," she said.

"On the contrary," Crowe told her, chuckling softly. "I believe I
had you. You see I've had this persistent dose of the clap that's
really stumped the pathologists. A really purulent and super con-
tagious strain of gonococcus. I wouldn't pick my nose or anything
on the way home." He waved. "Bye now. Come and see us."

He bought his cigarettes at the United Tobacco Store on the
corner, and they walked on down toward Morton. Warm for early
October. Even New York gets its Indian summer. Midnight, and
the theater crowds still thick. Two stumble-bums trying to punch
one another in front of the Voice office and a few fans beginning
to gather. The broken insect shuffle. Sounds of Sandy Bull from
an open window one floor above the street, Chuck Berry's
"Memphis" cutting the night over the jumble of traffic noise,
restaurant clatter, laughter and shouts of happy millions. On
Morton Street it was quiet. Peaceful. Quaint, even, in the soft

glow of shaded apartment lights, the grime tucked away in shadow. The sad little trees with their limp, sooty leaves looked almost healthy by lamplight. Up the steps of the apartment building and into the lobby. Paps yawned, tonsils vibrating. A girl was sitting on a bench under the row of mailboxes, suitcase on the floor under her legs, hands folded in her lap. She leaned against the wall behind her and slept. To his utter amazement Crowe saw that it was Sandy.

3

They sat on the couch in the apartment with the kitchen light on and Paps in bed. An FM station played "Appalachian Spring," there was a cigar butt in the coffee cup by the chair, and a strand of light poked its way through the part in the curtains, advancing, retreating with the slight breeze that struggled up from the street. Voices leaked through the sluggish air between the buildings. The hiss of steam pipes strained to catch up with the hot night. Crowe sat like a retarded ghost watching the shadows on the wall.

What he wanted to know, he had told her, after the initial flush and flutter of reunion, and after Paps had been properly introduced and disposed of, was why she had come. "It wasn't any good there alone," she had said. "I loved it but I was alone. I had to come to tell you I didn't mean those things I wrote you." Crowe had said he didn't understand exactly; that just because one was alone didn't mean one packed up and ran back home after six weeks unless one had specifically in mind something better to do. He was fishing, but she left his bait hanging. "I loved the place. San Francisco was just fabulous. But the University . . . I don't know. They threw all these requirements at me, breadth requirements you know, like, social sciences, humanities, pure sciences, languages, and hell, I didn't go there to have all that stuffed down my throat. I just wanted to take some courses in things that interested me, but I wound up in some dumb geology course and Chaucer and French 2, and I just kind of walked around for a month saying 'What's *happening* here? Why can't I study things I want to know instead of all this stuff somebody else thinks I *ought* to know?' but that was clearly a heretical attitude from the administration's point of view, so I dropped out." She made a grimace and threw up her hands.

He had told her he understood all that, but it didn't explain why she was in New York, since she could just have well have dropped out and gone to Galveston. "I came to see you, of course," she had said, and when he'd asked her what, now that she had seen him, she intended to do, she had simply shrugged. "I don't know. Go up to Brookline, I guess. Maybe get a job in Boston." That had not been at all what he wanted to hear, and so he had withdrawn and was sitting like a zombie in the semidark room refusing to talk or listen or participate in any way in reality. He was wondering if the shadow cast by the telephone looked more like an innocent party or a windy afternoon in March. Creeping visions of twisted rhyme on the apartment walls. Ground swell and a deer's flank in the purple damp of a redwood forest, and the line of a song going endlessly around in his head,

> *helplessly hoping her harlequin hovers nearby—*
> *awaiting a word.*
> *Gasping at glimpses of gentle true spirit—*
> *he runs,*
> *wishing he could fly,*
> *only to trip at the sound of good-bye.*

Finally, though, he reminded himself to attend the moment. What we need, he thought, is a drink to unsnarl the lines, and he rose, saying "You want some scotch or something? Beer?" and was completely taken by surprise when she began to cry without a sound, the little lines of tears tracking down her cheeks and catching the light from the kitchen along their path. "I don't want anything to drink," she said. "I just want you to tell me I wasn't wrong to come. Or if I was wrong I want you to say it now before I go to pieces."

"Pieces?" Crowe said. He noticed that she was wearing a blue linen suit with an open neck, that she had a suitcase and high-heeled alligator shoes. Wondered how many pairs of shoes can

one alligator hide? There was this man, see, who went into a bar
in Mississippi with an alligator on a leash. Why are you crying?
What have I done?

He made two drinks anyway, pulled the Murphy bed out of the
wall, lay down and closed his eyes. "I feel like a fish in a seine
net," he said. "Up out of the water and dumped into a hold with a
million others." He could hear the silk swish of stockings against
her thighs as she moved across the room. It reminded him of surf
on pebbles. When the sound stopped he knew she was standing
above him looking down but he kept his eyes closed and concen-
trated acutely on his performance. "Are you all right?" she
asked.

"Is that one word or two?"

"What?"

"All right. How do you spell it?"

"I don't know. a-l-r-i-g-h-t I guess. What difference does it
make?"

"You better go back to school. You better see if they'll rein-
state you out there so you won't embarrass yourself at cocktail
parties by not knowing how to spell all right."

"Hey, stop this, will you? I think it's a lousy time to be cute.
Can't you give me an answer? I just came three thousand miles on
an airplane and spent four hours sitting in the lobby of this building fending off a drunken super and scared stiff you might not be
here anymore, and all you do is . . . dump on me. I don't know
why?" She was crying again, and Crowe was ashamed of himself. He didn't know why either, except maybe because she
hadn't declared herself ready to move in with him or marry him.
"I'm sorry," he told her. "I'm glad you're here. I wanted you
here, I really did, but I just wasn't expecting it to happen. You
caught me off guard."

She knelt beside the bed and put her head on his stomach, and
he felt her cheek wet on his skin. After a while she took off her
skirt and jacket and lay down next to him. He offered her half of
the pillow. "I love you," he said. "Really. I'm overcome." He
meant it, he thought, but somehow it came out without much
conviction. Around midnight she got up and turned off the
kitchen light.

A car door slammed in the street below. Good night. Good
night. Lovely time. Clash of a missed shift and the engine noise
fading down the block. Steam pipes hissing. Refrigerator clicks on
with a rattling of its skirts. Fade out . . . in, to the hour chiming of
a church bell. Two hundred and forty minutes after twelve. Are
you still awake? I'm awake. Will you stay with me, Sandy? Yes,
that's why I came. Forever? Forever is a long time; who knows
about forever, but for now, yes. And what of those lies you could
not tell? That's my concession. It's about the lies that I changed
my mind; the little ones don't matter. We can make it legal, you
know, it only takes three days. No. Not now. About that lie I
have not changed my mind. When I know that it *is* forever, then
we can make it legal.

The refrigerator shuddered into silence. In the bedroom Paps
moaned in his sleep. Sunday morning. Out of film. Patterns on the
ceiling, dark stains of brownness, broken reeds lying scattered on
lamplight, leaping through the seeping. Shades sliding across the
room, and the church bell tolling one, two, three, four each other.
The song going around in his head again, the alliterative nonsense,

Wordlessly watching he waits by the window—
and wonders
at the empty place inside.
Heartlessly helping himself to her bad dreams—
he worries
did he hear a good-bye?
or even—Hello?

Are you still awake? she asked. I don't know. Do you want to
make love? I don't think I can. Shall I try and make you? If you
want. But he was more conscious of the weight of the sheet on his
legs than of the caressing and there was nothing he could do to
change.

She made him breakfast in the morning, and was relieved to find
him "ebullient and gracious and affectionate." The adjectives
were his. Whatever the cause of the night's jitters, they had passed

and he was being as clownish (and lewd) as ever. "Did I ever show
you my tattoo?" he asked while she was frying his eggs.

"You don't have a tattoo." She played the disbeliever.

"I do. I have one. Right on my bazooka. Done there for me by
a Chinese maiden in the formal gardens at the Pagoda of Sung
Yueh Ssu, using for her masterpiece only a nail punch and a bowl
of Basil's borsht."

"Oh that one. The one that says 'Shorty.'" She thought she
had him.

"Ah well, you've only seen it in repose. When it's on duty it
says 'Shorty's Super Conoco Service Station, Albuquerque, New
Mexico.' Why don't you come over here and see for yourself."

"I'm a dead woman," Sandy said, rolling up her eyes.

After breakfast she left for Grand Central and a train for
Boston to explain her return to her parents. She would tell them,
she said, that she was going to work in New York and share an
apartment with two girl friends. Crowe was to look for a place to
live, cheap but not too crummy. Paps, to whom he gave notice
during a second breakfast, was dubious. "There's no such place,"
he said, "but I know a few people. I'll check around."

Crowe retired to the couch and read the paper, looked at the
rent ads, found little to his taste. Called the two most appealing,
but one was rented and the other four hundred and fifty a month,
first and last in advance, a year's lease, no pets. He wondered if
he could maybe talk Paps into moving. Decidedly unlikely.
Dreary prospect, though, apartment hunting. Like that long, dull
section in that long, dull novel of William Dean Howells, a hazard
of something or other, where the walls were never the right color
or the kitchen wasn't laid out to suit or there weren't enough
windows. A hundred pages of tramp, tramp, tramp, and old Pro-
fessor Whosit marching through step by step, apologizing at every
intersection. *A tremendous force, you realize. Why, without his
stimulation and direction, Mark Twain might be only a very
minor figure in our past.* Tramp, tramp, tramp. A lesson there.
Let an agent find you a pad and you won't bore everybody with
all that local color later on. To the sport page. Trust Franny to
come up with something. Mustn't jeopardize the future of my
art.

Paps found a two-room place on Tenth, the sixth floor of a building that appeared to have survived the blitzkrieg and been moved stone by stone to the east village where it had been reassembled to assure ghetto dwellers everywhere that they had not reached the bottom. The buildings on either side of Paps's find were, in fact, lying in rubble. "Forty-five bucks a month," Paps said. They were standing in the street looking up at the roof line against a bruised sky. "Couple of kids from the print shop are moving out. They say the roaches aren't too bad on the sixth floor. If you don't leave food around."

"Forget it," Crowe told him. "The neighborhood is undesirable."

"Forty-five bucks a month."

"For five bucks a month I wouldn't live in it."

"Yassuh, boss. Well, you folks bein' quality an' all, I reckon you bess make inquiry up 'round de park. Suffin' in a small penthouse wid cook an' houseboy."

"I'll tell you what, Step, as temporary quarters it just might do. It just might, at that."

"You want to look inside?"

"I think I can imagine it."

Sandy went a little pale as Crowe, later that night, led her up the six flights of stairs. On the third floor a diseased cat, thin, patchy, left over from Halloween, slunk through a hole in the landing wall. On the fifth floor a young man with mad red eyes passed them, trailed by a sallow zombie in a paisley print muumuu and a fatigue jacket. She stopped and stared dully at Crowe, asked him for spare change. He shrugged. She went on without expression. Garbage in the hall and no glass in the landing windows. One naked light bulb per floor around which the moths fluttered. A cold forty watts. Not enough to kill. Bongo drums from 6-C and somebody groaning as if dying too slow. Crowe inserted the key into 6-A and they went into the sour darkness of the apartment kitchen. Groped for the light string that did its best to elude his sweeping hand, did its best to leave in obscurity the real inhabitants of the room. Crowe found the cord and pulled, heard Sandy gasp and shrink back, felt the prickles of his own skin, the lifting

of hairs on his neck, the flop of his stomach. "Oh my God,"
Sandy cried, backing toward the door. He hardly dared take a
step. The floor moved. The ceiling dripped. A seething tide of
roaches flowed away from the light, dropped from the enameled
kitchen table like ripe plums, scuttled along the drain board and
vanished into the sink, disappeared by the hundreds under the
rotting baseboards, piled up along the cracks in their haste and
formed a wriggling mass in every corner. Sandy making choking
noises in the doorway. Crowe transfixed. A roach fell from the
light fixture into his hair and he smacked at it with a shudder of
revulsion. Remained rooted to his spot. The bugs slowly evap-
orated into the walls. "Jesus," he said. "You ever see anything
like it? The d.t.'s." Sandy stared at him with wide, horrified eyes.
He made a quick tour of the other room without turning on its
light. More roaches. They crunched under his shoes. He opened the
bathroom door and nearly threw up into a toilet brimming with
urine and floating turds. Clogged, obviously, and never fixed.
Back into the kitchen and fled with a yell out the door, down the
stairs, into the street; half walk, half run across town, heading for
the clean clutter of Morton Street and a cleansing bottle of ale
from Paps's refrigerator. Sandy trails. Crowe hails. A cab. A hundred and sixty horses, yellow, fleeing the apocalypse.

Going up the elevator they looked at each other without saying
a word, breathing hard from their jog, feeling as if they had just
been delivered. Grateful. Then a fat roach crawled from under the
collar of Sandy's raincoat and fell with a brittle crack on the
elevator's linoleum floor. "Jesus, I'm sorry," he told her and
ground it to paste under his heel.

By the first of November Sandy had found a job as a sales girl at
Bloomingdale's, and Crowe an apartment in the building where
the Raos lived. In fact, it was George who got it for him. Small,
expensive, but clean. Bedroom, sitting room, large bath, a
reasonable kitchen. Newly painted, but unfurnished. Stephane
told Sandy she would lend her a few things until they got set up,
Crowe bought a decent mattress at a used furniture store, and they
moved in. He was a little worried about Stephane being so close,

but he figured he would spend his days in the darkroom or working on his book and Sandy would be there at night to ward off prowlers.

On their first night "at home" Paps brought over a second-rate girl friend and a third-rate bottle of champagne to celebrate the housewarming and his returned privacy. Crowe went out to the corner grocery and bought an even worse bottle to keep the first company. Somebody ordered pizzas. George and Stephane drifted up with a pint of Benedictine they said they couldn't stand, and the Crowe-Paps burlesque troupe who had no standards when free booze was concerned divided the bottle into two equal parts, added Coca Cola, and drank toasts to Franciscans, Dominicans, and Carmelites.

Sandy sat against the wall after the pizzas were eaten listening to the conversation without participating in it and without seeming to be quite aware of where she was. She stared at George who did most of the talking (Crowe and Paps concentrating on getting smashed), and Rao began addressing himself more and more to her alone. Crowe, tuning him in and out at various intervals, heard him ranging from the Arab-Israel war to A. S. Neill and the Summerhill School to Robert Lowell's latest poem in the *New York Review*. John Cage came up and George had a lecture prepared on Merce Cunningham, Buckminster Fuller, and Marshall McLuhan's influence on the work of Robert Duncan. Crowe yawned. Paps poured more Benedictine. "We're all just electric generators," George was saying, "and through the electronic media we're joined to the common nervous system. Man, it's the dawn of a new day of sensitivity where we're all involved with all other lives through our nerves, our electronic nerves." Paps announced his departure, gathered up his girl, and headed for the door. "Life is art," George said. "The environment is an art form." Crowe went to the bathroom. "Literacy is anti-environment," George told them. "Environmental control alienates man from his body and soul." Stephane woke up on the pile of cushions where she was sleeping. "Come on, Georgy Porgy," she said. "I feel an urge coming on that can't be satisfied in public."

"You see," George said, rising. "That's what I mean about

environmental control. That's the remark of a manipulated person. Why can't it be satisfied in public?"

"Because, honey," Stephane said, winking at Crowe. "I still like mine in private."

They lay in the dark on their mattress, a borrowed quilt over their legs. Sandy's arms were behind her head and Crowe knew her eyes were open. "What's the matter?" he asked. "You weren't much with it tonight."

"I don't know," she said. "I guess it's my turn for the blues. Just listening to everybody talk. Honest to God, I sometimes think there's no hope for me. I mean, my attitudes are such clichés, and I can't help it. You once called them a *Time-Life* gloss on the collective conscience of the disaffected."

"I never did," Crowe said, kissing her eyelids and brushing the hair away from her face. He suddenly felt butterflies in his stomach and wanted to bury his face in the warmth of her neck.

"Yes. I remember all your one-liners. But I get so confused, because I'm not even sure where my ideas come from. I mean, I'm afraid maybe I do get them from *Time-Life*; that the media really is my message."

"Wrong media," Crowe said.

"I'm not capable of thinking or feeling anything without making an analogy to something I've read or seen about how I'm supposed to think and feel."

"The manipulated woman. You become what you behold."

"When I'm really calm about it, I wonder just why I'm *supposed* to have an opinion about everything."

"Who says you are?"

"Well everybody. They're always asking you 'what do you think about the Beatles or capital punishment or geodesic domes or Mike Nichols,' and most of the time I don't think anything, not really, so I adopt somebody else's line and try to pretend I believe it, pretend I even thought it up myself."

"You and George Rao," Crowe said.

She kicked the quilt off her legs and he patted her thigh and she turned away a little to indicate it was an inappropriate gesture toward one who has the blues. "I think maybe if I could just create something, a book, a painting, a dance, anything, then I would be able to believe at least that I exist for some reason, that I have some existence beyond the space I take up, but even my attempts at creation are so clumsy and without talent that to try is worse than not to try because it just reminds me what a mediocrity I am, just a body, just an orifice into which the boys want to stick things." Crowe picked his hand off her hip where it had been snail walking toward the valley of the shadow. "You can put it back," she said in a tired voice, turning toward him, throwing a long leg across his. "It doesn't matter."

He dozed. Once he got up to to go the bathroom, once to open a window when the apartment got too stuffy. Sandy was awake both times, and her restlessness began to affect him so that he could not sleep. He suspected she would have preferred it if he had denied himself, remained celibate for just one night to prove in some simple-minded way that she was *not* just an orifice. Too late. Tomorrow he would seek redemption.

He got up again near dawn to shut the window, and when he lay back down her voice came out of the darkness. "Maybe we're all hollow. Maybe everybody is walking around just kidding themselves that they're so complex, so full of mysterious and unplumbed depths, untapped resources, unraveled puzzles. Maybe we are all just as vapid and empty as we appear." She sighed heavily. "Only I wish I could find a fresher way to express it."

4

Mid-November. Veteran's Day, as a matter of fact, and without deference to your indifference. Veteran's Day, and a veteran (one who has served long in a given activity or capacity. My dictionary has nicer pictures than yours) was how the brown cow had by now come to regard himself—insofar as the occupation of assistant to the photographer was concerned.

Start over.

The darkroom was dark. The work was dull. Crowe was bored. Boredom made him nervous because historically it had always led to the demise of whatever ambitious plot he had diddled his concupiscent soul into accepting as the year's game plan. He spent a great amount of time admiring the *Gymnogyps californianus* (Condor) that graced the margin of the page following the one on which he looked up concupiscent, two pages short, by the way, of another portrait of equally marginal interest, Joe Conradish, looking epicentic and mongoloid and probably sane. Desisted when reminded by a helpful editor and two critics (*kreticks 1. One afflicted with cretinism. Arrested mental development.*) that somebody would certainly recognize the imitation, rank it 3rd *Cru*, and that in any event a man's style is sacred and ought not to be profaned by second-comers or fourth-raters.

So he spent more and more of his time out with a camera, working on his book. Even there his enthusiasm began to pale. He was no Elliot Porter, Ansel Adams, Edward Weston, and it was clear, he told himself, that he was not going to be. He wasn't even an Aristotle Papanikolas. Looking at the work of Masters only depressed him because he couldn't come remotely close to it, couldn't *see* things the way they could, and it would take years of practice and hard work to acquire any proficiency at all with the eye, he decided. He didn't have years to spend. "I'm just not visually oriented," he told Sandy. "Language has always been my game, insofar as I have a game, and I can't seem to transpose a verbal image into a visual one. I mean, I can see how the world is, but I can't see how it's supposed to be."

"Why don't you go back and try writing again?" Sandy said.

"I don't know. It seems like such a phony thing to do. The world is so full of would-be writers it's embarrassing to even admit to anybody how you're spending your time."

"Well then I guess language is not your game."

"I don't know. Maybe I'll give it a go again, but I can't write and work for Paps too. He's complaining right now that we're getting behind." Sandy said nothing, but it was clear from the look she gave him that she did not regard him as overworked, and that if he was behind it was because he didn't make any great effort.

Later that evening as they were downing a few beers before bed, Crowe said, "Hey Sandy, what does Burt do?"

"He's the president of the International Machine Corporation and on the board of trustees of various other businesses. I don't know what all. He has many fingers in many pies. Why, you want a letter of recommendation?" She chuckled but Crowe did not, and when she saw that he might be serious, a look of real surprise came over her face. "You've got to be kidding."

"I didn't say anything."

"You don't have to. I see the handwriting on the wall, but forget it. The answer is just no. I couldn't ask Burt for a stick of gum, not now."

"What does that mean? 'not now'?"

"It means under my current housing arrangements. I can't be living with a guy, violating every notion of conduct that my father holds sacred, and then buzz in and hit him for a few favors whenever the picture looks dim. You . . . well Christ, you told me that yourself once; that if you're accepting somebody's money you're obliged to accept his rules too."

"O.K., O.K." Crowe said. "You're going off on a tangent. I didn't say anything." They drank in silence, listening to the squall of a baby in an apartment across the air flue, and the intervaled clunk of the water pipe as the Italian woman in the apartment next to theirs methodically rinsed her supper dishes. Crowe finally bent his beer can and looked over at his girl. "Hey San, you think if we were married your old man would make me a vice president of his big business like he did your stupid brother?"

"I think if we were married he'd probably disinherit me and murder you."

"How come?"

"N.O.C.D."

"What's that mean."

"Not our class, darling."

The more his job irritated him, the more the thought of trying once again to write appealed. Besides, Paps was becoming increasingly officious in his role as employer. *Why don't you get in here a little earlier? Come on, you're way behind on the Wilson pics. Jesus Christ, the Smiths will be divorced by the time you get proofs to them. You're going to put me out of business if you don't get with it.* He had even changed the lock on his apartment so Crowe could no longer raid his kitchen.

"The next time," Crowe said, "the very next time he gives me trouble I'm going to tell him where he can put his photography business."

He assisted fate by not showing up at all for two days. Paps was for once furious. "Jack," he said, "if you're not up to the pace maybe you ought to leave the field and let me get somebody I can count on."

"Right," Crowe said. "Over here in the big time it's more than I'm used to."

"It's small time, and it's still more than you're used to. Any time at all is more than you're used to." He ricochetted his palm off his forehead. "I knew I was just asking for it when I brought you in on this. Some guys never learn anything. I gotta call my shrink."

"Well, I'll see you, Francis," Crowe said. He picked his coat off the chair back and put it on. Liner torn. Arm went in the wrong slot. Back up.

"Where are you going?"

"I'm one who learns things fast. Like when I'm about to choke on weddings, parties, and babies. I'm leaving you, honey. I ain't grinding your coffee no more."

"What's happened to you lately, anyway?" Paps asked. "For a while you looked like you were really on top of it. The book and everything. You were doing some good stuff. You looked healthy. In control. Then your girlfriend comes back and you slide into the old pose. I don't get it. I'd think she'd straighten you out even more."

"One would think that," Crowe said, "if one were capable of thought." He had put his arm back in the same dead-end hole and in a fury he ripped the entire liner out of the sleeve.

"It's interesting to speculate on the duration of Sandy's tolerance," Paps said. "She's a fine, sensitive girl. I'm much taken by her and I'd venture to guess that you'll be a solo again before . . . let's see . . . March."

"Nobody gives a tepid fart for your ventures and guesses," Crowe said. "Nobody is interested."

"I suppose not," Paps answered. "Well, I've got to get to work. I hope you find what you're looking for, Crowe, though I think you ought to do a little more looking inside. And by the way, you didn't really need to fabricate this little scene, you know. No obligations. You could have just said you wanted out and given me a week's notice."

"And keep your hands off her. Nobody's solo yet."

Judas Priest, Crowe thought, going down the elevator. Everybody is full of advice for how to run my life these days. I can smell disapproval when I walk in a room. Sandy, and now Paps. Fuck 'em all.

Thanksgiving. Turning cold. Sandy home for turkey and parental appeasement. Obliging daughter. That makes it colder, Crowe thought. The wind begins to bite through the duffle coat. Ears become raw along the ridge and the nose leaks. Toes numb when the shoes are wet, and the shoes are always wet no matter how I hop the puddles. Out warm and dry to spend an hour or so at the Strand hobnobbing with the arts, and before I have walked two blocks my shoes have sponged water out of the air and it's squish-puck, squish-puck, squish-puck like two plumber's friends on their way to tea. Hideous city. Why do I stay? No closer to making it than I ever was! A photographer, for Christ's sake. An *ex*-photographer. A photographer's *ex*-helper. Some big deal. Some distinction. Got a fancy, rich girl who won't marry me and no job. At home the days are clear now, cool and sparkling, the hills beginning to green with the start of the rainy season. None of this penetrating, glacial cold. Brilliant purple wall of Bougainvillea climbing up the southern end of the sunporch where it would be nice to sit and bask in the warmth. Or have the flowers gone by now? Can't remember, but there was always something blooming around the garden. Dahlias, azaleas, clumps of Shasta daisies, pyracantha, camellias. We had oranges and lemons at Christmas. And sun on the sunporch. Wonder if the old house still has its glass. My old house.

My old house. He sat up suddenly in his chair. "Hey," he said out loud. "I *own* that house." He got up and walked excitedly around the room several times, following a light bulb in a pale, floating balloon. "I own it and the land around it, a couple of acres, a house, rundown, but still, given the out-of-sight value of coastal land, must be worth fifteen, maybe twenty thousand. Who knows, might be twice that." He toured the room twice more, went in the bathroom and peered idiotically into the mirror. "I'm a landowner," he told himself. "A property holder. I'm part of the establishment. Land holdings in California, Sir, which I am willing to part with for, say, thirty grand, and the answer is yes, I'll take a second mortgage for not more than half. Fifteen thou cash on the barrelhead and that ocean view is yours, my man, and you can sit right in your own backyard and watch the whales migrate. For fifty bucks I'll throw in the ghosts and the memories."

He mentioned his discovery to the Raos where he had been invited for Thanksgiving dinner.

"How come you never thought of this before?" George asked through the cranberry sauce and the Pepperidge Farm dressing.

"I knew it was mine, but I never thought about it in ownership terms. Since the old man died I haven't been there four times, and then just to walk around and wonder how he could have lived in it all by himself. I just never thought about it being valuable to me."

"What'd you think when you paid the taxes?" Stephane stood behind him and poured wine into his glass. Remove your tit from my ear, please, it impedes my hearing. Taxes?

"Taxes?" Crowe said. "I never paid any taxes. What taxes?"

"Property taxes. You have to pay taxes to the county."

"Nobody ever told me that," Crowe said.

"Maybe they couldn't find you. So after a few years they figure the place is abandoned and it gets turned over to the State and auctioned off."

"You think they'd do that?"

"Probably."

"How do you know about all these taxes and auctions and things?"

"It's the way they do it in my home state. Maybe California's different. You better write some real estate broker and tell him you want to sell and could he find out if you've got anything *to* sell."

"Yeah," Crowe mumbled. "I better do that. Christ, imagine, wiped out by the crash. Ruined before I'm launched."

In the New York Public Library he found a Monterey County phone book, looked in the yellow pages after rags, ranches, ranges, and razors. Real Estate. Homes. Acreage. Specializing in vacation properties. We work hard. We get results. We sell the earth. Disreputable occupation. Pratt Fall Realty, Sewer Creek Road. He wrote them a letter explaining his problem and requesting immediate attention. He was hoping, he said, to find a reputable contact who might be energetic enough to handle an additional two thousand acres of prime, developable land that his firm held in trust just north of Santa Cruz on Coast Highway One. While he had the typewriter out (Sandy's portable Olympia, complete with $\underline{\text{th}}$ and ∧ and ⅟) he decided to become, once again, a poet.

5

On the dark wood of a table lay a lined tablet of paper, its cover folded back beneath itself forming a grey bolster above the empty yellow sheets.. To the left a lamp with a solid navy shade threw a perfect circle of light on the table and a diminished, though equally symmetrical imitation on the ceiling directly above. From his chair Crowe looked straight ahead into the blank wall that divided the eating area from the kitchen. By turning his head slightly to the right, he could see the black hole left by the kitchen door, the corner of the room, and the front door with its brass chain lock and its police bolt; to the left the window that opened onto Mott Street, a rectangle of grey sky, a sparrow on its way south to City Hall Park.

On a dun day in December, with only a dozen shopping afternoons until Christmas, he sat at his table, pencil in hand, waiting for an idea. None came. The whole problem, he told himself, is that I can't let go of old mistakes, of those hundred and fifty pages of, for, and by the past already finished, washed up, and interred, that I've been hauling around these many months in an Eaton's Corrasable Bond box. Twenty-five percent cotton fiber, 75 percent horseshit. The manuscript, he knew, was terrible. What had been on his mind when he started now seemed banal and flat, the unmotivated rantings of an enraged idiot who could establish no meaningful relationships with anyone, who could perform no actions, who could not even violate his own point of view because he did not, in fact, have one. And yet he couldn't throw it away. I'm like that number in *The Floating Opera*, he thought, who pickled his crap in mason jars and stored it in the cellar.

He had worked hard for three weeks redoing those pages, cutting, adding new chapters, new characters, but when he had finished he was back where he had started. The story was still banal and flat, without point. He had no fresh insight to bring to it. His people bored him and their fate was a matter of supreme indifference. And so on that day in early December, when the trees stood out naked and black against the chiaroscuro sky, he had reached the end of his patience. The last drop of enthusiasm had been squeezed from his tube. Sandy came home from work to find him slumped in his chair with an Elgin, Royal Master Bonded Lead pencil, Number 224, driven deep into his heart.

Stop that. That's a flagrant theft.

He wanted only to sleep, and although this bothered him, he had, for almost a week, been unconscious fifteen, eighteen hours a day. Sandy came home from work to find an empty tablet on the dark wood of the table, the lamp shining hopefully in the twilight gloom, and Crowe out cold in the chair, newspapers around his feet, the ash tray upside down on the rug. Snoring. She took off her wet boots and hung her coat in the closet, went into the bathroom and drew a tub of water as hot as she could stand it, climbed in to soak away the chill of a five-block walk from the subway. Humming a Christmas carol. Turning on the hot water tap as the bath cooled. The sound of running water woke him and he got up, went in and sat on the toilet seat, looked at her stretched out in the tub and rubbed his eyes. "How's today?" he mumbled.

"Okay," she said. "Busy. God how I wish it would either snow and freeze or stop snowing. You should see the streets. Water ankle deep in all the gutters and cross walks. Taxis spraying slush on everybody. It's a mess."

"You get any cigarettes?" Crowe said.

"In my coat."

He went into the other room, took three packs out of her pocket and opened one. Pushed his gums with his index finger and tasted blood. Got to cut down. Mouth like kitty litter. Gums like silly putty. Think my teeth may fall out, as in the latest dream vision when I push from behind with my tongue and they all cant at right angles. Push them back and they crystalize, fall into the sink.

"Did you get some work done today?" she asked when he went back into the bathroom.

He lit two cigarettes and handed her one. "Some," he said.

She blew smoke over the water and watched it scud toward her feet, hit the porcelain wall of the end of the tub, and rise like a billow of steam into the atmosphere. "Crowe?"

"What?"

"Why are you bullshitting me? The carriage on the typewriter hasn't moved in a week."

"I'm a fussy man. I always return it to the same spot. Matter of order. Anyway I'm using a pencil just now."

She soaped her legs with one hand and held her cigarette away from the tub in her thumb and index finger. As if the Statue of Liberty had just fallen on its can into the Hudson River, Crowe thought. Must remember that image. Might be useful, you can't tell. "What's the trouble?" she asked. "Whither has fled the visionary gleam?"

"My, my," Crowe said, angry that she insisted on pursuing it. "We trot out our Junior College education; our spring term course in the romantics. But if we were really on top of that dejected ode we'd know the answer to our cute little question."

"Don't bite me, buddy. I'm not your muse."

"I think you are my muse. Maybe that's why I dried up. And my name isn't buddy."

Silence. Said that with a bit too much hostility. Forgot the humorous inflection. While we wait for the smoke to clear I'll peer into the looking glass. Compose an ode of my own. To the blackhead.

> *A man's time is spent indoors,*
> *Squeezing custard from the pores.*
> *Festering pustule in his grip,*
> *Letting fly the Ready Whip.*

Now I'm stuck. Begin again.

> *Twinkle, twinkle little sty,*
> *Like an eclair in my eye.*

"Stop that. Can't you do that when you're in here alone?"

"Look, I'm sorry," he said. "But I'm aware of my problems with the muse without having my figurative nose rubbed in it all the time." He turned away from the mirror, put his real nose up against the cold pane of the window and looked out at the snow caroming off the brick wall of the air flue. Mid-air swirls and eddies. Trapped in a Sisyphean cycle. Rise and fall. Never hit the bottom. Never hit the top. Through the bathroom odor of soap and shampoo the window smelled faintly metallic.

"Guess who came to see me today at Bloomingdale's," she remarked.

Crowe was bored. "I don't know, Chairman Mao. William F. Buckley. Aristotle Papanikolas."

"Well, him, but who else?"

"Him? *Paps?*" He pulled his nose off the window pane and turned around. "What the hell was *he* doing at Bloomingdale's?"

"Buying a shirt. Anyway that's not who I'm talking about."

"A shirt, my ass." Crowe turned back to the window. "He went there to check you out . . . to see if I'm still in the picture, the stinking, miserable, cocksman . . . the world's most *unsuccessful* cocksman, by the way . . . the masturbating pig, the drooling moron. A shirt. The slob hasn't bought himself a new shirt since Christ was a corporal, and anyway they don't *sell* shirts in the ladies lotions section, not the last time I was at Bloomingdale's." He sat down on the toilet seat to contemplate the treachery of Judas.

"My brother is who I'm trying to tell you about. He's been transferred to New York; lives in Brooklyn Heights in a fancy apartment, and he's getting married."

"Outstanding," Crowe said.

"He wants me to come out on Thursday for drinks and dinner to meet my future sister-in-law."

"Next to winning the New York State Lottery, I can't think of anything I'd rather have happen than to be invited . . ."

"Relax," she broke in. "He didn't invite you, since he doesn't know about you, you don't have to worry."

Oddly enough, Crowe was hurt. It occurred to him, moreover, that there was perhaps an opportunity, an opening, that was slipping out of his grasp, and that it might be well to cool the forthcoming insults and find a way to accompany her. Burt Junior was, after all, a vice president in his father's company and could eventually become an important ally. "How is Burt?" he asked with phony solicitude.

Sandy looked up from the bath. "He's all right," she said in a tone that indicated she saw through his interest. "That's two words. A-l-l/r-i-g-h-t-." He picked up a comb lying on the sink and began combing his hair down over his eyes. "You want to go, don't you?" she said, amused. "You actually want to go with me. I think that's hysterical." She began to laugh.

Crowe pulled the corners of his mouth down, raised his eyebrows and gave a shrug. "Weeell," he drawled, "you know. We sit in this miserable apartment seven nights a week without even a television set to separate us, and I like to step out now and then, even if it's only to your crummy brother's, because I can't stand to sit around *all* the time. And then I'd like to eat a meal you didn't cook for a change, just to give my intestines a rest, and look at a new face and see if I still remember how to talk to it."

"You'd be bored stiff," she said.

"Maybe. Maybe not."

"You'd have to wear a tie."

"I got a tie."

She sat in the tub without answering, thinking, weighing the pros and cons, and when it became clear to him that she was hesitating, it made him mildly sore. "What is this, anyway? What am I, a stud service or something, that I wait around here while the Missus goes uptown? Let's just not forget who came to pay a visit to whom and drop these airs."

"Don't be silly," Sandy said. "I just know you, and I know those people are going to be stuffy and conservative and snobbish, and I know how you behave when you get around that scene."

"I am not quite such a boor," Crowe said coldly, "that I can not restrain myself when social etiquette demands it."

"Okay," she said. "I'll call him and tell him I'm bringing a friend. But don't say I didn't tell you so when you get there."

Crowe was more or less mollified. He sat in the steamy gloom and watched a daddy-longlegs come goose stepping around the corner of the clothes hamper. When it encountered his dirty sock, it backed off revolted and detoured through a pair of rose colored underpants to an unknown destination behind the radiator. The creature reminded Crowe of his old boyhood chum, Jimmy Winklebleck, and Jimmy's idea of a fabulous sport for a rainy afternoon—cutting the legs off daddy, one by one, with a pair of nail scissors, the game being to degambitate the victim before it could reach the edge of a shirt-cardboard which served as an arena. Life, he decided was more or less like that unless you had special connections to the overseer. But maybe something would turn up at Burt's.

He was, characteristically, he thought as they were being introduced, the only one without a tie; a deliberate omission which Sandy had not observed until they were in the subway on their way to Brooklyn Heights. This in itself was of little consequence as far as he was concerned, but it set him off and as soon as he got to Burt's apartment he wished, above all, to be unnoticed. Among the half-dozen young up-and-coming couples, suited and heeled, barbered and coiffeured, perfumed and deodorized, he alone had not read the latest best seller, had not viewed the latest film rage, had not contributed any recent public service to the community. *Hair* he thought was something one found on the pillow in the morning. *Alice's Restaurant* was not in his copy of Craig Claiborne's guide. Tom Wolfe had died in the 1930s. He sat on the couch next to Burt's fiancée, his hostess, Trudy somebody or other, and drank too many old-fashioneds, letting the conversation wash around him and paying little attention. He wanted to get to Burt and somehow engage him, but Burt was a super-chef, it turned out, and was busy with his eggs and cheeses out in the kitchenette. "I really don't understand it," he heard Trudy saying, from a great distance, "the Negroes all *say* they want to go to college, and when we give them the opportunity, they aren't happy at all."

"Blacks, Trud," somebody quipped. "We don't call them Negroes anymore."

"They don't like the curriculum or the professors or the administration or the trustees or the requirements or anything. If anybody tells them to do anything they have a fit and walk off the football team. I mean, I'm bewildered. I'm as liberal as the next, but the way it looks to me, we give them everything and they spit in our faces. What do you think, Jack?"

There was a lull. Crowe suddenly realized she was addressing him, and that everybody was waiting. "I have no opinion," he said, hurriedly.

"Oh, but surely you must," she persisted. "You look closer to the problem than the rest of us. I mean, we're all squares." Everybody laughed. "Ha ha."

"No," Crowe said. "No opinion."

"Surely you must have some insight into the thing."

"Why must I?" Crowe said. "What's it got to do with me?" He felt that he was getting quite drunk. Noticed that the others who had been listening to the conversation now turned and began talking among themselves, and it was to him alone that Trudy continued speaking. He decided that Sandy was right, he disliked Burt's friends quite a lot.

"Well, we all live in the world, Mr. Crowe," she pointed out grandly. "We can't just ignore social problems and bury our heads in the sand."

"Why not?" Crowe said.

Trudy didn't seem to know. "We just can't," she said, after a moment of thought.

"I can," Crowe said.

"Then I feel very sorry for you." She seemed willing to change the subject, but Crowe was stung. Now I'm really pissed, he told himself. Now I'm involved in discourse. She had found the magic words.

"Why is that?" he said.

"That I'm sorry for you? Because I know your line and I definitely do not think ignorance is bliss."

"That isn't my line and you haven't answered the question."

"I think it must be very lonely to be cut off, to cut *yourself* off, from what is happening around you, and I think lonely people are unhappy."

"I see. And you probably also think, no doubt, that the attainment of happiness is a major goal."

"They say so."

"Ah, well, if *they* say so, it must be. Then a concern with the affairs of the third world is one road to happiness?"

"I'm not sure I understand . . . The third world?"

"The have-nots."

"I'm afraid I've somewhat lost the line . . ."

"You said you were sorry for me because to stick my head in the sand, as you so cleverly put it, was to be lonely and to be lonely was to be unhappy and to be unhappy was to be unattendant to life's major goal. I'm simply asking you if *not* sticking your head in the sand, that is, concerning yourself with social problems, that is, pondering why black students do not simper with gratitude when they receive a hand-out, means that you are not lonely and are therefore, happy."

Trudy shook her head. "I'm still lost. I think you're trying to confuse me. All I said was that to be aware of the world is to be alive, and I think it is a virtue to be alive."

"I think it's a virtue to be unaware and unalive. Maybe even an obligation. Certainly a right and privilege."

"Then I don't understand you."

"You don't understand black students either. You're only capable of assessing your world through your own experience in it, and your experience is not remotely similar in any way to a black man's. So it's rather idle for you to be critical of his response to his environment. Or of mine, for that matter."

Trudy was dumbfounded. In her world, people did not become belligerent at social gatherings, and if they did, sensible folks regarded it as their obligation to pour oil on troubled waters. "Ah well," she said as if hoping to dismiss the subject by agreeing with what she thought Crowe was saying. "Perhaps it's unreasonable to expect someone who has been oppressed for so long to be grateful for belated opportunities. Perhaps you're right, we don't give enough."

Crowe's waters were on fire. "*Perhaps,*" he mimicked, "it's not

an opportunity at all. *Perhaps* what you're giving is something of
no value. And *perhaps*, Miss, ah, Trudy, all those black-assed
malcontents find it a little bit distasteful to be given anything at
all by a white man. Perhaps they figure they got a right to it."

Now Trudy was angry. "Certainly they have a right to it," she
said shrilly. "But we've denied them an equal opportunity too
long, and when they get to college they're not prepared. They
can't keep up. We have to give them a chance, give them special
courses, things like that. You don't even talk to the point."

"I see," Crowe said. "Special courses. Like put them in bone-
head English, right. A segregated class, naturally, because we
don't worry too much if white kids are illiterate. Give 'em a
special math class in addition and subtraction. Maybe print their
diploma on black paper. Make sure they *feel* the distinction between themselves and the quality. Lower the standards. Dis one
fo' de men, dis one fo' de boys."

"Well then you suggest a solution," Trudy said.

"I have no solution."

"So you ignore it."

"It's not my problem. I don't hold anything back so I got
nothing to give away. Can't offend nobody. Not guilty of oppression *or* paternalism."

"You're still a member of the white race."

"Oh, man," Crowe said, raising his eyes to the ceiling. "Share
the burden, huh? I don't eat that pie, madam. I don't accept the
sins of the father. I didn't eat any apples, and I didn't sell any
slaves, and I disinherited the human race, red, white, black, and
green long ago, so you're on your own. Stay the hell out of my
garden, lady, or I'll sic my snake on you."

Trudy laughed as if it were all a huge joke, the fight is over,
one of the contestants took his marbles and went home. She rose
from the couch. "I think dinner is almost ready. Talking with you
has been edifying, Mr. Crowe. Really."

"It has?" he said, truly surprised. "I thought this was probably
the most vapid conversation I've had in months."

Her face froze.

"But might I add," he said, drunkenly, "that if your supper is as succulent as the cheeks of your ass, I shall ignore your foolish commitments and forgive you your vacant mind."

She gasped, turned toward Burt who was approaching from the far side of the room, a witless smile on his flushed face. Trudy's lips compressed with fury. "Will you ask this man to leave," she hissed, before she burst into tears and fled toward the bedroom. Burt looked confused, as if he should do something protective and manly but didn't quite know what. To Crowe the room appeared as a whirl of stunned mouths, O's for shame, faces by Edvard Munch. He moved unsteadily toward the door, fumbled with its automatic lock, and exited into the hall. As he waited for the elevator, Sandy came out and without comment handed him his coat. In the cab going home he realized she was crying, but what was there to say? So his behavior had been inexcusable no matter what he thought of Trudy. He hadn't meant to get in a silly fight and he really was sorry but it was a bit late for tears. Beside, he could live it down; he'd been there before. And anyway, what the hell. It seemed to him as if he were always getting pushed into corners lately. Sandy didn't actually *say* much, but he could see that look in her eye, that tighteness around the mouth, that air of preoccupation with practical matters that must be attended to— all those things that say "You're disappointing me. You're letting me down. You're not living up to your potential N.O.C.D." All those silent reproaches. He was damned if he was going to sit still and take it.

6

Another week gone. And there is a stupid fly sitting on the window sill rubbing its hands together like out, out damned spot. There's some sticky on me fingers that I can't get loose. Front legs go down and the hind ones up, rub a-dub-dub, over the wings and scratch the back. Itch like crazy. Buzz around the window pane, short excursion into the room, back to the window to a different pane and a brief hob-nob with death along the fringe of a spider web, then down to the sill to scratch some more.

She had told him she had to work late. There was a TV dinner in the freezing compartment he could put in the oven. He fell asleep thinking maybe he would put his head in the oven instead, and she woke him when she came in. As she wearily cooked his supper he started another row.

So you're not content living this way, it began. You'd like me off on the eight-o-five with my leather lunch pail, my rubber low cuts, my ear muffs? Work-a-daddy Crowe with an insurance policy and retirement benefits and time off for good behavior? And it took her awhile to connect this surly outburst with a week-old conversation. She set her jaw, told him she hadn't had that trip in mind, that she was content enough but wouldn't care to think "this" was the ultimate. "Since you bring it up," she said, "there are a few things I'd like to do with my life besides work for Bloomingdale's and come home to sit around a two-room apartment with a corpse."

"A corpse, huh?"

"Yeah. Right. A corpse. Now that I think about it, this place is a Goddamn mausoleum. We don't even have a radio. I come in and you're flaked out after your big day on the stone pile, and it's so freaking quiet I want to start busting things just to let myself know I'm not stuck in last week's dream trip. You grunt your way through dinner like Stanley Kowalski or somebody, only he at least put it to Stella once in a while; you're not even up to that. And when I turn my back, you're doing your thing again. Sawing z's." She ran water in the sink, holding her hand under the tap until the water ran hot, then put in the stopper and squirted soap out of a plastic bottle. Crowe considered her diction with distaste. Decided she must be picking it up from George Rao. George was undergoing a metamorphosis. Every time Crowe saw him he had become slightly more hip. He wore cowboy boots and leather vests to work. Somebody had just "burned" him by "ripping off" his car. Bad karma, that.

"I know it hasn't occurred to you," she went on, "but when I come home from work and find you sitting in the same chair I left you in, unshaved, half-dressed, the joint reeking of cigarette butts and garbage, I get just a little bit depressed about what's happening. I think, Sandy, this isn't quite so romantic as they make out in the movies, the gay newly unweds living in blissful, cold-water squalor—but in love and free. I think here I am, the cleaning lady, the cook, the whore, and I think, this is the pits. This is a dump, actually; I can put up with a dump if there's something to go with it, but in this particular dump there's only silence, just a hole in the middle of time. You want to know all the time why I don't want to make this legal, to marry you? Because I'm afraid this might be it. The way it is I can leave if I can't take it; married I'd be stuck. What ever happened to that red-hot career you told me in Martha's Vineyard was waiting for you in New York, the one you told me you couldn't go back to California because you'd miss out on? What ever happened to that? You just sit and look out the window."

"I don't just sit and look out the window, my classy little concubine," he said, really stung. Her mention of marriage had spiked him. "I do lots of things. Like I read the paper, make coffee, drink the coffee, walk to the can, take a big, busting country dump, make some more coffee, nap, prepare myself some lunch, nap, reread the paper so I'll be up on the current event, nap, and then you come home and I listen to your whining until it's time for bed. It's an occupation. It's a full-time job. So shut up."

She picked the breakfast dishes from the drainboard where he had left them that morning and slid them gently into the soapy water. "All right," she said dully. "I didn't mean it to come out that way. I just hate to see you sitting around all day in a funk. I don't think it's healthy, and it sure isn't helping our relationship."

Crowe lit his sixty-third cigarette of the day. "What makes you think I sit around all day in a funk?" Without prompting, his gums began to bleed.

"I'm not blind," she said, running the sponge over a handful of silverware. "And I'm not altogether stupid. I know your moods. The last time you smiled was on the Vineyard four months ago. And you would never then have pulled what you did at my brother's last week. Jesus. You're becoming a complete bird."

"Yeah," Crowe said. "I'm a bird of paradise."

The Vineyard. It seemed more like four years than four months. Or maybe forty years. Wandering in the wilderness. If he was lost then, what was he now? "You don't know from nothing," he said. "Inside I'm a canary. Inside it's all yellow and birdsong. I'm just experimenting to see if you can dissociate a mood from its expression. But inside, see, it's rainbows and ice-cream sodas and moonlight over the wood pile. You got the wrong fella. Me, I'm happy as a pig in shit. So lay off. If you think you've seen my bad moods you just keep nagging and I'll show you some worse."

Sandy said nothing. Drying dishes with her back to him. And after a few minutes he went out of the kitchen and lay down on the couch in the dark sitting room. To do nothing. That's not a bad occupation. If you can accommodate nothing, then let there be nothing. Nothing to think about, nothing to sweat, nothing to look at, nothing to hear. Nothing to eat. Ah. there's the rub. To enjoy nothing, you've got to eat and that means you probably can't do nothing indefinitely. He wondered why he had not heard from the Pratt Realty. Rao was probably right. The county had confiscated his land for failure to pay the property taxes. Outrageous. He ought to write the board of supervisors or somebody. I'm a citizen, I have rights. It's hardly my fault I was not contacted by the county assessor or whoever it is that robs the poor of their last crust. Ignorance of the law notwithstanding. If I leave no forwarding address it's only because out of a sense of civic duty I try to save the P.O. a little shoe leather delivering free samples of freeze-dried coffee, tiny tubes of tinny toothpaste, coupons worth a nickel on a box of Bisquick, advertisements for the car wash, the fried chicken, the drugstore penny sale.

He was vaguely aware of Sandy leaving the apartment. The only real mail I ever got, he mused on, besides rejection slips, was howdy from the draft board, and greetings from the President and the reserve unit telling me I owe them two more miserable weeks of my miserable life. I ask you. Who leaves a forwarding address?

And now they take away my land, my house; don't even send me a notice of public auction. He had a sudden, absurd urge to cry, managed to enjoin his tear ducts to leak, fell asleep feeling he was on a severely downward tilt.

I've got to go home again, she said. For Christmas, she said. Only for two or three days. I've got to do that much for my parents or they would get suspicious, not to mention terribly hurt. I hate to, really, it's a lousy time to leave you, but we can celebrate our Christmas early. Do up a turkey and everything. She had a little spruce tree in her hand with a plastic stand to set it upright on the table. Cut too early and already the needles were beginning to fall out. Maybe if we put it in water . . . *It's dead, for God's sake.* Well, it will last a little while. *It's a fire hazard.* Oh. Crowe, don't be such a glump. It's Christmas. We can string pop-corn around it and thread cranberries. *On the twigs? In two days most of it will be on the floor.* Well, I sweep the floor so don't worry about it. *I'm not worried about it. If you want to clutter up the apartment with your Christly totems, go ahead.* She went to the window and threw the tree out into the street. Curses from below and weeping from the bedroom. Crowe standing by the door yelling, "You really wrenched my organ with that one. You're a regular Ensign Pulver, you are."

I'm leaving tomorrow, she said. I'll be back on the twenty-sixth. There's food in the ice box, but I thought we could go out tonight. I wanted to do a turkey but . . . it seemed like we could maybe use a change, it being Christmas and all.

Go out? Go out why? A conspiracy to get me to move. It's a lousy night to go out. Snowing. Wet. Floods. High winds. Careenings of the globe. Let's eat home.

I've been working all day and I'd like a night off, okay?

No, it's not okay. I don't want to go anywhere. It's crappy weather and looking at a menu gives me ulcers. I can't make up my mind. I can't read a wine list. I don't know how much to tip. I'm incompetent, generally speaking, and I want to stay right here.

You're silly, it will be fun.

It will not be fun. It will be dreary. It will be inconvenient, expensive, and badly served. The food will be poisonous. Here I am trying to write and all you ever want to do is go out.

Write! Oh brother. Is that the joke of the year. I won't even dignify that claim with a reply. But I'll tell you something. I pay the bills here, Buster Brown, and so if I say we're going out, we're going out. When you're ready to get a job and become the head of the household you be sure to let me know and then you can dictate the program. Until then you can come along or starve, because I'm going.

Oh my, my. Now we're getting to the nitty-gritty, Miss Rinelander. Now our breeding is showing. SO WHO GIVES A FLYING FUCK IF YOU PAY THE BILLS? Who asked you to, anyway? Who asked you to come back to New York and needle me day in and day out? Who asked you to get all domestic and wifely and play house? Go on out and eat your dinner by yourself.

It's not going to be by myself.

Who's going with you?"

Paps. He was going with us anyway.

Oh he was, was he. How cozy.

I said all three of us were going.

Now it's just two of you.

Fine. That suits me fine.

I bet it does. You and national liberation front Paps can become real chums.

We already are.

I see. You stop by, no doubt, on your way home from work and get your apples juiced in old Pappy's press. He drops in to buy shirts at the perfume counter.

That's none of your business.

Now just a minute lady, it is my business. It is my Goddam business because . . .

Oh, why don't you shut up. Paps and I just happen to be friends. He's kind. He talks to me, which is more than you do. He likes me. He makes me feel like a woman, at least, and not a piece of garbage.

You are a piece of garbage.

You know, I think you're crazy. I think your brain has atrophied from too much sleep.

Izzat so? Well, let me tell you . . .

I think you need help, medical help. You didn't use to be like this. You weren't like this a month ago even. I thought it was just that the writing was going poorly and that when you got it going again you'd change, but now I think you're really sick.

The writing is going poorly. So are a lot of other things.

The writing, the writing. You're some kind of writer, all right. You know, I had a hot flash today when I passed a blind man with a tin cup full of pencils in the forty-second street mall. I thought to myself, Jesus, there's the perfect affliction for my man. I'm serious Jack, you really should have been born blind. All that pity, sympathy, charity—for a couple of pencils. No return requested. Instant compassion without the necessity for a response. I mean, you can just sit there behind your shades and be as hostile and bitter and expressionless as you please and nobody will ding you for it. You're excused. On account of physical defection.

She is dressing by the light from the closet. He sits in his chair watching arms butterfly to snap a bra and peach buttocks in three-quarter profile, wondering why is all this happening? I admit I'm a turd, but I'm under a lot of strain and she just makes it worse.

How does she think *I* feel about sitting here every day while she goes to work, especially when she comes home with the virtuous, smug, I'm really in charge here air, and that "really, Jack, I'm very tired, and anyway your stock is rather low on my exchange lately, what with you being basically a bum, so keep your hands off until I tell you it's okay." Haven't had a piece in eleven days. Count 'em. Cut off, I've been, and for what? Because I'm surly, she says, and that doesn't turn her on. Well, I'm surly because I don't get any. So there you are. Hungry for a bit of that peach.

She turns toward him, pulling on her skirt. "It's all the golden apples of the sun to you, isn't it Jack? You want them so badly, and when somebody gives them to you, they turn to ashes in your mouth. You decide you don't want them anymore. The dream is so much better than the real thing."

Come on. Do I deserve this? For a little writer's cramp and a month of ill temper? Maybe I do. What do I know anymore.

She pulls a sweater over her head, brushes her hair back with her hand, breaks out laughing. "That's funny. Life's number one lesson and I know it and you don't." She waves a pale finger at the table with its lamp, its tablet. "It's all right there in that empty pad of paper, that dusty typewriter, that pencil with the lead still sharp. You want to be a writer and I make it physically possible, at least, and you don't write. The hard part you don't want, or *can't do*, so you take it out on me. But I'm not going to let you do that, Crowe. There's only so much I'm willing to take."

I see now. I plead guilty, I concede. But I see now. You think I *can't* do it. You think I just might not have the stuff, and you've always thought that, wondered, been worried about hooking your train to a falling star, and that's why you'll live with me but won't marry me, and that's why you go around with this attitude of stiff independence that's calculated to bug me. You have no confidence, and without confidence, no respect, and *that's* what makes me a mean son of a bitch. I need a trumpet blower not a critic.

She rummages in a box for pearls. "So you probably wonder why I stay here, then? Why do I stay here? I don't know. I guess because in spite of it all, I still love you and I still believe in you, that you can change, that you can do everything you want to do, be everything you want to be, if you will. I stay because I go on hoping." She puts on her boots and takes her coat from the hook, slips into it and stands for a moment by the door. "Won't you please go with me? I'll wait for you downstairs in Raos' old apartment." Getting no answer, she steps out into the hall, leaving him in the quiet of his own wonder.

This is serious, he thinks. Take this seriously. A corpse she called me, and a corpse I am. Perambulating carrion. Should join a health club or something, swim fifty laps a day, play some basketball, jump rope, lift weights, jog. What I need tonight is a walk in the cold to revive me. Maybe a light supper in some quiet place with candles and a good bottle of wine. We could go up-town later and look at the Christmas lights around Rockefeller Plaza, have a drink at the CBS bar with all the well-heeled young executive types who meet there with their more or less flashy women and their loud tales of vacations on St. Thomas. Walk down Fifth Avenue window-shopping, and a late pastrami on rye and a bottle of Watney's Stingo at a place I know, off Thirty-Fourth Street. Get out of the Mott Street flea trap and into a little class. Up with the hustlers, the three-hour-lunch boys, the theater wheelers and show biz dealers. That make this town go.

He realized suddenly that she was gone. Grabbing a tie and his coat he went out the door, leaving it wide; down two flights of stairs to the Raos' apartment where he rang the bell, banged on the door, hollered "open up" until a woman with her hair so full of metallic curlers she looked like a Christmas tree ornament came out of an adjoining apartment and gave him the evil eye. "Nobody home," she said.

"Stephane's home," Crowe told her. "She's always home."

"Stephane ain't been here for two, three weeks, buddy," the lady told him. "The Raos moved out. Place is rented to a new guy with a funny name. Pappa something or other."

On down the stairs and out into the empty street. Gone, but she may have headed for the Spring Street station, and if I move fast, I'll catch her before a train comes. Like a madman he flies toward Lafayette and Spring, trying to put on his jacket while he runs through slush and patches of ice, no overcoat, no hat, mocassins on his feet, and a cold wind blowing through the open fly of his pants. Christmas trees in the apartment windows where it's happy and warm and smells of pine boughs. Colored lights twinkling red and blue and gold, and wreaths of holly, sprigs of mistletoe. Gone. The station empty as a tomb and colder. He stands there a minute, shivering, wondering, suddenly terrified by his own aloneness, then turns and goes back up the steps to the street. From a distant tower a carillon concert blends with the crunch of his feet on the scurf of snow, and at the corner of Houston Street a Salvation Army volunteer stands over a tripodded pot listlessly ringing a tiny bell that protrudes from the sleeve of her great, black coat. In a neighborhood gin mill with a spray starch Santa Claus stencilled on its hopeful window he orders rye and a draft, settles wearily down with the only other customer in attendance to watch a Lawrence Welk Christmas Special. Sing along with the bouncing cue. *Oh Come All Ye Faithful.* Miniver Cheevy, child of scorn.

7

She did not come back on the 26th. Nor the 27th. Nor the 28th. Neither did she return on the 29th. If Crowe had left the apartment more than once (to buy, repentantly, a forgotten present for one so near and dear) he might have seen her entering the building on the day after Christmas, he might have seen her on her way to and from work, he might even have caught her on the stairs carrying laundry from Paps' apartment down to the machines in the basement. He left only once, and then in the middle of the day. So he did not see her at all.

It was a long week for Crowe, longer than any he had spent since he had left California the summer before. Alone, and without the anticipation of interruption at the end of the day, he had absolutely nothing to do, not even wait. The manuscript had gone back in its box. His pencil lay underneath the table in a wafting bed of dust puppies and fluff. Even the ability to sleep had left him. His body, as if in retaliation for a long hibernation, had reversed its direction and he became an insomniac; spent long nights tossing on the bed, cursing a mind that would not focus on any particular object, would not follow any narrative line, and would not shut off. He drank hot milk, took hot baths, did push-ups, sit-ups, jump-ups, until his eyes bugged out and his face turned blue and the octogenarian below began pounding on the ceiling with her crutch. Still he lay with staring eyes, hot pillowed and sleepless, the emptiness beside him, for which there seemed no remedy, constantly on his mind. He had called the Rinelanders' house in Scarsdale when Sandy did not return, and had been told that she was working in New York, could be reached at a number on Mott Street. His own number. It did not occur to him to go to Bloomingdale's and ask for her there.

On the first day of the new year he had two callers; the first a special delivery boy with a letter from the Pratt Realty saying that they had looked into the matter of his property in Monterey, that there were some minor legal matters that could be handled by a title company and the payment of certain fees, and that they would be delighted to represent him in a sale. There were, however, no immediate prospects. Money was tight, interest rates high, nothing much moving these days. He should not get his hopes up. The house was quite run down, and only the land had real value. They would list the property and let him know if there were any "nibbles." He could, in the meantime, write the assessor's office at the county courthouse and clear up those legal snags. Crowe dumped the letter in the waste basket. Don't call us, we'll call you. Nibbles, schnibbles.

His second caller was Paps. Awkward at first, he came in as if he were avoiding an unpleasant subject that he knew he couldn't avoid long. It is my unfortunate duty to tell you that your little boy was just run over by a school bus, and incidentally, your X rays show thirty-four lesions on the linings of your lungs. Awfully sorry, pal, six months I'd say. "How you making it, man," Paps said.

"Making what?" Crowe told him.

Paps shrugged, sat down on the couch and cleaned the fingernails of his left hand with the thumbnail of his right. "I got to talk to you." Crowe slouched against the doorway of the kitchen and regarded his visitor with a gimlet eye. He offered no encouragement, and Paps, after a suitable pause, said, "You knew I moved into the building?"

"I heard," Crowe said.

"I needed more room. So when George and Stephane said they were leaving I grabbed it. They went to Oregon, by the way. They actually made the break."

"Wonderful," Crowe said. "What was it you had to talk to me about?"

Paps stalled a little more. Regarded his nails. Scraped his cuticles. "Sandy," he said finally. "You see, she started dropping in on her way home from work to talk—about you, mostly. The troubles you were having, the way you were getting more and more down. She wanted to know what to do. I didn't really want to stick my nose in it, and I didn't have any ideas anyway, but I figured just having somebody to talk to about it would do her good and I'd be her listening post if that's what she wanted. The more I listened the more I began to like her until one day I realized I was really hung up." He stopped and blew his nose, either to let that sink in or because he was embarrassed. "We started talking about a lot of things, got to know each other much better, even went out a few times to get something to eat. To put it to you straight, I really got knocked out by her." He began cleaning his right nails with his left thumbnail, waiting for Crowe to offer a comment.

"Let's get to the point," Crowe said.

"The point is not easily got at," Paps replied. "It's complicated. As I've said, Sandy really got to me. I'm as lonely as the next guy, and it turned out we were helping each other just being together now and then for a little conversation. A physical thing it was not, but after a while it began to be clear to us both that it was heading in that direction and it wasn't going to be long before it was. We talked about that too, and then I asked her to leave you." He looked up from his nails, again waiting.

"And?" said an exasperated Crowe.

"And she wouldn't. She couldn't make it over the barrier. She said she couldn't figure out why, but she loved you."

"Yes, well she loves me so much," Crowe said, "she hasn't been here for over a week." He was about to add that they were in the same boat when Paps said, "I know. She's been downstairs at my place. In the spare bedroom."

A police siren went by two blocks away. The kitchen clock hummed. Somebody's radio was playing too loudly. For the first time since before Christmas Crowe was tired. He wanted to lie down. "Then, what in Christ's name are you doing up here? You don't have to ask me for her hand, you know."

"I'm just getting to the point," Paps said. "I told you it's not simply put. Sandy is a very confused girl at this juncture. She thinks you don't want her. Now if that's true, then everything is very easy. I do. I think she could feel the same about me, maybe does already. I want her to go to California with me, but she can't make up her mind, can't let go, and I can't force her. If I could, the way I feel now, I would, but then I guess I wouldn't really want her that way. And I didn't come up here to ask you to *tell* her to go . . . I don't know where you stand in all this . . . I came up here to ask you to tell her *something,* to give her a way to think through her unhappiness, give her back her life, whether it's with you or with me, that doesn't really matter, what matters is Sandy."

"Your altriusm is moving," Crowe said. "Now if you would kindly remove your tokus from my couch and walk it back downstairs where it belongs, it will save me the trouble of throwing you out."

Paps was calmly annoyed. "Don't you ever take anything seriously? I think I could probably give you an argument, if I wanted to."

"I doubt it," Crowe told him. "It would be, in any event, an argument you would lose."

Not to be diverted. "May I tell her you'll talk to her; tell her to come up here?"

"Christ," Crowe exploded. "What are you anyway? Her pimp? I don't care what you tell her. I didn't ask her to leave in the first place. If she wants to talk about it now, that's up to her."

Paps smiled. "I'll take that as acquiescence, if nothing stronger." He stood up and put his hands in his pockets. "I wish you bad luck," he said, heading for the door. "My altruism extends only so far."

Crowe remained against the door jamb. It was nearly dark and the pilot light from the water heater threw strange flickerings on the patterned linoleum of the kitchen floor. And where am I now if she *doesn't* come up? he wondered. In a way he was enormously relieved. She was not, as he had feared, gone for good. If they talked and he told her he wanted her back she would maybe come back and that would be that. On that score he was easy. On the more abstract question of its desirability, and in the completely shadowed area of his moral responsibility in determining her choice, he was less quiet. But who could allow himself to be usurped by a Greek photographer with a private income? It was, when you thought about it, briefly, beneath contemplation, and Crowe thought about it only briefly. He must have, he decided, those golden apples of the sun.

He went to the closet, fished around behind a pile of shirts on the top shelf, brought out a small box of black velvet, and put it in his pocket. He thought it a little small of himself to be aware of it, but he knew when he gave her the contents of that box, her Christmas present, she would be overcome by the realization that he had not forgotten—had, in fact, gone to considerable thought and expense to find something that would please her. It was a sign that he cared. She might weep, for once, for joy.

In a tasteful little restaurant on Waverly Place, with candles and cannelloni and a bottle of 1959 *Côte de Nuits*, with preliminary apologies for reprehensible behavior and spiritual turpitude out of the way, with forgiveness and reconciliation just around the corner (he hoped), he gave her the box, unwrapped (he regretted) but somehow more impressive therefore, and she mimicked with iris and tear the sparkle of emeralds on golden posts that lay against white satin on the inside. "How beautiful," she whispered, reaching for her ear lobe to remove the plain silver hoops she wore.

The moment coiling back upon itself in circuitous intermission. We are too overcome to say more.

Crowe eased back in his chair feeling pleased with himself, swirled the last of the wine in his glass, inhaled its fragrance, and drank. He raised two fingers to the discreetly hovering waiter, mouthed Cognac, and took from his pocket a good, if not great, cigar. "You shouldn't have," she breathed, radiant because he had. "They must have cost a fortune." He waved the cigar in a gesture of expansive indifference, reflecting that depending on how you looked at it, it had been her money that had paid for them. He preferred to think of it as the last of his earnings as a photographic technician. "They matched your eyes," he said. "I couldn't resist."

The waiter brought their cognac and Crowe nestled his in a warming palm, anticipating its sinus-tingling bouquet. In translation, the restaurant, with its gentle hush, its silver and crystal gleaming in the aureole of a single candle at each linened table, its comfortable casing of dark red walls and carpet, fairly lulled one with sensibility and good fellowship. "When you were gone," he lied, "I would get them out and drown myself staring into their depths. Like those volcanic pools at Yellowstone, so brilliant and deep you just want to dive in and drift to the bottom. Never come up. Jeweled sleep, like your eyes."

Or something like that. The more he mellowed the less sense he made, but it hardly mattered. He had scaled the north face, reached the col just beneath the final ridge, had only a small patch of ice to cross before he stood at the summit.

They left the restaurant, walked the eight blocks down Mac-Dougal to Prince, until the tips of their ears began to ache and the moisture in their noses to freeze, and caught a cab across town to Mott. In the foyer of the apartment house Crowe stopped to remove his coat and gloves. "There's a small item we haven't touched on," he said. Beware of the avalanche. "We haven't discussed your present accommodations."

Sandy leaned against the wall, watching her shoes as she moved one foot back and forth over the nap of the rug. "Well," she said, looking up at him, "at the moment I'm living—alone—in the spare room at Paps's. I've been trying all night to think of what to tell you I'm going to do, and I can't, because I don't know. Tonight was wonderful. You haven't been like this for a long time, and I'm just a little bit afraid that if I move back in, it will all stop and you'll go to sleep for another six months."

He started to protest, but she put a finger on his lips and stopped him. "Living with somebody who closes you out is worse than not living at all. It's like there's always a carrot dangling in front of your face, and the faster you run after it, the faster it moves away. Better to have no carrot there at all, because then, at least, you aren't always reminded of how hungry you are. I'm just not sure of you. You can be mighty persuasive when you want something, and mighty careless of it when you have it."

He started to interrupt once more, but again she stopped him. "Something began to happen to me a few months ago. I found out I'd been telling myself I was so sure of everything, how I felt, because I wasn't sure at all, and because I'd put myself in a position where to back down was to admit to having been foolish. I had been telling myself that I was right to have left school, lied to my parents, set up housekeeping with a man I wasn't married to," (Whose fault was that? Crowe thought sourly) "taken a dumb job selling cosmetics instead of becoming a teacher the way I always wanted—telling myself this was all O.K. because to deny it was to really bring an end to my world. This is going to make you mad, I know, but it was really Paps who pointed out the ways I was kidding myself. I started going to talk to him to keep myself sane and because I didn't really know anyone else in New York. He convinced me that there's always another chance, another way not yet tried; that if one road ends in a blind alley, you can back up and take another."

"What makes you so sure it's a blind alley?" Crowe said. "I don't see what it is you want."

She shifted her weight to the other foot and fooled with the clasp of her handbag. "Look, I don't know anything anymore except that I can't stand to be alone. With you I was always alone. I don't know how I feel about Paps, quite, but with him I'm not alone. I know where he stands, and I know what I can count on."

"That sounds comfortably dull."

"Maybe so. But it's something. Anyway, I don't think you give him much of a break. Some of his ideas may be screwy, and the things he wants to do a little far out, but at least he's not guilty of complete withdrawal. There is movement in his life."

"Yeah," Crowe said. "There's movement in a clock's pendulum too. Anyway, you don't have to tell me about Paps. I've known him a lot longer than you have."

"I wonder," Sandy said. "But we're getting side tracked. The question is you and me, and I'm trying to explain some of the things I think about. I don't want to fight, Crowe, we've been doing that long enough, and in a fight I'm *always* going to be the loser. When it comes to jamming the air waves you're unprecedented. I could never get at you because you'd just throw up a smoke screen of gibberish and rhetorical nonsense. So let me stay on the point. You asked me indirectly if I'm going to come back and live with you, and I'm trying to give you an answer. I want to stay by myself for a while until I can work a few things out. If you really do want me, let me have a little time. Respect *my* needs for once."

"By yourself. With Paps to help you through the tough parts."

"Paps is gone until Thursday. He's in Philadelphia seeing his lawyer about his . . . financial affairs, I think he called them. He really is planning to take off for California."

Crowe took his coat off the bench and pushed the elevator button. There was, he decided with rare beneficence, no point in tearing a hole in a perfect canvas. The evening was pure. The painter had the work clearly defined in his head. Tomorrow, or the next day, would be soon enough to begin transforming art into life. "I'll see you up," he said.

She smiled at him, thanking him for his trust, his patience. "If you'd like a night cap, I think maybe there's something in the cupboard we could have." Laughing at him, at herself. "That's how they always do it in the movies, isn't it?"

"But of course," he said with a bow. "A night cap is just the thing."

They had three, and then Crowe went up two flights to his own bed. On the way out, and without thinking why he did it, he flipped off the lock button on Paps's door.

In a jumbling head, tumbling, rumbling, fumbling for consciousness, he slept and did not sleep and dreamed and believed. Thinking, I can't find the handle. In this cockeyed world where it snows up as hard as it snows down. Where somewhere around the third floor of the building the flakes get caught in an updraft by her window and go back past mine with the same grimy velocity they fell. I cannot climb aboard. I am the man who loved and lost. It is not uncommon for the man who has loved and lost to be depressed. Would accept this gloomy vision and even transcend it, were it not for that third dimension to oppression. Don't know why I lost. Strike that. Don't know why I wish to lose. The drifting away of love is somehow connected to everything else that has gone by, like snow flakes, but it is no more clear. Somewhere during the race I tripped, or fell down, or was pushed, or some sneak painted an extra lane leading out of the stadium while I was puffing over on the back stretch. Myopic, I am. Worse than myopic. Blind. Ran right out of the arena and never knew it until I found myself in the parking lot.

Who is that clown who sits in cockeyed suspension peering at the wedding invitation, the synthesis of woe, that lies on the dark wood of a table where a book once slept? A ridiculous invitation from the other side. Silkscreened, misspelled, multicolored. Like a poster for a rock band. There will be a conception before the ceremony. You are urged to attend the honeymoon. A trip to the far reaches of a gray continent where light, sight, and sound explode in a world of shattered images and illusions and shock waves of amplified noise. And why, pray tell, did you send me this farcical announcement of your final union with insanity? Why send me your obituary? I'll go to Bloomingdale's and buy the most cube-shaped casserole they sell and send it to you. For Sandy, from Love to Squalor. A pot for your garbanzo beans.

Is it possible to be so infatuated by a cliché? Lining his soulmates up in front of a mile-long mirror, as my old man once lined me up, and I see a rainbow turned to dust, swirling vapor turned solid and blown like powder in a wind storm. A mile of pontificates. A mile of Jesus Christs wearing haloes of flies. Can they walk on water? Can they raise the dead? Can they return you from the dream dump where your eyes stare vacantly from a wreckage of flesh and bone? They cannot. They are themselves the risen dead, come back to tell us all.

Perhaps it is nothing more than time that has put me down; that metamorphic river of dreams turned to nightmare and finally to insomniac horror as I sprawl in my stuffed chair listening to the metronome of my pulse counting cadence through the night. From the windowshade a light filters in, ghostly shapes slide along the parlor walls of the old weatherbeaten house—messengers whose voices have been lost in combat with the keeper who marks the score sheet. How much they could reveal to us who are still wandering through the wilderness of our dreams. I hear rain striking against the window and the boom of surf on the point. I am melancholic, bilious, and old. I am a lugubrious belch. I am the afterword to a sour stomach: the preface to nausea. I am stuck in ruts I can hardly span. Shaped in an alien mold. Hunched with the weight of righteousness. My spinesack bulges with the aphorisms of honesty and industry. My soul is bleached in the chlorinated bathwater of my childhood faith. Or is it my faith in childhood? My feet are splayed from traveling in the rut of the road most taken. And I reject it. I despise it. And while I reject and despise, I nail the soles of my shoes to the subfloor and howl for the carpenter to sheet up the walls.

Who is that clown who sits day after day in his prison of dullness, eating peanut butter and whole-wheat bread, dreaming of forests and cool brooks and picnics in the meadow with the breeze gently stirring through the grass and the perfume of clover in the air? On the wall there is a travel poster that instructs him to see Vermont and previews a lake in the Green Mountains with a happy couple sailing a Sunfish out toward a cover where the pines open up and the sun shines through. With magical ease I transport myself to its shores—to an afternoon of sun and cloud and sequins on the water—back to a frozen point in time when I was blissfully happy with a moment in the present, and the past and the future were not only irrelevant but inconceivable. The bed on which I lie becomes a patch of close-cropped grass, and down through the shimmering leaves of a birch tree the lake flows peacefully off into the distance and hides itself behind the fold of a hill. A weasel pokes its whiskers into a corner of my memory, and ducks back behind a swaying branch. I have not had many such tranquil moments, Sandy, real or imaginary.

And how, in God's name, could you marry, could you have married, could you intend to marry, anybody with a name like

Paps? A tumescent nickname. A bulging offspring of Aristotle Francis Papanikolas. Paps who suckles the hydrocephalic souls of the hopeless and homeless. That social paraplegic. That primitive pigmy from the primeval forest. That missing link. My old buddy. I'll write your epitaph, my old buddy. I'll tell you what you destroyed in the name of Eros and Libertas. The wallflower grows under your nose. The wildflower has become a weed.

He rose with a yell from the bed, found himself standing in the middle of the room, wringing wet, completely without mooring, in an uncontrollable rage. He was shaking and sweat stung his eyes. The more he rubbed them clear, the worse the stinging became. She had lied. He knew she had lied. She had fooled him with her talk, her plea for respect, her request for time. It had all been a ruse to put him off, a sop to hold him at bay a few days longer while she planned her escape, while she screwed Paps into total compliance and made him flee with her to California. She was down there now. With him. Mindless with lust. Wrapped around him in squirming confidence of her victory. Well, it wouldn't work. He'd kill them both. Break their backs like a trout, a knee between the shoulder blades and a swift backward yank of the head. He sought in the dark for his underwear, found it, put it on as he hopped toward the hall.

Her door was open. She had forgotten the police bolt and had gone to bed assuming the regular lock was on. Crowe stepped from the brightly lit hall into swimming blackness, waited a few minutes until his eyes adjusted. The window slowly emerged out of the night, the corner of a table, a stand-up lamp, the sofa, the bedroom door. He thought for a moment that he was back in the darkroom, watching a print take shape in the bottom of its chemical bath. Only reversed. Black paper turning light. He moved quietly across the room, no longer sure what he intended to do when he reached that door, paused to listen to the regular expulsion of her breath, two breaths, panting mouths, animal grunts. Total silence. He pushed the door with his toe and stood looking at himself in the dresser mirror, an inky silhouette against the opening.

She was alone. He could see from where he was standing the outline of a single shape beneath the sheets, and for a moment he thought he would turn and slip out as quietly as he had come in. He had been wrong, had been wrenched by his dream into a pathological state that had now passed because proved pathological, and the only sane course was to retreat. She would never know. Their agreement would remain intact. In a few days she would come back. To stay and be discovered would be to destroy all faith.

He went in cautiously, slowly, along the foot of the bed, moving toward the side. She stirred in her sleep, muttered something as he stood frozen, then her breathing went on, even, calm. He moved again, one step, another, filled with tenderness now, aching to touch her, to express somehow in something other than words the feeling of yearning, adoration, devotion that swelled inside him. He was beside her, looking down at the dark tangle of her hair, her face barely visible against the paleness of the pillow, thinking how even more beautiful she seemed in sleep with the tiredness that had lately come into her expression gone, and her mouth slightly parted so that her teeth gleamed in a thin line between her lips. She slept naked, one shoulder uncovered, and impulsively he bent to kiss the shadowed juncture of her arm and breast.

She woke with a sharp intake of her breath and her body convulsed away, then froze in terror. "It's me," Crowe said, reaching out to soothe, to reassure, to catch his balance. She struck at his hand with a frightened cry, tried to scuttle out of bed away from him. He grabbed her, saying, "It's me, Goddamn it, it's Crowe," and then again, and then over and over, pulling her back half in anger at her persistent refusal to wake up and acknowledge him, and somehow kissing her neck, her shoulder, her breast, while she struck at him with her fists. Because she fought, his anger returned; he struck her and then he was on top of her, viciously pinning her arms with his arms, her legs with his; smothering her struggle, her disgust, and feeling her writhe beneath him in an attempt to get free. Her movements drove him on, increased his need, and ignoring her furious demand that he stop, that she hated him, that he revolted her, that she had no protection, ignoring her crying when finally she gave up, quit trying to resist his weight, his insistence, his own fury, and lay as passively as a rag doll, he forced her knees apart and entered her; she, dry and tight and dead, crying why couldn't you˙wait, why, why, why, why, and still crying after what seemed like hours later when her body betrayed her and began perversely to respond as if in some dim recollection of love and in spite of the outraged mind that no longer controlled it. His orgasm, when it came, was an explosion of agony that left him sick and unrelieved, and when he stood up, reeling, clutching his bursting head in his hands, she lay without moving, her face turned away, her eyes closed. He stumbled from the room and fled up the stairs. In the bathroom, from disgust, hatred, self-loathing, knowing that he had for no reason but malignant perversity hit absolute rock bottom, he heaved his insides, and went on heaving, dry, empty, unable to produce anything but a thin, watery bile.

In his delirium he spoke to her saying, *I cannot blot it out.* A smell, a song, a corner cupboard in a furniture store window near my apartment—they all bring back the house, the lake, the girl, the time when times were good. Do you remember that house, Sandy? Large, comfortable. Stuffed couches, armchairs, a. brick fireplace big enough to hold a camp meeting, corner cupboard with the funny old enamel knobs that kept falling off and rolling down into the floor registers, fake antique hutch, dry sink, newly lined with copper and used as a bar. Do you recall how many times I stood in front of that sink mixing martinis, manhattans, daiquiris, biting the filter tip of my cigarette between my teeth like Mr. Cool, the movie actor, who flipped your mind and made you think of love. I remember. How many times did we sit on that porch that smelled faintly of creosote and leaf mold, watching the sun disappear slowly into the bosom of the mountain over near Stowe? How many times did we watch a cold moon slip down behind those same hills in the early hours of the morning as we lay dreaming on that antique sofa, waiting for the alarm clock to shock us into consciousness and send you slipping back to your father's house through the misty dawn. I am romanticizing the romantic. I can hear your soft breathing. In the moonlight that floods my dreams I see your hair spread out over the pillow. It all makes me very sad. And now I have done this.

When, two days later, he finally found the physical strength and the courage to approach Paps's apartment, to try somehow (he had not the remotest idea how) to make amends, Sandy and Paps were gone. The super was there spreading canvas on the floor in preparation for painting. He simply shrugged and raised his eyebrows when Crowe asked him "where?"

"Told me to give you this," the super said, handing Crowe a manila envelope. He opened it to find the passbook to a savings account at the Bank of America with a four-hundred dollar balance, and a small, black, velvet-covered box, which he did not bother to open.

Part 3

THE DREAM DUMP

1

On a sunny morning near the end of June a blue Renault, circa 1957, with a finish like peanut brittle and a hundred-dollar price tag still painted on its windshield (Crowe had paid seventy-five), rattled down the coast highway from San Francisco toward Monterey, rods knocking, tappets tapping, rear end howling. As it squiggled by on misaligned tires, a turkey buzzard, perched by the side of the road on the carcass of somebody's cat, paused in mid-morsel to watch and wonder.

The trip, being necessarily slow and cautious, gave the operator plenty of time to plan his attack, to arrange his arguments, to consider alternatives, and prepare to counter unforeseen events. He did none of these. He had, in fact, no specific plan, no excuse, no reason to be; only renewed hope and regenerated optimism for the possibilities of the future. He was back in California. Had anybody asked why, he could not likely have told; could only have offered mysterious and evasive mutterings about spiritual urges, vague beckonings of the past, cravings for forbidden fruit, the need for redemption. Metaphysics. If anybody had asked how, he would have told them, with concealed though not inconsiderable pride, that he had, out of abject hopelessness and self hatred, transformed the jagged edge of despair into art, had written a love story of considerable length about a disaffected eastern girl with money and background and a dissolute western boy with nothing much but the hungries, and miracle of miracles, had sold it to a ladies' magazine for a whopping two thousand dollars. Unlikely story, but true. And no less unlikely, he told himself, than the three nearly completed stories traveling comfortably in their manila envelope in his suitcase, all of them promising, and all of them better work than he had ever done before. It was perhaps because of this "breakthough" that his heart was light and his head at ease. You can only stay down so long.

Instead of considering his destination and its implications, he watched the country pass by; country, it occurred to him, in which he had grown up but to which he had not given a thought in some time. He left Golden Gate Park and headed south toward Daly City through funky housing developments built on the tops of hills that had been carved off and used to fill in the valleys. As he neared the cutoff to the coast the entire community stretching away below him seemed to be sitting on a precarious foundation of loose adobe that would, if given a good quake shake, slide right down into the bay. Ah the wonderfulness of a Dolger Home, he thought, amused; the pink plaster Dolger shack with the thin shake roof and the sinking foundation, the plate-glass window, and the perpetual view of the fog sweeping up and down the street, kindly obscuring the property owner from all the other pink plaster shacks that surround him for miles in every direction. But what the hell, Crowe thought, a home is a home.

On the western slope of Daly City the houses were perched up on terraced hills, picture windows facing the sea, heavy curtains drawn from dawn to dusk against an ocean glare that transfers the water outside to the eyeball inside. At a stop light he watched a pale woman in a terrycloth robe and curlers come out on her overhanging porch and call down through the sunshine to a paler child playing with his army trucks in the ice plant beside the freeway.

Once past Pacifica the coast is hardly inhabited for miles. On the one side it drops abruptly into the ocean; on the other it rolls away in pasture and fields of brussels sprouts, rises to oak-dotted knolls, and then still higher to forests of pine and redwood. Occasionally he passed a small ranch with a row of cypress protecting the whitewashed buildings from wind and Pacific storms. Barn fowl scratched in a yard fenced with escallonia and juniper. Hanging fuchsia obscured the kitchen windows. A hawk's wings were spread and nailed to the side of the barn; a superstitious ritual to ward off others of its kind. Out on a headland a farmer was harrowing a field, raising a small cloud of dust that trailed behind him.

Lordy, lordy, how easily I put all this behind me, he thought. How easy to erase what touches you most. My problem in a nutshell. Twenty minutes from the scene of the crime and here I am in empty country completely untouched by the crawling idiocy on the other side of the mountain. Twenty miles from the city and I'm passing through land where coyotes and cougars still feed on the rancher's calves, and a quail's worst enemy is a coon. What kind of a fool would run from this?

Fifteen years ago on a pre-dawn morning in June we came with wet suits and tire irons to one of these rocky points where the low tide uncovered a rare shoal; searched frantically an hour or so for abalone, until the tide started in again and the crevices where crustacean like to hide were once again submerged in surf. Spent the morning cleaning our catch, cutting the black-rimmed flesh out of its shell, scraping, slicing steaks, pounding the rubbery meat until it was soft and ready to be fried over a driftwood fire in a battered pan filled with butter. Poetry on the palate.

Two girls hitch-hiking south from Pescadero reminded Crowe that he had not come to sight-see and wallow in the past. In another hour or so he would be standing on Sandy's threshold obliged to explain his odd, unannounced appearance at the portals of Papanikolas's paradise, because she would know he had not come out of curiosity or for old time's sake. He had belied his capacity for sentiment too often. He decided he could only tell her the truth—insofar as he understood it himself— could only tell her that he had come back to the country where he now knew he belonged (the year in the east had taught him that much), to a piece of land that had been his father's and now was his and that some internal twitch told him he should, being thirty-one years old and getting no younger, restore and inhabit. He could tell her that settling down meant to him a wife and children and (here came the sticky part) he wanted, if there was any way possible, to erase those months in New York, to wipe the slate, to forget the past (since he could in no way explain it), and go back to an earlier time. He wanted to be all the things he had not been, agree to all the things he had side-stepped and put off. He could do it now. He knew, he would tell her, that he was asking the impossible, that he had been given a second chance, and a third, and a fourth, and that he had no right to ask for yet another, but he was going to ask it anyway. People could change, and he would, indeed, already had, as the copy of his printed story and the three nearly finished manuscripts in his suitcase should show. To ask another chance was all he could do. The rest was up to her.

A few miles north of Santa Cruz he passed Año Nuevo island where he and Jimmy Winklebleck used to go when an unusually minus tide would occur because the whole reef connecting the island to the mainland would emerge and few abalone hunters had combed the area. He remembered watching the seals body-surf on two lines of breakers that rolled in toward the reef from opposite directions, meeting in the middle in an explosion of white spray. It had been that experience that had left him yearning all through his high school years to be a marine biologist and study animal behavior. Another road not taken, he thought sadly. A few miles south of Santa Cruz he passed the exit to La Selva State Beach where he used to dig late for Pismo clams out on the sand bars, up to his waist in surf and sunset.

About an hour later and ten miles up the Carmel Valley he spotted the turn-off to Tassajara. From there the road wound through a canyon between ungrazed hills of dry grass, mustard stalks, and thistles, over a ridge and down into another valley thick with poison oak, coyote brush, and sage. He passed an abandoned gravel quarry where two boys were shooting with .22's at a row of cans set back against the cliff. They turned to stare at his rattle trap car and he was afraid for a moment that the temptation might overcome them to put a few holes in a moving target, but after eyeing him for a moment, they went back to more stationary objects. He drove for another ten minutes, and then, as he came over a low rise, saw a collection of buildings off to the left, about three hundred yards beyond the dry creek bed that paralleled the road—a house, two or three sheds, a tired barn with most of its roof gone, a variety of collapsing fences. A mailbox at the end of the driveway said Papanikolas.

The only sign of habitation was a Volkswagen bus parked in the middle of the yard. Bare dirt everywhere, a few zinnias struggling in a planter box by the house, a half-dozen begonias in pots along the porch rail, a willow tree beside the barn, an avocado tree between the barn and tool shed. Otherwise the surrounding land was without planting. The hills, which would be green in winter and patched with lupine in spring, had turned brown, and the entire valley simmered in arid heat.

Crowe pulled up by the barn and stepped out of his car. A calico mutt ambled out of the shade, tail wagging, and sniffed his pant-leg. Nothing of interest. Piss on it anyway. Establish claim. Crowe's booted foot shot out and dumped the dog on its side where it lay yelping with outrage. Interrupted by a flea. Began a furious chewing of its left flank. From the barn loft there was a flutter of pigeon wings and he could hear a radio playing somewhere in the house—the only real indication that the place was not abandoned.

Nobody answered his knock at the door and he wandered around to the side of the house. Behind it there was a garden that he had not seen from the road, still in its infancy but growing and obviously well tended. A girl in a long sack dress and bare feet was thinning shoots of corn, working from her knees, her copper hair falling long and straight toward the earth as if it might take root and form a permanent arch over the plants beneath it. Crowe did not need to speculate on its owner's identity.

She straightened up after a while, brushed her hair back with a muddy hand, and then, catching him in the corner of her eye, turned toward him with a startled expression. With the sun at his back she could not recognize him at once, but rose to her feet, clumsily, saying with an easy laugh, "You took me by surprise." Crowe, to *his* surprise, to his complete amazement, to his utter incomprehension, saw she was pregnant.

There was, it seemed, an endless suspension of time during which he stood leaden stomached and stupidly gaping at the vague reflection of a form his memory could not alter, his mind trying desperately to rewind, to erase the last hundred feet of footage so that he could come once again around the house and encounter her tending her garden—along the banks of the Connecticut river, the sun filtering down through the maples, the cows grazing in the pasture down by the spring. We'll have corn, beets, beans, peas, radishes, tomatoes, potatoes, squash, and Black-seeded Simpson. No children. Children are later. We'll have walks in the woods and a moonlight swim in the brook. We'll have spring in Europe, summer in southern France, winter in the Alps, fall in Cuernavaca. Children are definitely *de trop*.

"Oh God," she said, pressing a hand to her breast, her face a composite of disbelief, distrust, uncertainty. "What are you *doing* here?"

Perhaps it is just that the face itself has changed, grown pale, lined a little around the mouth, and the hair lusterless, not terribly clean. But the eyes—wider, greener. They seem eternal, ingenuous, Elysian. He stared into them, trying to focus his mind on the present. "To see about . . ." he began. "I told you my father's place in Monterey." He stopped, aware that he had garbled the syntax but unable to rephrase his remark.

"You're living . . . in his house?" she asked, the words coming slowly, without reflection, as if she were not conscious of having said them.

"Not living. I'm here to see what to do about it. Fix it up, maybe." He was rushing things, he knew. Her condition threw him. And so he shut up and they were silent again, like two people who have just met, each trying to think of a polite but intelligent question that will stimulate conversation, each aware that the long pause growing between them was making the situation more awkward, more artificial, more impossible.

"Warm today," Crowe said, and regretted it.

"How did you find . . . ?" Sandy waved her hand at nothing in particular.

"I guessed, more or less." He looked around at various rows of tiny shoots in the garden, trying to keep his eyes off her stomach. "How's Paps? Francis, I mean." He wondered why the nickname sounded inappropriate, almost insolent.

"Everybody's gone to the beach," she said, moving toward the house. She went slowly up the porch steps, using the senile railing for support. It wobbled and threatened to collapse. At the door she stopped and took a deep breath. "Three months to go yet, and I think if I get any fatter I'll pop."

In the kitchen it was cool. The doors and windows were open and a light breeze blew through the house. The radio continued to entertain itself in some other room. Sandy went to the refrigerator and took out a quart bottle of ginger ale, held it up and raised her eyebrows in a silent question. Crowe nodded and while she poured two glasses, he looked around. In the corner of the room there was a litter of kittens that suddenly reminded him of another litter, years ago, in the old house in Monterey, and for a moment he was revolted by the thought of those cats; fish food, packaged in burlap, flung into the Pacific by a demented screwball who could not stand their mewing and their refusal to acknowledge the kitty litter. Still, he was not a cat lover and he considered with distaste the faint odor of feces that rose from their lair. Under the eaves outside the kitchen window there was a swallow's nest and the parent birds were flitting in and out of their adobe home.

"Are you still living in New York?" Sandy asked. "Mott Street?"

"Until about two days ago."

"Did you drive out?"

"Flew."

Silence. Obviously she wondered how he afforded a plane ticket. Crowe smiled. "Small breakthrough," he said. "I exorcised the demon sloth when you left me—I guess that jolted me pretty good—I started to work like a madman to prove to myself I *wasn't* a madman, not all the time anyway, and . . . well . . . things sort of panned out, I sold a piece, wrote two or three more . . ."

"That's wonderful," Sandy said, clasping her hands together, "I knew you could, if you just would. Oh, I can't wait to read it. What's it about?"

Crowe was considerably lifted by her enthusiasm, but he didn't want to appear overly proud of himself. "It's about thirty pages," he said.

"I see your humor is as sanguine as ever."

"I see your vocabulary has improved, if without much precision."

"It's the company I keep," Sandy told him with just a touch of sarcasm. "They talk more than some of my older acquaintances."

"Yeah," Crowe said. "Well, I gather there's more of them now."

"There are six of us here now," she said, pleasantly, as if she were being interviewed by Lawrence Spivak and wanted to project in the face of hostility an image of calm beatitude. "We think maybe two or three more are coming in September, which will be groovy because there's a lot to be done. You know, fixing up the house, mending the fences, planting, working the garden, taking care of the animals."

"A regular Brook Farm," Crowe observed.

Sandy shrugged, sipped her ginger ale and regarded him over the edge of the glass. No Lawrence Spivak was going to shake her faith.

"You know there's never been a Brook Farm in the history of mankind that made it," Crowe went on.

"Made what?" she said, and laughed.

"Survived."

"So what does that prove?"

"Doesn't *prove* anything, except it would seem to suggest that your chances of pulling the whole thing off are statistically not good."

She looked rather bored, as if success or failure had never been a real consideration. "The chances of transplanting a human heart were not very good . . . statistically. But somebody did it. Anyway, nobody here is very much concerned about ideology or statistics. This isn't exactly a commune, you know, it's just a place to live for as long as you feel like it, and a place where everybody can do what he wants in his own way without having to justify himself to any social or economic or political establishment." She got off the stool on which she had been sitting, took a carton of milk from the refrigerator and poured some in the kittens' dish. Then she straightened up, and still holding the carton leaned against the sink, looked at Crowe. "Jack, why did you come here?"

He wished that on his way down the coast he had considered more carefully the best way to play his role, but then, he reflected, it wasn't really a drama anymore, the theater was closed, the box office dark, and on its window a sign that said *sold out—all future performances.* "I don't know that I can explain it very exactly," he said, deciding to remain honest for once. "Lots of reasons, I guess, but none of them too clear. My old man's house sitting there empty and falling to bits was one. But mainly there was you. I realize it sounds pretty hollow to say that I felt you were owed an apology . . . hell, much more than that . . . supplication for forgiveness, even though I don't deserve it. And there didn't seem any honorable way to do it without standing up and giving you a chance to slug me." He got up and walked to the kitchen door, stood looking out into the sunlight, talking more to himself than to her. "I left here in the first place looking for something . . . proof of a theory . . . I don't know what to call it exactly . . . roots, traditions, established modes of culture that I wanted for some reason and figured I could find in the east. Stability. It all sounds very puerile to me now, and it is, because I was blaming my location for an inner vacuity, for a lack of will, an inability to work out any form of self discipline, a weakness for the ho-daddy life style. You've got to grow up here to understand it, and even then it's hard." He paused, aware that he was making a speech, but unable to stop. "I was running away from one myth—California as panacea—to another myth that has something to do with the east as a place where one finds a pedigree. I read too many books when I was a kid. Too much Henry James and Edith Wharton and Henry Adams. I mean I could only relate to life through a literary analogy. Sort of like Mark Twain hungering all his life after a social milieu where Lowells speak only to Cabots and Cabots speak only to God. Wanting to be what you're not. Wanting what you don't have. Only, as you know, I didn't behave any different in the country I ran to than I did in the country I ran from."

He stopped talking and leaned against the door jamb, looking out again over the garden toward a sagging whitewashed fence in the middle ground, the soft, brown rise of the hills in the distance. One of the kittens walked through the saucer and stood mewing in its own damp tracks, shaking first one foot and then the other. Sandy suddenly discovered the milk carton that she was holding against her breast with both hands, set it on the counter while she picked the cat's dish off the floor and put it in the sink. "I don't think I agree with you," she said. "Maybe if you grew up out here it's that way, but if you grew up in the east changing your geography does a lot for your head."

Crowe shrugged. "One man's meat," he said. He turned from the doorway and came back in the kitchen. "Maybe so. At any rate I see it's done a good deal for your stomach." He tried to say it lightheartedly and did not altogether succeed.

"Geography is not responsible for my stomach," Sandy said pointedly. He missed the point, and she did not elaborate. The radio provided background for an extended silence during which they both focused their eyes on their shoes, a Miro print on the wall, two flies noisily fornicating on the counter, a book of matches on the stove, a thumb tack and a calendar on the door, and then, finally, each other's faces. Solemn façade. Volcanic beneath the crust. "You don't look so good," Crowe croaked.

"Flattery will get you nowhere."

"You look tired, worn out."

"I am." She patted her stomach.

"But still beautiful."

Raised eyebrows. "Not dissipated?"

"Just a little."

"Degenerate?"

"Vaguely."

"Dissolute and wantonly self-destructive?"

"That's it."

We're turning this into a joke.

"Been dropping too much monosodium glutamate. Gotta get straight." She smiled then, relieved maybe that some obscure barrier had been crossed. "It's funny," she said. "I'm really glad to see you. I wasn't, but now I am."

Crowe took out a pack of cigarettes, offered her one, and when she shook her head put the pack away. "I was afraid you hated my insides. You have every right to."

She stopped smiling then, and looked at her hands. "No. Not really. I did for a while . . ." She smoothed her dress over her stomach. "But there wasn't any percentage in that. Mostly I was just sad. You're always sad when something ends. But hating isn't an end. Maybe being pregnant keeps you from hating things."

Crowe winced. He wished she would not remind him so frequently of his losses.

Sandy brushed her hair away from her face. "Lately," she went on, "I found myself thinking about you quite often. Nice thoughts. Like when I go out to the coast and spend the day just wandering around the rocks and tide pools, or when I go into Monterey and see all those old adobe buildings up behind the main street with the courtyard gardens and crumbling walls. I think about how here I am and here you were, and it's kind of sad all over, kind of fate-laden or something, that we couldn't be here together. When we were together we were really heading in opposite directions."

Crowe changed his mind, took out his ciagettes again and lit one. "That could be remedied," he said.

"It's like that joke," Sandy went on, "about the two carloads of musicians, one from California and one from New York. The California bunch want to get where the recording studios and industry wheels are, so they're driving east. The New Yorkers want to get out where they think the real music action is and the hippest audiences, so they're driving west. And when they pass each other in Kansas they lean out of their cars and shout at each other 'go back, go back.' That's what happened to us in a way. Only I did go back once, and it was a mistake. Now you're back." She didn't say whether she thought that, too, was a mistake.

"Except the situation is a bit different," Crowe said, decided he had to know. "You're married now, and safe from the devil's clutches."

"Married?" Sandy looked at him puzzled for a moment, then glanced down at her stomach. "Oh that," she laughed. "Well, we were going to, but when I discovered I was going to have a baby we decided to put it off until . . . the future."

Crowe couldn't decide whether he was happy she wasn't married or unhappy that she had planned to be. "Isn't that kind of backward," he said. "I mean usually you hurry it up to give the kid an honest name."

"Getting married would not exactly have accomplished that," she said, once again pointedly. Once again he missed the point. "Anyway, it's not important."

"Sandy," he blurted. "What *are* the chances?"

She looked at him for a long time, perhaps not quite understanding the question at first and then, having understood, unable to make a simple reply. The clock hummed, and it seemed to Crowe that finally she was about to answer when the sound of a car with a broken muffler violated the hot quiet of the valley. Immediately she gathered the glasses and put them in the sink, threw the ginger ale bottle in the trash. Her sudden activity betrayed her nervousness and Crowe knew that the car was coming to the house and that it contained Paps. He cursed the intruder silently, and wondered what kind of scene lay ahead, what version of his sudden appearance Paps would accept, and what, if anything, they would say to each other. He was trapped, however; the broken muffler had already turned off the main road and was approaching the house. There was nothing to do but play it out. Leave the opening move to the opposition. Best offense is a good defense. "We'll see," Sandy said with her back to him and in a voice so low he was not sure she had really said anything at all.

The dog was barking in frantic recognition, joined after a minute by two more. When the engine stopped, the barking stopped. Crowe sat tilted back in his chair, his arm on the kitchen table, listening to the shouts of three or four voices and the slamming of car doors. "Here Sally. C'mere Humbert, you silly son of a bitch. Bones for Bowser. Git it." The sound of yelping and running feet as something was thrown against the wall of the barn. And then human feet on the porch, kicking the front door open, clattering in over the board floors of the living room like a barbarian horde in a temple. Four persons, actually, only one of whom paid any attention to Crowe.

Paps came in the kitchen with grocery sacks in his arms, executed a conventional double take at the man tilted in his chair against the wall, and then set the groceries down slowly, carefully, as if he thought Crowe might be holding a gun and did not want by any sudden move to precipitate a hasty assassination. Crowe tilted forward and the chair legs scraped loudly in the hushed kitchen when he stood up. "Hello Franny," he said.

There was a moment of indecision and then Paps said, "I'll be damned." He stepped forward and extended an uncertain hand, apparently still unconvinced that Crowe was not homicidal. "Where'd you come from?"

"New York."

"Sure." Paps didn't seem to know what else to say.

"You were right. It's a lousy place to live."

Paps looked at Sandy and then back at Crowe, searching in their faces for some hint of what had passed before he had returned. Crowe was rather surprised to find that it was he, not Francis, who was on top of the situation, and although he was beginning to feel a little arrogant, a little like the black knight appearing at the joust and casting his gauntlet at the feet of the simpering prince who thinks he has just won the hand of the king's daughter, he also felt a little sorry about what was happening to his old friend. Paps had never been devious or sneaky and he deserved to know the ground on which the contest was to be fought, if indeed a contest *was* to be fought. I'm getting ahead of the script, Crowe thought. Becoming the author of this tale and not just a character in it. He reminded himself of where arrogance had gotten him in the past and knew that it was a pose he could no longer afford—not with Sandy, not with anybody or anything that touched her. It was, in fact, a pose he no longer seemed to cherish. Anyway, Paps was not a weak sister anymore, if he had ever really been. He had come to grips in the last year with what he was about, what he wanted, what he believed in, and he had never been the type to back off in a fight. If Crowe still thought him a little short on originality, he no longer underestimated his capability to defend what he thought was his. That unswerving generosity was deceptive.

Crowe was about to remark on the estate, to observe that it

was a welcome change from the lower east side, when the others came in with a gunny sack full of abalone, a case of Coors, and three gallons of Red Mountain burgundy. Paps introduced him to a pale haired young man with ice colored eyes named Chadwick, and to the thinnest girl Crowe could ever remember meeting, Linda Grimes. She was as tall as Sandy but could not have weighed over a hundred pounds. Her brown hair, which hung half way down her back, straight and the texture of milk-weed fluff, simply added to the impression that she enjoyed at best a tentative and temporary existence in a world of gravity-governed mass. "Hi," she said, and the faint expulsion of breath in her greeting caused the hair around her face to lift, float up and away like a feather in a vacuum tube. "My pleasure," Crowe said, to which she faintly smiled.

At the sink the fourth member of the group, Willy Wonder, was emptying the abalone out of the sack and trying to pry them off each other's backs. "Mutherin' muscles got a sucker on 'em like a magnet," he said to anybody. On his right foot he wore a specially constructed boot, heavily built up in the back. Crowe later learned that he had once been a fast draw and trick shot specialist in some Nevada ghost town, but that his trigger finger had achieved a degree of independence, had revolted, as it were, from the parental restraints of thumb and palm, and in his final performance Willy's gun had not cleared leather when the recalcitrant finger constricted and shot off his heel, leaving it smashed like a clam in the dust. Willy had grey hair and was closing in on his fiftieth birthday. He half turned from the sink and showed Crowe a mouthful of badly stained teeth by way of a greeting.

As it turned out nobody in the group had any idea what to do with abalone. They had taken the shellfish illegally from the rocks at Point Lobos on the advice of some passing poacher who had told them where and what but not how. Grimes thought you boiled them. Willy Wonder was of the opinion that unless they were cleaned first, they would poison the eater, and that the shells had to be removed to get at the guts. He wanted to bust them with a rock. In the midst of a heated argument during which Willy began to use a lot of bad language, calling everybody down for a collection of low life, rum bellied, fuckheads, Paps told everybody to pipe down. "Crowe probably knows," he said, turning. "He grew up on this stuff."

"Sure," Crowe told them, happy to be included. "You need some sharp knives and a wooden mallet and something to pound on." He explained how to work the knife in between the meat and the shell until the muscle that connected the two was severed, how to scrape the black rind from the edge and slice the meat into thin steaks, how to pound it until it was tender without tearing it to bits. They took the abalone outside to an old workbench where he demonstrated, and everybody set to work. Willy Wonder, however, amputated a half-inch of thumb and had to be retired; grumbling, before he marinated everything in his blood. When they carried the huge platter of steaks into the kitchen where Linda Grimes and Sandy were heating oil in the biggest frying pan available, Paps turned to Crowe and said, "For once you fell in at the right time, Jackson. Would all have been wasted without you." It was, or so Crowe chose to take it, a tacit invitation to dinner.

After they had eaten they sat out on the back porch groaning under their load of abalone, french bread, and braised leeks, passing the jug of Red Mountain and watching the light fade. The tops of the hills were still golden with sunlight, but in the valley long shadows were forming and the air, though still, was cool. Willy Wonder lay prone on the boards, one arm over his eyes, his bum foot hanging over the edge, belching periodically and recommending each time that they vote on it. Chadwick, who had hardly said anything all evening, was reading a tattered Zap comic, and Linda Grimes, when she heard Crowe had just come out from New York, was telling anybody who cared to listen about a trip she had once taken to Fire Island with two faggots from Yonkers. All that's missing, Crowe thought, is Teeterass and Ringworm.

He was beginning to find the whole situation uncomfortable and faintly depressing, since he did not yet have a picture of his relationship to its parts, and he was wondering how he could gracefully remove himself to the kitchen where he could hear Sandy doing the dishes, when he noticed a squat little figure in a baseball cap slide out of the tool shed by the garden and begin to work its way over to the porch. Grimes' monotone monologue droned on. The baseball cap was reversed, with its bill bent up in back and held there by the elastic strap of a pair of ski goggles through which its owner was peering like a wary animal. No shirt and no shoes. Patchy areas over the chest that looked like skin grafts. Mostly stomach. High altitude flight pants, leather outside, fleece inside, held up by red and blue suspenders. From beneath the cap greasy hair hung like a black fringe on an awning, and there were perhaps a dozen hairs on either side of the upper lip that offered to pass for a moustache. Crowe was completely intrigued, in a detached sort of way, marveling at such excessive grotesquery and amazed that his companions paid it no attention, though they obviously saw it. Or perhaps they didn't. Perhaps it was only an apparition. Shellfish had been known to give him trouble before.

Cap and awning sidled up to the edge of the porch and stood staring at him from a distance of no more than two feet. Malevolent, pig eyes. Odor of wood smoke and stale sweat. He jumped perceptibly when it said very loudly, in a child's voice, "What's this guy?"

Grimes broke off her story long enough to say "He's O.K., Bird," then went on crossing the ferry from Brown's point to Fire Island Pines. Chadwick went on reading. Willy Wonder belched and said, "let's vote on it." Crowe had an impulse to touch the stomach resting on the porch to see if his finger would poke through and prove the whole thing an illusion. "WHAT IS THIS GUY?" it said again, louder, nastier.

Paps, who had been dozing with his head propped against the wall, opened an eye. "It's O.K., Bird," he said. "He's a friend of ours. He's going to be around." Paps took his eye off Bird and focused it on Crowe. "Aren't you? I mean, I don't suppose your habits have changed, have they?"

In the yellow lenses of the ski goggles Crowe could see his own face reflected . . . and distorted . . . so that it looked curiously like *Bird's* face. After a moment the cap and flight pants stumped away into the garden where their owner stretched out his arms and stood on hyponastic legs pretending he was a scarecrow. Bad pun, that. But he *had* given Crowe a scare. "Who in God's name is Bird?" he asked Paps.

"Nobody knows. He just wandered in one day and he's been around ever since. Lives in the woods most of the time and watches the place." Paps raised himself to a sitting position and folded his arms on his knees. "He pulls that 'What is this?' business with anybody he hasn't seen before. He thinks he's our watchdog or something."

Crowe thought a minute. "How does he live? I mean, you bring him in the house and everything?"

Paps laughed. "He's an outdoors watchdog."

"I see," said Crowe.

"He has lean-tos here and there back in the brush. Snares birds, mostly. Quail and stuff. He's got a .22 for rabbits, but mostly he eats birds. Willy called him the Bird of Paradise one day and it stuck."

"I'd think he'd give you the creeps."

"He's harmless." Paps picked his nose with his thumb. "It's Sandy he thinks he's protecting. She saw him first, talked to him, gave him stuff to eat, and I guess he figured that since she didn't get hysterical or faint or anything, like most women would if they came on him in the woods, that she's the Madonna and he's the guardian angel."

The Bird of Paradise continued to glom Crowe with the stink eye from his perch in the garden. The sun had gone well down and the night chill had set in. Willy Wonder and Chadwick went inside. Paps and Crowe sat silently on the porch watching out outbuildings grow less and less visible. Pale, whitewashed fences showing against the dark rise of the hills, and then only the stars to mark the separation of ridge and sky. "You didn't answer my question," Paps finally said. "You staying on a while?"

Crowe knew that the moment had arrived. "You extending an invitation?"

"I extend an invitation to everybody," Paps said. "Which shouldn't come as any surprise to you. And I hold no grudges either, if you're wondering about that. The business in New York was between you and Sandy; before my time you might say. Only there is something needs saying if you're going to be around. I don't know what she's told you since you got here, or if she ever wrote you about the baby, but if that's why you came I just want to make it clear that you're welcome to everything around, as long as you pitch in, *except* Sandy and the baby. My scotch and my grub is one thing, but neither Sandy nor the kid are yours anymore, and if you got any bright ideas about taking off with them you'll have to run over me to do it." He cleared his throat and squinted out into the night. "I kid you not, Jack. I'm not as passive and obliging as I used to be, because I've got something that matters at stake now."

Crowe looked for a long time at the new Paps, squatting now in the rectangle of light cast through the kitchen window, and tried to organize a variety of echoes in his head. "This baby," he said, "I don't think I quite . . . that is, what do you mean *neither* is mine anymore?"

Paps turned his head slowly, pulled his lower lip through his teeth. "Ah well," he said softly. "So you didn't know." He wiped his hand across his mouth. "I never laid a hand on Sandy until two months ago." Crowe's face felt frozen. "It took her that long to get over your parting shot. In a way, my friend, assuming the child outlives the parent, she'll never get over it." He rose to his feet, took a last look at the dark valley, and turned into the doorway. "Anyway," he said, "there's no need for anybody to dwell on it."

When the moon came up over the barn bringing with it night shadows and the long howl of a distant dog, Crowe was still sitting on his legs on the porch, motionless, unaware of the shrill chirp of the crickets and the sudden flicker of the silent bats.

2 Time begins to lose its edge. Mornings, afternoons, Tuesday, Thursday, Saturday blend into one ceaseless flow of aimless chores, meals, conversations, rests. Redwood stakes appear in even, broken, even, broken lines from the ridge of the barn, and a rototiller digs up an acre of new ground. Collapsing fences straighten up here and there. A cut in the chicken wire around the hen yard heals, and a sobbing toilet on the second floor swallows an emetic, finds new courage to go on. Chin up, pal. Grin and bear it. We all choke daily our *tartine du merde*. Corn shoots pop up in the new ground and stand at attention in even rows of ten guarding the tomato and the bean. A lamb grazes at tether waiting for a reclining roll of chain-link fence to stretch itself around the patient posts resting at ease in their unfilled holes.

Nothing ever gets finished. Paps is the camp counselor for all projects, and he instructs, supervises, does most of the work himself, and then quits before the job is done. Something else is always more pressing, more worthy of his organizational skills. So the barn gets half of its shingles, and the toilet has its tracheotomy but continues to leak, and the corn field gets planted but dies from inadequate care, and the fence posts go up without boards or wire and keep nothing in and keep nothing out.

Through all of this Crowe remained a kind of participating consultant and passive observer, unable to act upon his original plan, unable to abandon it for a new direction, unable to reintroduce either the subject or mood of that first day's encounter. It was not simply that he lacked confidence or that he was unwilling to suffer the consequences of a rejection (though both of these were true and he knew that failure would require his departure); he lacked also the opportunity. There was always somebody else around. And Sandy, either by accident or by design, managed to avoid the chance isolation that would permit him to press his case. To his nightly anguish she continued to share Paps's bed (though he could not think of a legitimate reason why she should not), and if she had given any thought to that hushed "we'll see" that she might or might not have spoken in answer to his hurried question concerning their "chances" during their first conversation, she gave him no indication. And so he waited. And the longer he waited, the more soporific and undirected he became. His single progressive act in all those five weeks was the settling of the tax problems on his father's house, and the legal establishment of himself as its owner.

Because all projects on the farm had a beginning and some-times a middle but never an end, his sense of time, that depended to a certain extent on a completed past, disintegrated. And so it was that he found himself one late morning in late July sitting in a stuffed chair in the living room staring at a County Bank calendar hanging by the kitchen door and wondering what had happened to the last two weeks—how they had managed to pass without a single incident impressing itself on his consciousness. Sandy was standing in the doorway, leaning against the jamb with her arms folded on top of her stomach, watching him peer blankly at the calendar, and he added a few additional items to his wonder—how long had she been there? how long had he been sitting in that chair? and how long could Ali Akbar Khan play in the bedroom upstairs before his strings rusted and his bridge collapsed? He was not sure, in fact, that he might not have just arrived.

"Can you take me into Monterey?" she said. "There are some things I need to do."

Crowe gazed at her mindlessly, hearing, but not quite able to understand the request. "Where's Paps?" he finally said.

It was Sandy's turn to stare. "Where have you been?" she said incredulously. "Everybody left for Morro Bay at four this morn-ing for the photography field trip. What's the matter with you, anyway? Franny's been talking about it for a week. The gallery in

Carmel, that's going to handle his stuff—remember? God, you're getting to be more of a zombie than ever."

"I forgot," Crowe said. It wasn't true. He hadn't even been aware of the last week. He stood up, mildly surprised by the stiffness in his legs, considered for a moment how they had gotten that way. "Get your hat," he said, giving up.

It was an hour's drive from the farm into Monterey, and for most of it they didn't say much. Sandy sat uncomfortably in the tiny Renault with her knees pressed against the glove compartment, leaning toward the open window. The exhaust fumes were nauseating even with the air circulating through the car. "What we need here," Crowe said at one point, "is good old Burt's Cadillac." Sandy grunted. "Speaking of good old Burt," Crowe went on, "does he know where you are? How you are? I mean, that he's about to be a grandfather?"

She spoke without turning her head. "I wrote them. They communicated their outrage, and that was that. I haven't heard from them since."

Crowe drove insanely fast until they hit the Carmel Valley road and it occurred to him that the constant swaying and skidding around corners might be making her ill. Then he slowed down to thirty miles an hour and blocked traffic for a half mile behind. When she spoke again it was to continue her last remark, as if she had been brooding on the subject for the previous twenty minutes. "They informed me that they had given me everything a child could possibly have and that I had failed them; that I was a wanton, willful, contemptuous sort of person, undeserving of the privileges of a respectable home and a devoted family, and that, for the present, at least, they could have no further commerce with me. That was Burt's phrase. No further commerce." Crowe laughed and Sandy shrugged. "I think maybe they're right," she said. "On their terms I did fail them. But then I think that parents are like any other kind of friends. Sometimes you figure it's not worth keeping up an acquaintanceship, and you let it drop."

"I think that's a crappy way to look at it," Crowe said, his mood suddenly changing. "I think maybe all those things they said are just their inept way of saying how much they care."

"Please. It's too hot for preaching."

"I mean it. They're totally bewildered. To them somebody who would just throw up everything, the comforts, the education, the gentility that they worked hard to provide and go and live in a foreign country like California with a lot of freaks is just a total mystery. They're scared, and they think if they take the hard line and cut you off, *you'll* get scared and straighten out." He paused, then added, "They might be right, too."

Sandy regarded him with wide eyes. "Well I'll be damned," she said. "Where did you pick up all this girl's school guidance counselor shit anyway? You, of all people, can't believe what you just said. Straighten myself out! What *is* this?"

"Look," Crowe said, "tell me the end of the story. Tell me how long you think the hearty pioneers are going to go on tilling the soil, harvesting the crops, huh? Nobody out there is exactly Henry David Thoreau, you know. Not even Paps. He may have changed some but not that much. So how long? Two years? Three? Maybe only one? And then what? On to the next adventure? Like maybe buy a boat and cruise down to Tahiti? I once lived with a bunch up in Santa Cruz who tried that. They thought I was a real heretic when I wouldn't go. Of course none of them knew a halyard from a sheet and they got as far as Point Conception before they ran onto a rock and sank, but two of them actually lived to carry on the dream. One was in the can in Acapulco when last heard from, and the other is living with his mother in Beverly Hills."

"So?"

"So wake up!" Crowe banged the heel of his hand to his forehead, lost control momentarily and swerved onto the shoulder. "Jesus! I tell you I know what I'm talking about. I've seen it all before. I've been a part of it all before—when you were still in bobby socks and high collars. It comes to smash. Nowhere. Nothing."

Sandy was quiet for a while. Then she said, "Well if that's all, why are you here? *Again.*"

Crowe kept his eyes on the road and chewed at some dry skin on his chapped upper lip. "I tried to tell you," he said, "when I got here, but I didn't find the right combination, or you didn't have the receiver on, or something. I'm here because I followed you. I followed you because in my inept and crippled way I wanted to ask you for another chance, but I haven't been able to bring myself to ask because I have reason to believe that I may have lost that right back in New York. It's a very circuitous problem, you see. But I also came because I wanted to try to convince you that living this way is a mistake. It softens your head, your will, your drive. It's noncombative."

"You of the mighty drive."

"I'm trying, Sandy. For once I'm trying."

In Monterey they stopped at the medical clinic where Sandy had an appointment with her doctor, and then at the Rexall Drug so she could get a prescription filled. Crowe waited in the car at both stops and indulged himself in the fantasy that he was a golf pro from Pebble Beach interrupted on the 18th tee of the Bing Crosby Pro-Am (which he was of course, winning by seven strokes) to rush his lovely, young, pregnant wife to the hospital where she was about to make him a proud father. Decided his son's first present would be an electric train. Because he had never had one himself.

When Sandy returned to the car there was sweat on her lip and her temples were damp. "Okay," she said. "Let's get out of this bathtub." Crowe started the car, she put her arm out the window, snatched it back irritably. "Goddamn it, I thought Monterey was supposed to be cold and foggy in the summer."

"Where to?" Crowe asked, ignoring her mood.

"How about Tahiti?" She opened her bottle of pills and swallowed one. "I'm done. Home, I guess. Unless you have a pressing engagement."

"You want to see where I grew up?" It was an unpremeditated question. Crowe was struck by a sudden urge to visit the homestead, to show its possibilities to his girl. Perhaps only to delay going back.

She hesitated for a moment, then, "All right. Sure. Long as we're home by dark."

He headed the car out of town on a new road that by-passed the old cannery and followed the coast through a residential

area. Then he turned inland for a few miles, and wound back
out toward the point. Grassland replaced houses. Wind breaks
of cypress. Banks of purple flowering ice plant spilling down to
the road. Cooler out of Monterey, with a southeasterly breeze
blowing off the ocean. White caps. Crowe began to get excited.
They passed landmarks that were unchanged since he had been
a boy, and he heard himself telling Sandy about people and
places and things that had happened . . . once upon a time. This is
where Jimmy Winklebleck got socked in the ear with a dried mud
ball that put him out for six hours. We had a fort over there by
that oak where we used to go and pee in a 7-Up bottle and dare
each other to drink it. Nino Feterre screwed his sister in that
horse shed over there while we all stood around cheering him and
bidding for seconds. And that's the house on the hill where the
guy would always shag us off on Halloween, so we crapped in a
paper bag and set fire to it on his front steps and watched him
stomp it out from behind the bushes.

"What an idyllic childhood. How come you never talked about
all this before?" she said as they parked the car beside a long field
that sloped gradually down to the sea.

Crowe shrugged. "I forgot about it. We can walk to the house
from here. Through the field. It's just beyond that rise." They
followed a cow trail through the dry weeds splotched here and
there with patches of yellow mustard and clumps of pampas grass
until they reached a broader path that paralleled the bank of the
eroded cliffs. A gnarled cypress along the edge so black it emerges
even on the darkest night. This is not night. Against the blueness
of the sea the black, twisted trunk stands like a jagged hole in the
middle of space. This is not space either. Nor is this present, but
past. He stopped and looked back along the path, then inland
toward the hills. "I used to come here about this time of year,
maybe a few months earlier, looking for the red-winged black
birds' nests in the grass. Wanted to see the eggs and all before the
farmer plowed." The wind billowed Sandy's skirt and blew hair
across her face. A hundred feet off shore three pelicans flapped
gracelessly by. "I used to hide in my room with the pillow over
my head when he'd plow. You could hear those birds, hundreds

of them, bewildered, flying over and over the sod, crying for their unborn young."

"It sounds horrible," Sandy said.

"Yes," Crowe told her, as he went up the path. "It was. After a couple of years there weren't any more redwings around here. Sometimes I still dream about them."

The house too, was unchanged. Dark shingles, blackened by the years; brickwork in ruin; the unboarded windows broken by passing kids; the porches sagging and their carved railings kicked loose by those same kids. Crowe knew. He had participated in a few demolition derbies himself when he was a boy. They walked through the tangled front yard where blackberry vines and wild morning-glory had wrapped choking tentacles around everything, went around the side to the back and in through the broken door of the sun-porch. The place had been looted; nothing left but the litter of destruction. Furniture gone, dishes, pictures, rugs, even the ancient washing machine with its mangled rollers through which his mother had squeezed the various uniforms of his life— the diapers, the short pants of his first five years, the brown corduroys of the second five, the blue cub scout shirts and the khaki uniform of the boy scout, the number 11 jersey and white toreador pants with the red stripe of his junior high football days. The emptiness of the house and the complete disintegration of its finish in just a little more than a year hit him with a peculiar force. He wished he had never left it, or had come back sooner. It was as if nobody had *ever* lived there; nobody that he knew. He could not picture his mother working in the midst of that broken lath and plaster, that torn and watermarked wallpaper, that warped and heaving floor. He could not find the old man dozing in front of the parlor fire in the early dark of a blustery fall evening. Worst of all he could not find himself. All the crawlways of his childhood had been erased.

The absent washing machine left the biggest hole in the texture of his past, and he stood looking at the four rusty indentations its wheels had made in the linoleum of the service area, remembering the way he had been endlessly entertained as a child by watching the rollers squeeze moisture out of a T-shirt or a pair of pants or a towel, spitting them out like pressed tongue into the waiting basket below. That image stayed with him. He knew he was being sentimental, but nevertheless, the loss of the washer made him extremely sad. It had been one of his security objects, he recalled, like the smell of fresh bread and the singing of songs and a story before bed—all of them without substance but the machine. Now it too was gone. While Sandy went upstairs to explore, he went outside and sat on the steps.

Later, after she had come down and told him there was nothing left in the upper rooms but more peeling wallpaper and more broken plaster, they sat on the grass behind the house and Sandy made a necklace out of periwinkles. A slight haze had moved in from the ocean, and a fog bank, still several miles off shore, rolled in toward the land like a mountain range, gray-white between the blue of sky and sea. When I was a boy, he thought, I used to wish I could fly into that muffling blanket and disappear slowly like a fading shadow, like Invisible Man making a ghostly exit. Goodbye. You can't catch me here. Even the noise of your calling dies quickly in these walls. Gone to the haunted country, a sly spirit blown seaward, a memory drifting out with the tide's ebb.

"What happened to your parents?" Sandy asked.

"My mother died when I was about eighteen or nineteen. I'm not even sure of what. Some kind of heart disease, they said, but I think it was probably just lack of affection. If you think I'm self-centered and taciturn, you should have seen my old man. He blew himself up about five years later on his boat. Fuel got into the bilge and when he hit the starter, *ka-blawee.*"

Sandy did not ask for further details. "What are you going to do with this house?" she said.

Crowe decided it was now or never. "I'm not sure," he told her. "What I'd kind of like to do is fix it up and live here. Write. Keep a garden. Stuff like that."

"I thought you were telling me earlier that tilling the soil was an absurd ambition."

"That's not exactly what I said. I'm not looking for a half-dozen partners and I'm not under the illusion that one can live entirely off the land either. I think maybe I'd like to go back to college and finish up, get a teaching credential, find a job in one of the local schools. That would give me my summers at least, and without a lot of expenses I could save up enough to take a year off now and then, work on a longer book. I could do stories in between."

"So what's stopping you?"

"Nothing, really. I kind of wanted to see what you thought of the idea, whether you thought maybe it might appeal . . . I don't know, I'm just still thinking it out."

"Why me?" she said. "Oh, Jack, just listen to yourself. 'I'd kind of like this and maybe I'd do that and if I went there then I could maybe come here.' And you want me to clap my hands and join up. Don't you *see*? It's just the same old shuck, the same old con job you're doing on yourself, always planning, never *doing* any of the things you plan. I've been that route with you, and it ended in nothing, and I absolutely couldn't stand it again, I couldn't, really. I'd die."

"People change," Crowe said.

"Oh sure, people change, but I don't see any evidence that you have."

"I settled the problem with this house. The taxes and all. I own it now, in my name."

"Well, that's wonderful. In five weeks you've managed to devote one afternoon to the grand scheme. What happened to the other thirty-four?"

"You know, you brought all this up, Kiddo," he said, sourly. "You *asked* me what I was going to do." He began tossing pebbles at an oil drum on a cradle beside the house. Sandy picked more of the blue periwinkles and hummed softly to herself. Her passivity suddenly infuriated him. "You really think," he said, "that that collection of kooks out there is any kind of place to wind up? A fifty-year-old derelict with half a foot, an albino mute, a consumptive lesbian, and a witless gargoyle who skulks around in the woods masturbating into his baseball hat? You think I'm kidding? Well I'm not. I've seen him. You may think he keeps his eye on you out of hare-brained devotion, some kind of Quasimodo and La Esmeralda trip, but I assure you that the single desire in his dim little brain is to get into your pants as soon as he can figure out how to woo you away from our 'leader.' "

Sandy looked up slowly from her growing chain of periwinkles. "Oh brother" she said. "Let's be honest, at least. Quit pretending you're trying to save me from a fate worse than death. You want me to come here with you because you can't stand the idea of my finding somebody else's offering better than your leavings. You're doing this to me, not because you want me, but because in your insecure and rootless world your power to make people *react*, even negatively, as you so cleverly showed at my brother's house one night, is the only thing you've got. It's your identity. Without it you don't exist. And because making people rise to you is your only way of saying 'I am' you have to keep testing the strength of their commitment." Her poise was leaving her; her voice was unsteady. "Love, trust, respect, acceptance—that's not enough for you. There has to be a contest. You have to keep probing the limits, because the only way you can gauge the meaning of a relationship is to strain it farther and farther toward the breaking point. When it does break, you're really happy because you can start the game all over." She had, by now, worked herself into a state. "You bastard, it's your strategy to always appear inert, always let the other guy make the opening move so that you never have to feel responsible for having initiated anything. That's why you've been here for five weeks without having spoken to anyone, except in passing, about *why* you're here. Waiting for the opening." She stopped and wiped her face with her skirt. "I've got to admit it, though, I've got to hand it to you. I look at you and I think about what you *could* be and I really have to fight myself not to give in. Only I'm not going to. Not this time."

Crowe stopped throwing pebbles and stood up. He looked down at her on the grass, at the stubborn set of her mouth, at the puffy eyes and shiny nose. It made him mad, this refusal to recognize that he had changed, that he sincerely wanted to start over and that he needed help—her help and his future son's help. He'd even be happy with a daughter. "Why didn't you ever tell me who the father of that child is?" he said, pointing at her stomach.

Sandy raised her eyebrows. "Why should I have?"

"Not to was dishonest."

"Dishonest hell." She got to her knees. "Not to tell you was not to give you an opening. That's why you wish I'd told you. So you could have thought 'she's telling me because she expects me to do something about it, so whatever I do or don't do I can lay on her because she brought it up.' But I didn't want you to do anything about it, Jack. All I wanted was for you to stay the fuck out of my life."

"I can't do that," Crowe said. "And I don't believe you really want me to."

"Believe what you want."

"Let's go back," he said, exasperated. "It's a cold wind blowing."

He came to doubt his prognosis in the days that followed, though he continued to watch and wait. Sandy didn't avoid him or seek him out, and he had half expected her to do one or the other. She seemed to consider the matter of their relationship settled. He was no different in the new arrangement than Willy Wonder or Chadwick or, for that matter, the Bird of Paradise. Just a presence. Just one of the team. He was thinking about it one hot afternoon, lying in a rotting hammock he had strung between the trunk of a willow and the tail gate of a dilapidated wagon parked by the barn and engulfed by the tree's foliage. With a little pruning he had made himself an area nearly ten feet square, completely surrounded by a curtain of drooping branches, so that lying in his hammock with his eyes half closed, he had the illusion of being wrapped in a green gelatine capsule through which nothing but a distant, watery light could filter.

He was thinking that maybe Sandy had actually, unbelievably, rejected him once and for all (and the thought made him both miserable and furious) when Willy Wonder parted the leafy curtain and squinted in at him out of bright sunlight. He stepped inside, letting the branches close behind him and stood looking around as if his eyes couldn't adjust to the gloom. "Hey," he said after a while. "All right. This here's a time."

Crowe regarded him through half-closed eyes. "*In Xanadu did Kubla Khan a stately pleasure dome decree,*" he said.

"You got dope in here?" Will asked.

"*Where Alph, the sacred river, ran through caverns measureless to man down to a sunless sea.*"

"Oh shit," Willy said. "Poetry."

"Poetry," Crowe agreed. "Inspired by dope, Willy. You're not without perception there. In fact, your comment suggests a remarkable literary sensitivity for a man of your, ah, academic limitations. You perceive in a mere two lines that somebody, poet or reciter, must be stoned."

"How come you know that kind of stuff?" Willy asked. "Poetry."

Crowe dropped one leg out of the hammock and gave himself a little sideways shove. His hands were crossed on his stomach and he closed his eyes. "I learned to read," he said. "*A damsel with a dulcimer in a vision once I saw. Fed on honeydew and drunk the milk of Paradise.*"

"You puttin' me on?" Willy asked.

"Yes," Crowe said.

Willy sat down and propped his back against the tree, wiggled around until he got comfortable. "You want some corn?" he said, producing a milk bottle of clear fluid from under his wind-breaker and holding it up to show.

"Corn?"

"Moonshine."

"Where in God's name do you get moonshine around here?"

"I got a friend," Willy said.

"Give it here." Crowe unscrewed the cap and stuck his nose in the top. It smelled like paint thinner but he took a swallow to find out. It wasn't. He shuddered, gave off an acidic belch, and handed the bottle back to Willy. "You got some friend," he choked. "One or two friends like that and you don't need any enemies."

"Good, huh?" Willy grinned and took a swallow himself.

"*Good?* Listen, I don't want to appear ungrateful or anything but that's the worst horse piss I ever drank." Crowe shuddered again, and held out his hand for the bottle.

They swapped drinks, Willy Wonder leaning against the tree telling Crowe how he had discovered late in life that he had a natural affection for all God's creatures and had hung up his guns not so much because he had blown half his foot off but because the noise they made disturbed the ecology, and Crowe swinging slowly in his hammock thinking with less and less clarity how he might overthrow the world, establish himself as spiritual counsel to a colony of lotus eaters, when the branches parted again and the Bird of Paradise put his head in. Crowe was by this time so precariously balanced he fell out of his hammock. From his knees he looked at Bird, screwed up his face in a grimace of revulsion. "Jesus," he said. "Genghis Kahn. Kubla Cohen. Beware the flashing eyes, Willy, the floating hair." Bird came into the bower and squatted on his heels, his eyes shifting back and forth between Willy Wonder and Crowe.

"What's that," he said eventually, pointing at the milk bottle, now almost empty.

"Thas panther pee," Willy said thickly. "You can have some."

Bird shook his head and stared at Crowe, still on his knees with his face cradled between his forearms muttering into the dirt, "*A damsel with a dulcimer . . . an Abyssinian maid . . . singing of Mount Abora . . .*" He raised his head and looked at Bird. "How about it, chicken delight? You ever see any damsels with dulcimers? Any Abyssinian maids?" He rolled over on his back laughing "Sure you have, you sorry freak. Right over there in that run-down house, right? The fiery hair, the emerald eyes, the alabaster breasts, the proud beauty. Tee-hee. It's her music that builds your dome, little birdy." He rolled over and crawled across the dirt floor under his hammock until he was only a foot or two away, peered into Bird's nervous eyes, and shuddered again. "You know what, Bird? You remind me of an asshole after a Mexican dinner. You look like an implosion in the stain factory." Bird, if he understood, did not show it. Crowe sat back and began to grin. "How that poor captured Princess can be tragically, secretly, hopelessly in love with a mistake like you is beyond us all, beyond us all." Bird eyed him suspiciously, and Crowe backed away in mock surprise. "Why you knew that didn't you?

What's that? Come again? You didn't? How could you miss it, man? She's sweet on you. Listen, she tol' me," he moved closer, almost whispering, confidential, "she tol' me that if she could just think of a way to dump Pappy why she'd glom onto you like a hair in the butter dish. But *he's* keeping her captive, see, even though it don't look like it, and she can't figure any way to get loose so's she can run off with you."

Bird still didn't say anything and his expression didn't change, but his eyes flicked and slid off sideways. Crowe was drunkenly amused by the fairy tale running through his head, the toadlike creature harboring an impotent lust for a beautiful woman who, if she could just free herself to plant one kiss on his revolting face, might transform him into a glowing prince. "All you got to do," he said, "is slay the fire-breathing dragon, grab her by her golden fleece, and walk off on the water." He reached over and snapped one of Bird's suspenders. Bird winced and rubbed his chest. "How about it, Sir Gawain? That's not much. Nothing to it. Just lop the head off the old Green Knight."

"Knock it off," Willy Wonder said. "He don't even know you're kidding."

"Naw," Crowe said, looking slyly at Bird, "a smart fella like him? Sure he does. You know I'm kidding you, huh Bird? Hydrocephalus hasn't damaged your brain, has it champ?"

"Cool it," Willy Wonder said. "It's lush making you feisty. He ain't done nothing to you you should burn him that way. Man, if I'd known you were gonna get all uptight and mean I wouldn't 'a laid any juice on you."

Crowe climbed back into his hammock. He was on the ragged edge; either he had to get sick or pass out and sleep it off. Decided the latter course was the neatest. As he drifted into unconsciousness he heard himself telling Willy Wonder that some behavior was motivated by a concern for aesthetics and that Bird was an abomination before God, an assault on the dignity of mankind, and ought to be erased for being criminally grotesque.

"You're a cruel bastard," Willy Wonder said. It was the last thing Crowe heard. "You're a miserable, cruel bastard."

cypress at the cliff's edge, and see it looming there, black and forbidding, out of the darkness, its roof line, dormers, and chimneys describing an unsymmetrical cut-out in the star littered night around it.

As he stood there listening to the hum in his ears a voice, muffled by time and incredible distance, hollow and without timbre, but warning, threatening, called to him. A voice like his father's, but altered, as if it came through a congesting fog. It called him again, closer and more distinct, but still as if through a heavy wall. And then again. Suddenly he became aware that his mind had drifted off and that he was still standing in the same spot at the edge of the shadow of the barn. The voice was Paps's, coming from inside, insistent, telling him to hustle, and he ran around to the door that led into the old stable, slipped through and picked his way between the junk toward the flashlight beam on the other side.

Paps was standing there just in front of the light that Willy Wonder was pointing into the corner of the barn, his face a mixture of anger and disgust. In the corner the chicken thief was huddled, stark naked except for his baseball cap and the hairy awning beneath it, the corpse of a Plymouth Rock hen clutched in his lap. The chicken's head hung down on the salt and pepper speckles of its breast. The Bird of Paradise glowered but as usual said nothing and made no attempt to move. Willy kept the light directly in his face and Crowe could see the hate glittering in his eyes. "The bastardly idiot," Paps said, "has been buggering our chickens."

There was no doubt about it. The Bird still had the hen impaled, and he did not seem about to relinquish her until whatever sorry summit he sought to climb had been reached and conquered. He glared at them defiantly, without blinking, as if he expected the poisonousness of his gaze to cause them to shrivel and expire. Crowe looked at Willy Wonder standing there above the flashlight, his embarrassment obvious even in the periphery of its cone. He looked as if he were pretty sorry about where he was.

"I heard of screwing sheep," Crowe said, "and Ike Snopes

had a fondness for cows, but chickens?" He looked at Bird's frozen, glaring face and wondered if this was really happening. Decided it was even if it wasn't. "What now?" he asked.

Paps gave a grunt of disgust. "He's killed it. We're too late to do anything about that."

"He don't seem too upset over it," Willy Wonder said. "How you gonna keep him from doing it again?"

"Yeah," Paps agreed. "How? I don't know." He took a few steps forward, staying carefully to the side so as not to block the light. Sweat trickled down his side and along the indentation of his spine, and his biceps jumped every few seconds as if he were flexing them in his anger. "Hey Bird," he said, none too gently, "put that hen down. That's a very bad thing you're doing there." No response. Bird didn't move a muscle. "Come on now," Paps enjoined, "I don't dictate your taste in pussy, but you can't do a chicken like that. They die. Only crazy people do things like you're doing there." Still no response. Bird looked like a cornered animal about to explode in a fury, and Paps, perhaps thinking that if he moved in close enough he might get clawed or bitten, stepped back and took the lead pipe from Crowe. Then he walked directly up to Bird and stood over him with the pipe half raised. "Listen Goddamn it," he said, his voice trembling now, "you leave off on that stuff. You want to go around putting it to animals that's your business, but you can't do it here. I don't know what you do with 'em when you're finished up, but we lost five in the last two weeks and we can't afford it. We need 'em. So lay that hen down and get your ass out of here, and if I ever catch you at this again I'll throw you off the place so fast you won't know which way you came from."

"Well now," Crowe said, surprised. "That's a surly speech for such a tolerant cat."

Bird looked up at Paps for the first time, moved his loins obscenely and let his mouth go slack. Paps raised the pipe higher. "I'm warning you, you freak," he yelled, but Bird just clutched his love closer. When the pipe came down and caught him right above the ear he went over with a grunt, sprawling on the rotten boards with the chicken still impaled like a tea cozy over his genitals. Paps grabbed it by the neck and in one motion flung it across the barn. He spat in revulsion, motioned Willy to shine the light on Bird while he checked to make sure he was still breathing, and then they went out through the barn doors into the moonstruck night to clear their lungs and exchange glances of complete bewilderment. "I shouldn't have done that," Paps finally said, shaking his head. "It doesn't mix with peace and fellowship. Brings everything down." He looked over at Crowe. "You don't agree, do you. You think love is mostly violence."

Crowe smiled and gave no answer. Don't lay it on me, he thought, you said it.

"Well," Willy told them, "I reckon we won't lose no more stock. But I reckon when things come to this pass it's just Sodom and Gomorrah around the corner. I seen it before. Thing like this just leads bad to worst."

3

August. The temperature is incredible in the valley. The sun, straight up in a flat white sky, glares down on the yard. From a piece of corrugated tin lying beside the ramshackle porch, thermal waves rise a dozen feet in the air, distorting everything behind them—the hills, the sagging fence, the pathetic avocado tree with its drooping leaves—everything yellow and wobbling in the refracted heat of the scorched earth. In the six inches of shade along one edge of the tool shed three of the dogs lie panting, eyes closed, absorbed in their total discomfort, seemingly aware that there is nothing to do but wait for night. A hawk circles over the dry hills, motionless in the act of gliding, as if it is the earth below that slowly revolves while he hangs in suspension, a fixed point against the sky. He, too, seems to be waiting for something to snap, something to break the spell, something to tell us that yesterday was not, and today is an illusion.

Yesterday Sandy sat on a hard-backed chair on the porch, hugely pregnant, knees splayed, fanning her swollen belly with the hem of her dress. Occasionally she wiped her forehead with the back of her hand, ran it along her thigh where the cloth was already damp and discolored, took up the hem again and resumed fanning. In the doorway Chadwick sat drinking a beer and humming tunelessly to himself, and behind him, inside the house, the eternal radio was blaring, is blaring, acid rock from some station in Salinas. Nobody is listening. Nobody is here to listen, but then nobody ever seemed to listen. By the time the sound reaches the porch it is absorbed into the general oppressiveness of the afternoon. Until the announcer comes on during the commer-

cial break and delivers, in a mixture of honky-cracker, hip-spade
lingo, an ad for some kind of paste that will dissolve your mind
along with your pimples, you are scarcely aware of any noise but
the pounding of your head.

Out in the yard, in the empty back of a Volkswagen bus, a
recent arrival at our holy retreat, our little community in the
Santa Lucia mountains, sat framed by the open doors, fiddling
with a piece of electronic gear which he had dismantled and could
not remember how to put back together. He called himself The
Last Hair, and claimed to be an unemployed TV repairman.
"Lost my gig," he said, "on account of people would call and say
'Last Hair, my tube's on a bummer,' and I'd motor out and look
at the snow storm and the color of darkness and I tell 'em 'you're
bad-tripping your own set, man, they ain't nothing wrong. You
just looking at it weird. You don't need no TV man, you need a
shrink.' So I get the boost. What a rip." Heat didn't seem to affect
the Last Hair. He tinkered and talked to himself. In the house
Aretha Franklin sang "Chain of Fools." Or is she singing it
now?

How long ago was it, Crowe wondered, that I woke on a cold,
fog-swirled morning and found myself trying to roost in that
farmer's hen house in Watsonville, clucking away in the aftermath
of nitrous oxide, benzedrine, and moon stroke? How long? One
year? Four? It is as if my sense of time, like the landscape
around me, has warped in the heat. The past is an old phonograph
record left under a sunny window. Bubbles and bumps. Hills and
hummocks. In the playback the needle jumps to the beginning and
wobbles over and over in the little valley. Where it is hot. Hot and
pale. Like wheat sheaves and the dried husks of corn. Where I
cannot put together one single consecutive thought—only observe, disembodied, sight unattached.

The real blends with the surreal, the unreal. It seems to him
that the recent past, even the not so recent past, has all been a
fantasy, an extended vacation in the brain-pan, a fiction, if such
a thing exists; that, in fact, he never left California a year ago,
never exchanged the west coast for an eastern seashore, never
succumbed to the tantalizing *Saturday Review* classified ad for a

1786 homestead with 300 acres of pastures, streams, woodlands —only the historically interested need apply: this property holds special interest for the rootless, distracted, irresolute who seeks a stable environment with a two-hundred year dossier. In fact, in that New England dream, he never met, loved, let slide through his clumsy fingers the girl, woman, mother-to-be who sat fanning herself on the porch (was it only yesterday?), and whom he came here two months ago, he of all people, to "save." He made it all up. He is still in that farmer's yard. The chickens are pecking around below him at bits of corn and gravel as he roosts on the rail, waiting for the sun to go down.

The afternoon wore on, as it has always worn on. Yesterday he picked a book out of a carton by the steps and tried to ignore the heat by reading.

The Sense of an Ending: Studies in the Theory of Fiction
by Frank Kermode

On the flyleaf it said:

Property of Sandy Rinelander
University of California, Berkeley
English 234: Tues. and Thurs. 3-5.

And on the first page Aristotle said:

"Time cannot exist without a soul (to count it)." He started to read Chapter One, which was entitled "The End" (later, he thought, I will be accused of making all this up) but in the second paragraph Mr. Kermode began, "You remember the golden bird in Yeats' poem," and there he bogged down. He did not remember. He tried. He conjured up holy fires and burning gyres, but no golden birds. Only chickens. Clearly, he remarked, I suffer from an infection of the inner ear.

Paps came out of the house, leaned against a porch column, and scratched his stomach. He asked what time it was; seemed in a sour mood, as if he had just awakened from a sweaty nap and found himself with a headache. The tracks of a bedspread were imprinted along one side of his face. Warp and woof, corrugated, like cube steak. Crowe told him time could not exist without a soul to count it, and Paps suggested he have carnal relations with himself. Dull humor for a dull afternoon. "You ought to be doing something," Paps said. Odd disclaimer of guilt-by-associa- tion. "Get off your dead asses and do something with the day. I mean, it's hot. So what? You come on like it's some kind of personal outrage."

Nobody bothered to respond and Paps continued to scratch himself. Then, after a while, Crowe said, "Where I recently come from they've got air conditioning for days like this."

"Is that right?" Paps said. "Air conditioning. So you won't wilt the lace on your panties, I expect. Huh?"

"I expect," Crowe said, too hot to bother to get involved. Chadwick snickered.

Paps squatted down holding on to the post and looked across the yard. A fly crawled from his T-shirt to his neck and he waved it away. "You know," he said irritably, more to himself than anyone around, "that's the whole trouble. Everything in this world is air-conditioned, purified, and wrapped in plastic. Chlori- nated, dehydrated, synthetic, quick frozen, and instant."

They are playing Muddy Waters now.

"Inspected, selected, detected," Crowe said, picking him up, "ninety-nine, one hundred percent pure of everything but a few little chemicals that promote color, destroy flavor, disinfect, and then kill you. I mean, the residues pile up in your system there, the chlordanes and the DDT's, and pretty soon you don't feel so good anymore, and your digestion craps out, and your bowels turn to stone, and you're running down to the health clinic every week with pains in your chest, fuzzy vision, paralysis of the liver and bacon, sinus trouble from too many tokes on the air-condi- tioner machine. I mean, that's where it all ends up. You choke on your own bullshit."

Paps gave him a hard stare. "That's right," he said. He let go of the post and picked his front teeth with a paper match, in- spected what he dislodged, stood up.

"Which is why we're out here, right?" Crowe went on. "To get away from all that. To find a way to live that feels right . . . some kind of *organic* relationship with the land . . . a way to *inhabit* the earth instead of just trespass on it. I mean, like that's what it's all about, is it not? To find some rhythm to our ways and days?"

"Amen," Willy Wonder said.

"Shut up," Paps told him, aware now that Crowe had been putting him on.

"Peace, daddy. Amen. You the chief, we the Indians. If you say so, that's what we here for."

"I didn't say so. He did," Paps muttered. "And don't anybody strain himself. Around here work just takes care of itself, as you well know. I mean, I don't want you to bust any organs or anything." He stepped off the porch and went over to the tool shed, jerked open the door and disappeared inside. They could hear him in there banging around, dropping things, and then he came out with a hammer and a crowbar in his hand, a carpenter's apron on with its pouch full. He headed toward the pasture fence that they had started repairing in anticipation of buying a couple of beef cows, stopped on his way past the porch to deliver one last soliloquy. "What I mean to say is that if it gets hot and we turn on the air conditioning, creating thereby an artificial atmosphere, well then, ladies and gentlemen, we have circumcised our pride, our self-respect, and surrendered the right to scorn an establishment way of life. Amen."

Crowe smiled. Old Francis. Not to be undercut.

Sandy and Chadwick watched Paps go down the road, looked at each other and shrugged. Crowe went back to his book, trying this time the last chapter. It bore the title "Solitary Confinement," and was prefaced by a quotation from Philip Larkin.

> Truly, though our element is time
> We are not suited to the long perspectives
> Open at each instant of our lives.
> They link us to our losses. . . .

Again he bogged down, got fixated by the first paragraph, started thinking about his losses, found that since there had never been gains to which to contrast them he could not recall any. Mr. Larkin's terms are meaningless, he thought. Particularly his allusion to time, which is distinctly not my element.

Aimlessly his eyes drifted to different points on the surrounding hills: a cluster of oaks, a terraced slope of dead vines, the dark slash of an arroyo filled with coyote brush and manzanita; then on to farther hills bleached pale and smoky in the heat, their summits barely visible against the washed-out sky. The smell of tar weed and oak mold, dust, and the excrement of barn fowl was thick and cloying in the still air.

Willy Wonder broke in on Crowe's musing with a surprised grunt. "The Bird is back," he said in a low voice, and looking up Crowe followed his gaze over to the barn where a figure was lurking, spying on them really, poking his head around the corner, pulling it back, peeking out again. He did it twice, three times, before he finally realized he had been observed and came out into the yard and shuffled over to the lee of the tool shed. It was indeed the nameless mutation. He still had on his baseball cap and his ski goggles. He was still shirtless, but he had exchanged the fleece-lined high-altitude flight pants that once covered his grotesque undercarriage for a pair of Ivy League Bermuda shorts —on him, a costume even more absurd than its predecessor. Blood from the wound he had received when Paps laid him out with the pipe was still clotted in the greasy hair beneath the cap, and his face, always malevolent at best, was more vicious than ever. In spite of the heat Crowe felt a cold prickle run through him, as if he had encountered afresh a creature whose essence was completely corrupt. So grotesque was the Bird that it was difficult to believe in his reality. He seemed more a walking exemplum, a metaphysical metaphor for rank evil than a creature of will and substance.

"My God but he really is awful," Linda Grimes said. "I just got to say it."

"I wonder where he's been for the last week?" Chadwick said.

"Paps didn't tell you?" Willy Wonder asked him.

"Tell me what?"

"About the other night we caught him in the barn balling a chicken?"

Linda and Sandy looked at Willy Wonder as if he had just

passed a rat sandwich and asked them to sample it. Chadwick was clearly skeptical. "Chickens are not built like that."

"I don't know nothing," Willy protested, "but you can't find no other way to tell it what our man there was into. Paps busted him upside the head to make him leave off. Which is why he ain't been around for a while, seems to me. I wouldn't come back a'tall."

Although Crowe waited expectantly, Sandy offered no comment. Chadwick, seeing that Willy was serious, shook his head and said, "Too much."

Later in the afternoon, around three, it began to cool a little. Sandy fell asleep in her chair; Chadwick went inside to play his guitar and the blaring radio was replaced by some not very accomplished flat picking in the style of, and inspired by, Doc Watson.

Weary of sitting, Crowe got up and walked down the road toward the echo of hammer blows, crossed the plank bridge that spanned the creek, and wound his way through scrub oak, poison oak, and live oak to the pasture where Paps was working on the fence. There were quail feeding through the brush along the rim of the creek, and although he couldn't see them he heard their continuous rustling as they fanned away from his approach. Across the valley a doe and two half-grown fawns stood under a clump of trees, ears cocked, their attention all on the man working down below them. A family of jay birds screamed at one another in the woods behind, and he wonderful if in their apparently boundless outrage one had ever contracted an ulcer, a heart condition, a sour stomach.

Paps stopped hammering when he came up. He dropped his tools by a post, stretched his back, and Crowe gave a mocking check to the barbed wire Paps had restrung. "Pretty tough," Crowe told him. "Not bad for a city boy."

"Of course," Paps replied, obviously in a better mood than he had been in earlier. "That's because it's a solo performance. Solitary confinement. Too many cooks spoil the broth." He flipped Crowe the hammer. "If you promise not to tell a soul I'll let you help."

So for about an hour they worked along the line, Paps catching the barbs in the claws of the crowbar and drawing the wire tight around the posts, while Crowe pounded in staples to hold it. He realized that in spite of the heat it felt good to be moving, to be flexing a muscle, to be working up a sweat, and he realized also that he was not so soft as he had been when he had come to the farm two months ago; that the tire around his waist, acquired in a year of sitting on his behind, was almost gone; that his legs, which he had come to regard as infarcted appendages, useful only for propping him up in elevators and subways, no longer ached and trembled after a day's work. His nose, constantly irritated by smog and chemical dust, accustomed only to unmentionable smells, had cleared up, retooled. Now it remembered only wild oat and mustard grass. Even his sweat tasted clean.

Eventually they reached the corner by the creek and knocked off for the day, gathered up their tools, and stood for a moment looking at their work. "It's a great little valley, huh?" Paps said, in a moment of sentiment. Crowe opened his mouth to agree, but Paps went on. "You remember when I was living in San Francisco, before I went to New York, and I used to come down here to this country and camp for a week at a time? I got where I loved it so much I either had to be here or not think about it, and since I couldn't quit thinking about it . . . well, I just had to be here." He fished a roll of Lifesavers out of his pocket, picked the lint off the top one, offered it to Crowe. "In six months we haven't done so bad. In fact, we've come quite a ways. Most everybody has pitched in; they see what I'm trying to build, even if they do fade out once in a while. It takes us all a while to shake off the propaganda we've been fed ever since we started the first grade— about how the end of everything is economic and about how if you're not working *for* somebody or *employing* somebody you're un-American and probably retarded and ought to have your beatnik ass run out of town. I mean, even people who don't buy that crap and who have nothing but contempt for everything their parents and their school teachers have ever told them are subconscious victims of the same propaganda. They don't know where they're at. They don't know anything better to do. So they're standing around miserable and complaining, with daddy's latest bank draft in their back pocket, burning a hole in it, which they're aware of and which doesn't make them any more comfortable. And they're joining the revolution because they're pretty sure they can't make it in their old man's world and it's an easy way to pass the buck and pacify the social conscience at the same time."

"You've got it all worked out, do you?" Crowe said.

Paps put another Lifesaver in his mouth and offered the roll to Crowe. "We'll see. All I know is I'm living the way I want to, and I'm hoping to show a few other people that it's a perfectly viable way."

Crowe found himself wishing that Paps would quit making reasonable speeches because he had come to the farm with theft in his heart and the long-standing conviction that Francis was an unimaginative thinker who was as soft in the head as he was in the heart. Now his preconceptions were getting scrambled.

"Sandy says you're talking about fixing up your father's place and moving into it," Paps said as they started back. "That sounds like a great idea."

"Yeah," Crowe said. "Well, so far it's just talk." When he offered nothing more, Paps let it drop. Crowe wondered what else Sandy had said.

"Listen, I am absolutely famished," Paps said, breaking into a trot. "Let's go and really do up a feed, supper on the ground. Do a real banquet outside by the Willow. Eat everything in the house."

"Why not?" Crowe told him. "What better end to this miserable day?"

When they were back in the yard Paps called everybody out of the house and lined them up on the porch. He paced back and forth in front of them like a drill sergeant reviewing the troops. Even the Bird of Paradise, who was still lurking around the tool shed, was ordered into the ranks. Paps seemed to accept his return with the same equanimity he showed toward his absence. The Last Hair shambled over from the Volkswagen bus and stood at attention on the top step. Chadwick and Willy Wonder leaned against the wall and the girls sat in the chairs. Looking over this crew Crowe was again struck by the disparity between their appearance and their talents and the way of life to which they had supposedly dedicated themselves. He wondered what the pilgrim fathers would think of this incarnation.

"All right," Paps said, in his best military voice, "you people there, now, what's happening is we're about to celebrate the first annual half-anniversary of our venture in this valley, and how we're going to do it is we're going to have a community feed, right now, tonight, at o'eighteen hundred, out here in the boondocks in the dirt with the ants and the flies. So I want total cooperation from all parties of the whole . . . total cooperation . . . because some of you have been forgetting what it is we're here for and have been backsliding into old ruts of noninvolvement and the let Colonel-Sanders-do-it,-I-don't-want-to-get-my-fingers-messy-in-the-chicken-fat syndrome. Willy Wonder, I want you to get wood for a cook fire out here, and stones around it to rest a spit on. Chadwick, you get that redwood table out of the barn, and benches and that five-gallon cask of vino primo in the cellar. Sandy and Linda, we're going to need salad and cut up those melons and bake potatoes and anything else you can find in there to heat. Last Hair, you bring the speaker out from the living room and hook it up on the porch so we can have us a little raga during chow, and . . . let's see . . . Bird, since you're so fond of fowl-play, heh heh, you come with me and we'll select a succulent hen to sacrifice. And I do mean sacrifice, because this is a ritual occasion consecrating hallowed ground, and we must be neither squeamish nor ignorant of the total process involved in the preparation of our victuals." Crowe watched Bird's face. He blinked his reptilian eyelids once, slowly, and that was all. "How'd I do?" Paps said, walking over to where Crowe was standing.

"Very eloquent, Francis. Very eloquent. Churchill himself could not have done better."

"I trust when it comes time to ask the blessing, you too will rise to the occasion."

The sun is behind the hills now, heading for Japan, but the land reluctantly yields its radiance, the light fades slowly and the valley changes from the color of ripe melons to early corn. Mauve shadows appear, lengthen, melt into a smoky dusk that will linger for several hours before the smoke turns to ash and then to cinders.

They lounged around the yard, drinking wine, waiting for Paps. The smell of baking potatoes drifted out from the kitchen and the table was piled with food; chard, carrots, scallions, tomatoes, apples, a huge pottery bowl of salad, four kinds of bread, a rhubarb pie. They lacked only the main course. And then it appeared, dangling upside down from Paps's hand, its wings flapping without enthusiasm, a low, crowing moan of despair escaping from its craw. Paps walked to the center of the yard, held the hen high above his head and gestured for silence. "Our valedictorian," he said, with a slight bow in Crowe's direction, "will now give us a few words."

"Yes. Well, ah . . ." Crowe began, "unaccustomed as I am . . . we meet here on an historic occasion, friends." He glanced over at Sandy sitting on the top step of the porch. "We are about to launch the revolution to abolish plastic plenitude—right here in the midst of our small pluralistic society of populists. We are about to reimmerse our hands in the dirt, the grime, the blood, the guts, and the stink of life. We are about to proclaim the reopening of an old frontier, where a man, if he wanted Chicken Delight, went out to the hen house, grabbed himself a Plymouth Rock, wrang its neck, ripped out its smoking heart, tore off its feathers, rammed a spit up its ass, and cooked the little darling over a hickory fire. In the merest twinkling of an eye."

Paps waved hatchet and hen over his head and did a little dance. All watched with a kind of horrified fascination, waiting for the beheading. Crowe went on.

"I mean, nobody except for our esteemed leader handles the unpleasantries anymore. Your run-of-the-mill housewife couldn't clean and pluck a chicken if her ovaries depended on it. It all comes wrapped in a baggy and she doesn't have to feel it, look at it, think about it; just hands it to the spade in the white coat and he deals with it out in the kitchen and brings it back all nice and golden brown with giblet sauce and roast potatoes and asparagus with hollandaise. No commitment, you dig? She doesn't get involved. Just sits down in her polyethylene, push-button automatic shift dining room with the Muzak whining in her transistorized ears, and eats."

The chicken, patient enough during this speech, suddenly got one leg free and began to thrash around again. Paps handed the hatchet to the Bird of Paradise standing behind him while he tried to get a hold on the errant claw so that he could trip the bird over on its side and cut its head off. Linda Grimes tittered and shivered. She had never watched an animal killed. It suddenly seemed incredibly hot again to Crowe, and through the sweat blear in his eyes he too watched the struggle, fascinated, entranced, only vaguely aware of the real spectacle going on at the sacrificial altar. The Bird of Paradise was idly directing at the back of Paps's head little gestures with the axe, as if he were measuring a block of wood that he meant to split into kindling. A comic pantomime unrelated to the business at hand.

"So what it's all about," Crowe went on when Paps had the chicken back in control, "is that we hereby proclaim a moratorium on the bad supermarket trip, an end to all the Safeway, A & P, 7–11 Speedy Mart shoppers out there in the land of Saran wrap; an end to the part-time housewives with bouffant hair and wall-to-wall tans, with the flabby shanks puddling away under Capri slacks, pushing carts up and down the aisles, a sticky kid with a runny smile parked in the rumble seat stuffing himself with Froot Loops while Mom tosses in the instant coffee, tea, and milk, instant breakfast, instant potatoes, instant six-pack of premixed cocktails." The Bird of Paradise continued to draw a symbolic bead on Paps's head. Does nobody notice this? Crowe wondered.

"Right on," Chadwick yelled.

"An end to your hopsack hubbies with their continental vents, sclerotic arteries, and varicose veins, belching Alka Seltzer on the terrace while they wait for their instant supper, muching Tums and Rolaids and Maalox as they drag their jellied decrepitude upstairs to plop it on the posturepedic. An end to it all. An end, an end." He reached up a hand in silent supplication; then turned to Paps, saying to the crowd as he did so, "We will now have the benediction."

"Let us now, most heavenly and merciful father," Paps intoned, imitating Crowe's style, "offer up the soul of this thy most louse-ridden servant, and ask that ye grant to us who are still on our pilgrimage glory everlasting through the soil we till, for in the words of your own illustrious son, 'he that soweth little shall reap little; and he that soweth plenteously shall reap plenteously. Let every man do according as he is disposed in his heart, not grudgingly, or of necessity; for God loves a cheerful giver.'"

He extended his arm up and back, the fingers of his hand partially curved to receive the helve of the axe and, before any of his tribe, scattered around the yard, dulled with wine and the flow of Crowe's rhetoric, could open their mouths to cry out, and with a heavy *chunk*, rather like the sound one might expect if one chopped into an overripe melon, received instead its blade into the crown of his skull. Just that sound . . . a cosmic pause . . . and then Francis, in one violent motion, like a poleaxed steer, fell forward through mortality, into the dust, and died instantly without convulsion. For a moment the hatchet remained in place, like a Hollywood stage prop attached to a warrior's wig with papier maché and wire ribbing; then it fell out of the parted skull and released a single rush of blood that sprayed the ground in front of the corpse for several seconds before its force subsided and left only a mixture of fluids and membrane percolating down through the spongy hair and away into the dirt.

4

In a small and crabbed hand he wrote on the yellowing pages of a spiral notebook, *One should not love a place*. Star gazers are mad; captives of illusion; capable of eating dirt and rolling in the grass; given to talking with trees and flowers, writing poetry, and singing to their serial selves. I have found in my wanderings that people are inconstant and destructive, that things either break or wear out, that all one is left with is a distant place. What I wish is that I could go back. Back to a different sea. Back to a greener Pacific. Back to a younger coast range where as a boy I walked over foothills of oat and lupine and poppies, unencumbered and unaware. The country there is wild, and except for a few wandering cattle trails along the rims of canyons, uncharted, unclaimed, unseen even by the scattered owners who live in more accessible areas of the western coast. Less private areas of my dream. There I am free of carbons, hydrogens, nitrogens. Free at last of the metabolic machinery that traps everything in time and space. Free of creation. I am disembodied. I am a voice unattached.

Sitting in the heat in the open doors of the Volkswagen bus, head aching, empty, utterly bewildered. Except for the dogs and the hawk and the chickens, he was alone. Chickens. It occurred to him as he watched the hawk circle high overhead that the chickens were probably the object of its vigil. All that stood between their brainless pecking and their savage extinction was himself. A parable, he thought, but Lord God I didn't mean it to happen that way. How could I know that in a stupid joke, a mindless teasing of a poor, befuddled idiot, a seed could be planted that would grow into such monstrous, hyperbolic craving.

Although nearly two weeks had passed since Paps's murder he was still literally shaken. The simple fact of his accessory guilt would not fade from his consciousness for a single moment, and the obvious manifestation of that awareness was physical disability. Except when he wrote in his notebook his hands trembled constantly. He could not hold a coffee cup without spilling half its contents. To light a cigarette was a matter of supreme concentration. He could not keep anything down but liquids and a few uncooked vegetables.

Why he stayed on the place he could hardly say. It seemed important, somehow, that the garden be watered and the animals fed. There was nobody else to do it, and an act performed, any act, helped keep him from going stark raving mad. Chadwick and Grimes had disappeared together the day after the inquest and the depositions had been taken. Willy Wonder had hung around a day or two longer and then he also vanished. The Last Hair had not even waited long enough to pick up his belongings.

So for the time being it was up to him. When Sandy got out of the hospital, he reasoned, she might conceivably want to come back, though he doubted it. He doubted even that she could sell the land, since she and Paps had never been married and she would have no legal rights. She might have been able to claim it for her child if she could convince the authorities that Paps had been its father, but the child was dead, premature and stillborn. If the doctors had allowed him to see her the matter could have been discussed, but they had denied him access to her ward, informing him that she was partially paralyzed and in isolation, a temporary condition they hoped, but one that should not be aggravated by unnecessary reminders of what had recently occurred. They would advise him, they said, of her condition and he could speak with her as soon as it was physically and psychologically possible. He had not been to the hospital since, feeling that he had intruded too often already. But on the chance that something might change he stayed on at the farm, working in the garden, caring for the animals, shaking and brooding in the hot sun.

Everything remained exactly as it had been on the evening of Paps's death. The table out in the yard still piled with food, the wine barrel, now with its perpetual cloud of fruit flies. The speaker out on the porch, the doors and windows of the house open, and the blood stains in the center of it all, blackened by the sun and gradually fading under a thickening layer of new, powdery dust. Because he refused to go into the house Crowe had moved into his willow hideaway behind the barn, sleeping in the hammock and brewing tea over a rusty grate he had found in the hen house. He needed no more. The quarters were temporary; only until Sandy recovered and would no longer need a caretaker.

Eventually he developed a routine and followed it religiously. Rising at dawn he would wash his hands and face in the horse trough, fill the bucket for the lamb to drink, throw out some grain for the chickens, and go to the garden for a day's supply of tomatoes, carrots, and lettuce. Then he would return to his hut and build a fire to heat the tea water, eat, and lie in his hammock until the sun was high enough to warm the valley. The rest of the morning he spent in the garden, weeding, thinning, staking the bean and tomato vines, spreading compost. He built himself a makeshift root cellar—three bales of hay set corner to corner, a few boards, and a load of dirt for a roof—and he could keep his overabundance of produce for a long time without its rotting or growing soft. He rearranged the tool shed, sharpened hoes and shovels, trapped gophers, sprinkled snail bait—anything to fill the mornings, to keep busy. In the afternoons, after a lunch indistinguishable from breakfast and after an hour's rest, he repaired fences or collapsing parts of the barn. At dusk he drank more tea, ate more vegetables, and sat staring with hypnotic fascination at the coals of his small fire until they winked out. Then he slept. He read nothing. He heard nothing but birds, animals, and insects. He saw nothing but the task directly in front of him. Time passed, and he did not notice. Only in his journal, written half to himself, half to Sandy, did he allow himself to think beyond the present moment.

There is a special place, he wrote, near the Carmel Valley. A ridge with a view of the bay to the north and a canyon choked with manzanita and scrub oak to the south. With my magic glass I can just make out the wharf in Monterey where my father's fishing boat is moored and the pier near the old Cannery Row with its restaurants and bauble stores selling everything from fish chowder to Mexican serapes: a string of bells, coral and shells, an ashtray with a view. Memories cluttered like a whirligig of picture postcards. Street scenes from New York. Vermont woods in the fall.

It is the hawks that I mostly watch; soaring without effort on the updrafts that sweep over the mountains, hovering high over the ridge with only the barest trace of movement, then diving into the chapparal after a rabbit caught napping in an open bed of grass and sun. Explosion of fur. Wings beat the still air. The carcass, bloodied and limp, suspended beneath the bird as it glides away toward a private cliff where it will feed and rest.

Always I went up the hill slowly, carrying my lunch in a brown paper bag in one hand and a cheap, low-powered spy glass in the other—a small dark speck from the hawk's point of view, winding back and forth through the thick meadow that rolls in windblown waves up toward the ridge. I stop to look back at the sea and the uneven line of breakers that separate the foothills from bay, then go on in a zigzag ascent toward the ancient white oak on the crest. The wind dries the sweat on my back and the touch of my still wet shirt is strangely cold. Foxtails catch in my socks and make my ankles prickle. Sometimes when I reach the top I climb the tree and watch the canyon from its lower branches, straddling a limb and resting my telescope on a gnarled fork beyond my outstretched body. Sometimes I just lie on my back and look at the cloudless sky through the fluttering shade of a spring afternoon. An old gopher snake, the six-foot granddaddy of all gopher snakes, lives among the roots of the oak, and I watch his slow, powerful undulations through the grass. I pick him up and stroke him behind the head, and he wraps himself in coils around my arm. Docile and noncommittal snake. Too big to be the prey of any circling hawk. Too old and wise to be concerned about a boy who comes to eat a peanut butter sandwich at his doorstep.

In New York, Sandy, I lived on peanut butter. Intrusive recollection. Through the dirty window of an apartment on Mott Street I ate peanut butter sandwiches and watched the snow drift between the buildings. There are conceptual problems when one is reduced to mere consciousness.

And in the spring lupine and a hundred other flowers cover the hill. In a penny arcade on Third Avenue there is a booth where one can fix a flower to a small piece of white paper and imprison it forever behind a thin skin of translucent plastic. One can imprison a driver's license, or a draft card, or a social security number more easily, but I prefer a flower. There are many ways to solidify the documents of one's self. I discovered that during my sojourn in the East. I learned how one becomes flat and without substance. A voice only. A mind unrestricted.

In summer the hill is dry and the color of toast. The grass crackles and pops as I move through it, and on a hot, still day it seems as if a snap of the fingers could cause the whole earth to burst into flame. Everything beyond the hill shimmers through waves of heat—the sea, the mountains, the headlands stretching away to the south, the hawks gliding high over the canyons on vague and impossible drafts. It is a water color on which the paints have run—blurred lines, boundaries without definition. An occasional wind through the grass is like the rustle of sheaves in a dying corn field that some New England farmer has been slow to harvest. Along the Connecticut River Valley the farmers are just cutting their second crop of hay as we drive down through Vermont on our way to Martha's Vineyard. There are apples ripening in the trees and the clouds, floating high overhead, cast their shadows across the pastures on the other side of the river. There is the hint of fall in the air, and we are prospective buyers looking for a country home where we can plant our garden and raise our children who will know the difference between dirt and ashes, soil and dust. You do not like beets. I want a cow.

The fall of the year is heavily overcast. Lead clouds rise out of the sea and pass overhead in unbroken waves toward the mountains. I can see nothing in the canyon but a tendril of fog working its way inland, and Monterey is obliterated by rain squalls that streak the north-west sky. I stand beneath the ghostly oak and watch the mist swirl over the ridge, and when the first drops reach me on the wind I sit up in the highest fork of the tree and wait for the clouds to swallow my imprint against the closing darkness. In time I will go down into the canyon and follow the path that leads out the headlands and along the cliffs to the coast highway leading south. But I will come again, when the winter has passed, to watch the seasons. Nothing changes on my hill but the colors of earth and sky.

One mid-morning in October Crowe looked up from the rhubarb he was thinning and watched a gray pickup truck turn off the main road and ease its way through pot holes and ruts toward the house. He contemplated disappearing into the woods and decided not to bother. What difference would it make? Instead he went around the house and met Willy Wonder as he stepped from the cab. He looked older, grayer, his weathered face a little more weathered. They regarded one another for a few minutes, and then Willy leaned against the fender and looked off toward the hills. "Howdy," he said.

Crowe nodded.

Willy scuffed in the dust with his toe. "Wondered if you was still around. Just came by to pick up a few things."

Crowe nodded again. "Been looking after the place," he said.

Willy turned slowly around three hundred and sixty degrees, as if he were the official inspector. "What for?" he asked.

"For Sandy," Crowe told him. "She might want it when she gets out of the hospital."

Willy Wonder scraped a discolored incisor with the finger nail of his index finger and watched Crowe curiously for a moment. He sucked some saliva through the gaps in his teeth. "You seen her lately?" he asked.

"No," Crowe said. "They wouldn't let me until she got better."

Willy picked his teeth for a while. "She got better," he finally said, flatly. "She's been out of that place more than a month."

Crowe was stunned. "You've seen her?" If he had thought about Sandy at all in the past weeks it had always been in the context of a hospital bed out of which she could not escape without official sanction. He had somehow expected them to let him know when she was to be released.

"Sure. I seen her," Willy said. "I been working for a lettuce grower in Salinas and I seen her in town at a place called Boob Hill."

"Boob Hill?"

"It's a rocky-roll, titty place. You know, one of them topless joints where you can dance. They got the girls up off the floor in bamboo cages in each corner. Go-go girls."

"Go-go girls? In Salinas?" Crowe's voice shook. He didn't believe Willy.

"Yeah," Willy said. "It ain't much of a place, but it's a job, I guess. They got her in a pair of gold pants, tight, you know, on account of I guess she's still stretched from the kid. Only she ain't got nothing on the top and that's all them boys look at. It ain't a altogether classy joint." He took a pack of cigarettes out of his pocket and offered one to Crowe who refused it with a shake of his head. He couldn't focus his eyes and thought maybe he was going to have to sit down. Willy looked away and sighed heavily. "It's a hard road," he said. "Some people just unlucky, you know, and there ain't a hell of a lot you can do for it." He lit his cigarette. "Naw Sir, there ain't a hell of a whole lot a fellow can do. I'm sorry, man, but that's where she's at. I talked to her a while, only she's sort of out of it and like she didn't really want to see me much." When Crowe only stood staring dumbly down at the dirt Willy began to get fidgety. "I got to pick up a few things," he said, moving away from the car toward the house.

For five mintues Crowe remained rooted to his spot, feeling numb and queasy. When he became aware of the sun beating down on the back of his neck he shuffled away toward the cooling shade of his willow enshrouded hammock. Willy Wonder left without saying good-bye.

The road into Salinas from the south. Winding through low hills, headlights glaring in the pockets of fog at the bottom, leaping

ahead at the top to illuminate a black stretch of road that disappears once again into swirling mist. Poorly banked curves that are
hard to negotiate when you are driving too fast and find yourself
into them without warning. A deer bounds across the road and
disappears over the bank. The eye of some night animal gleams
briefly at the farthest reach of the lights, vanishes into the low
brush inside the road.

At the outskirts of Salinas he reduced speed and followed what
appeared to be a main artery into town. Several miles of tract
homes protected from highway noise by a six-foot redwood fence.
There was no highway noise. Crowe's was the only car abroad.
Rows of street lights illuminating deserted streets. Most of the
houses dark though it was not yet midnight. The fence continued
and he began to wonder if he had missed a turn, by-passed the
central district. Looked for a gas station to ask his way, but there
was no gas station. And then, before he knew it Highway 68
coming from the south ran into Highway 101 and he had to
turn—right, he guessed, because the lights were that way, and he
drove for a quarter of a mile until he saw it. Boob Hill. Formerly
Boot Hill, until the hillbilly clientele changed its mind and found
bellies and breasts and rock music more enticing than buttons and
bows and down-country fiddlers. It was clear that the T in boot
had been replaced with the B in boob because the neon was
brighter in that final letter.

Crowe parked in the lot behind and sat in the car for a moment
to steady his nerves, then got out and walked around to the front
to the vinyl padded doors with their brass upholstery tacks and
palette shaped brass handles. A signboard announced an all topless review with polaroid snapshots of the caged attractions inside. Underneath in silver glitter it said "Sounds By Mr. Clean
and the Uncalled Four."

Inside the air is damp and heavy. Faces shine wet with perspiration out of a colored darkness. Unattached limbs flash, gyrate in a
fleeting light, disappear into the shadows. A grinning set of teeth
sidles by, a light touch on his arm, and someone leads him to a
table near the band. A match flares out of nowhere and ignites a

floating cigarette. His head rattles, warps with the strain of sonic blasts from an electric organ. Thought shatters. There is no build up to this insanity, no crescendo, no developing intensity, just an instantaneous blasting of noise, a tidal wave of sound that rips through everything in its path. From the far end of the room the amplified shriek of a flute weaves in and around jackhammer explosions of electric bass, guitar, organ, mouth harp. The man is beating holes in his skins, striking fire from his cymbals. The grinning teeth slide past, back to their original post. He feels his scalp coming loose from his skull and slipping down over his eyes. And high in the corner, a red spot washing her twisting, jerking, half-naked body—Sandy. Face set in expressionless boredom, eyes near closed and unseeing. Now and then when the sideways wiggle of hips and shoulders is changed to a high stepping, forward, backward jerk, she tosses her long burnished hair in a sweeping, elliptical arc over breasts still heavy from motherhood, blue-veined and swollen in spite of the make-up and the rosy light. He knows the movements of her hips and pelvis and the mimed action of her dance; knows the reality of her suggestions, and he cannot watch longer. The illusion is far too close to the now denied reality.

The flute is stuck on a piercing dog whistle, barely audible above the frantic drive of the hard rock rhythm blaring out of hundred-watt amplifiers. The roar and squeals of electronic noise loosen the bowels and they rattle in their gut-sack like marbles in a Bull Durham bag. Time slips a gear. Sixteenths become eighths and then quarters, halves. The light reddens. On the wall above the weaving shadows of the musicians and the naked dancers oily bubbles erupt; floating, burgeoning, spreading out in clouds of color; spinwheels of green and yellow, and the oil spits and pops on the hot glass of an opaque projector transferring molecular panic to the wall. . . . Look back and still she bops her suggestive dance, staring vacantly at him now, without sign of recognition, chewing gum . . . veins and arteries superimposed on twitching cells and the whole image seems to expand and contract with the beat of the music. Suddenly he is peering into a blurping cauldron in his skull, pipe lines, conduits of sticky purple, pulsing, weaving like sea grass in the ocean's swell, and his joints are paralyzed and his spatial awareness wrenched from its mooring . . . she stands slightly sideways, away from the dancers on the floor, the oglers at the bar, the table drinkers, slightly toward the wall and his single vantage point beside the crepe paper palm tree, and she chews her gum with half her face, the other half frozen in the perpetual sag of paralysis from which she has not recovered and will not . . . and when he steps through pink polka dots that drip like melting plastic down the boards to the floor to evaporate beneath his feet, when he steps through a chain link mesh of ozone fog to call her name up at her through the lower bars of her cage, to tell her he has kept the house, the garden, the livestock, and that he will go on keeping it, asking nothing but the chance to give her back life if only she will quit this hideous place and come home; to tell her that she was right, he is a spoiler of that which he most loves, but love her he has and does and will, asking nothing now but the right to repay and serve: when he tries to climb up to her to shake the bars and force her to know him, to say something, anything, the bouncer comes quickly from behind the bar saying behave or leave and he can hear people laughing, see them turning in their seats, shaking their heads . . . there's always some screwball . . . and so he has to plead from his chair, beg her, for the love of God to have pity, there is nothing, nothing he will not do, cut off his head and hand it to her on a pike if that will somehow atone even in part for the misery he has brought her. She looks down and for an instant stops chewing on that gum while she searches his streaked and collapsing face for God only knows what, and then she looks away, without acknowledgment, without expression, without any sign but boredom, languor, depression. Her limbs flash in the sweating light and her jaws begin once again their slow, bored, grinding movement.

He sat cross-legged on the ground in front of his small fire watching the flames eat through the center of a thin, straight fruitwood branch about four feet long and perhaps an inch and a half in diameter. It was growing dark under the willow and the fading evening outside barely penetrated his arbor, turning the light faintly greenish like the inside of a wine bottle. His eyes traveled up the trunk of the tree, noting each bump, each indentation, each twig; up to where twigs became branches and hung down with slender grace under the lacey weight of their leaves; up to the densest part of the foliage where the heat from his fire had scorched those leaves and caused them to shrivel and turn brown. Then he lay on his back staring above him, listening to the voices that hummed around him, waiting for night. *Don't cry lady, I'll buy your Goddamn violets, don't cry lady I'll buy your pencils too. When I passed a blind man with a tin cup of pencils, she said, I thought to myself there's the perfect affliction. . . .*

When night came, and he could no longer see anything beyond the periphery of the fire, he threw on more wood and took his spiral notebook out of the knapsack he had earlier packed. His pencil was dull but he sharpened it enough with his thumb nail so that it would write. TO WHOM IT MAY CONCERN he put in block letters at the top of the page, and under that *The paths to Zion mourn, for none attend her sacred feasts.* Then he began his own lamentation.

Three million years it has taken. Once I drifted in salt and murky sun along the currents of the North Atlantic. Once I wallowed in the swamp mud of a receding lake, hungry for breath, thinking dimly of a future dimension. Once I lived in the trees and swung from the creeping tendrils that veined the forest. Once I had flesh and bones, teeth, hair. Three million years, but I am free at last; free of creation, free of carbons, hydrogens, nitrogens. I am God's ape making dreams out of the fragments of a disinherited mind.

At the end of a crooked alley in my blackened brain there is a patch of blue ocean, sky, a cloud, a sea bird crucified against the late afternoon. The sun is burning low on the western edge of the world, and soon I'll be in darkness. Thirty years I have wandered in the wilderness. I catch the scent of cypress blowing seaward on the wind, and I remember an afternoon and a boy who lay under an oak on the bank of an inlet and sought the pattern of his days in the tapestry of foliage and shadow that moved, feathery and light, before his upturned, half-closed eyes.

The sun becomes waterlogged and sinks below the refractive waves. For a time the coast is gilded in the alchemy of twilight. The sea eddies around the rocks, sweeps in toward the cliffs, and disintegrates in a burst of rainbow spray. A tanker glides south on the vanishing horizon and is swallowed by the approaching night. I do not see this. Like everything else, it takes place in the security of my imagination and memory. A hawk soars over fields of lupine and poppy; an effortless flight on the wind currents from the surrounding canyons. It ascends into the last of the sunlight and is lost for a time. Then, in the upper regions, away above the world, it reappears, a tiny speck, a minute flaw against the enclosing blue, drifting ever higher into the unvaulted space beyond the sky.

There is a highway near the inlet, a highway that leads inland from the coast to Salinas where it meets U.S. 101 and thence both north and south along the western half of the San Joaquin Valley. And along that highway, just at the outskirts of Salinas, there is a newly remodeled barn full of dreams, Miltonic fantasies, visions of Bosch, Brueghel, and Blake; a rock and roll palace of mottled green, bordered on the north by a Taco Bell, on the south by an Episcopal church and graveyard. Nothing is happening yet. Nothing is ever happening but the things we invent. The dancers have not begun the dance. The musicians are still asleep. Only a few early arrivals from who knows where drift around the parking lot. A girl laughs hysterically from the back seat of a car. In the shadows of memory, beside the old church, I wait calmly for the dancers and the dance. Calmly, I insist. I am not afraid. No trepidations. No queasiness. No fear. I am not afraid. I knock dreams off the headstones in the adjoining graveyard as I wait—calmly. Fungo flies into an outfield of the past. Hallucinations. Thoughts dispossessed These are my only sure possessions.

There are monuments for heroes in old burial grounds on Martha's Vineyard where we once spent an afternoon. Monuments for men who went back into the sea from which we all come. Went with struggle, with Herculean efforts to outrun fate, but without a whimper, without a sneer, without regretting the pattern and circumstance of their lives. Agh! I am an incurable romantic. They whimpered, no doubt, but death absolves. In the mid-September twilight I walk along the road to Gay Head through a rolling fog and count the graves that pop in and out of the mist. They tilt. They fall forward on their faces. No semblance of order. Only the comfortable dignity of age. A horse wanders from its pasture and begins cropping the grass around a headstone. On the weathered and pockmarked surface crossed harpoons have been carved, with marble rope descending into marble tubs at the pedestal. Twelve names have been chiseled in the stone—interment by proxy, no actual corpses being present. But no matter. Their ghosts are mine, their valor my despair. If I had lived in another time I might have been like them. Or if I had possessed even then my suicidal streak I might, like Ahab, have transferred self-loathing into hateful vengeance. The day of heroes is gone. Evolution has trebled the ego, just as, in the misty past, she trebled the size of our brain and allowed us, after a million years of waiting, to dream and to hope and to be afraid.

It is no longer too early. The heavy beat of *Mr. Clean* causes the glowworms on the building to pulsate. Do I dare go inside? Even from this safe distance? I am not so young anymore. Thirty years of searching, and there comes a time when a man is too old, too tired. The cars that drive up are disgorging children; thin-legged, careless, feverish. How long have I paddled in their leaky canoe? How many castles have I built in their sand? I am an old castle maker now, unfit for active duty. The highway in my head is bounded by swooping telephone lines that dip and rise and flash past on the broken rhyme of yesterday, the day before. Perhaps the freedom ride ends in a collision, but it grows too late to become concerned with dangers. I follow my elusive hawk. And there will be time . . . how is it? . . . for a hundred visions and revisions. I have spent my life searching for an island out of time, and what have I found? A grave. And beside it, in the parking lot of my mind, a rock and roll palace. In this case, one and the same. An apt metaphor. The rain that once made the grass grow now carries mud into the drainage ditch along the highway. Algae grow in little pools of seepage. The long course of evolution is traveling back.

But there is time. The boy I envision passing along the road with his long-haired, long-limbed girl seems unaware. In his tight pants and high-heeled boots, his silk dueling shirt and brocade vest he is of another era . . . an eighteenth-century fop on his way to the sporting house . . . but he is unaware. In another half-century he will be smacking his woman with a club and glowering at the mystery of fire through the tangled mat of his hair. But there is time for all that. Nothing changes but the population. Today is yesterday and yesterday is tomorrow, and time is only a frozen moment remembered.

But there is something askew. Once you have traversed the landscape of your mind, conquered the frontier of your reality and come upon the sloping, seaward drop of the farthest hills there is only the flat face of the waters from which you came. My hawk has escaped through the iridescent film of space and there is only the crystal emptiness of the sky.

I am almost finished. Thirty years in the wilderness, the sun burning with effusive waste, burning the skin black, burning in the backyard of the brain. I am parched. My lips are cracked and bleeding; my nerves twisted, frayed, torn. I ache again for the blinding flash of night and mortality. There will not be time . . . except to spit out that sun and grind it under the heel of darkness. Time is a river that flows in devious channels. Its alluvial banks are forever crumbling, reforming, crumbling again. It makes its bed and refuses to lie in it. You push out toward the middle, intending to float peacefully along on your back and watch the trees and sky drift past, and suddenly you are wallowing in mud, thrashing in the reeds of a paleozoic swamp, coughing up the ooze of another day and age. You sink slowly into the quagmire of your past and it is too late. Your nose and mouth fill with silt. For a time your eyes continue to see and you can watch the river moving farther away. Then they too are sucked under and you lie in a winding sheet of thick black mud, wondering, for a few brief moments before you are dead, what happened to that warm, preconscious day of your youth when you floated under the willows and saw the sun and sky through a green curtain of leaves.

He threw his pencil into the fire and watched its yellow paint bubble, turn black, and burst into flame. Rising to his feet he held the notebook in his hands for a long time, looking at it as if he were unable to decide how it had come into his possession and, now that it had, what he was supposed to do with it. Then he tossed it, too, into the coals. "What I'm going to do," he said out loud, shouldering his pack and making his way from under the tree toward his car, "what I'm going to do now . . ." Stopping, unable to think of an ending, or even the *sense* of an ending, only beginnings, places to go that would lead, he knew, to the same inconclusion. "What I'm going to do . . ." A faint, rasping snore through the cosmic silence. ". . . is light out for the territories. Wherever they are?"

He shoved his pack in the trunk of the Renault and got in. On the front seat the large, gray mother cat whose kittens he had seen playing on the kitchen floor the day he had arrived rose up in a slow Halloween arch, stretching and yawning, rubbed up against him and then curled back down into the warmth she had left. "It's not Eldorado, Pussycat," he said, taking her face in his hands and turning it to him, "but you certainly have green eyes." He turned the key and after a moment of grinding effort the engine started. "And who knows, maybe if we both go and we say the square root of life is nine, who knows but one day we might just get a letter in the mail that says, not 'Dear Jack' or 'My Darling Crowe', but 'I tried for a long time not to write this.' Who knows how things come to pass?"